Pam Moses was born in the West Country. Her career has included working as a commercial artists' agent out of Dickensian premises in Covent Garden, and as an art buyer for an advertising agency, and for the Arts Council. After marriage (to one husband only) came her long-standing love affair with estate agency, a willingness to move house frequently and a magical sojourn in the Middle East. She has written articles, mostly on cats or antiques, for various periodicals and *The Kennington Lion*, her children's play, was professionally performed in London and the provinces. She now lives in East Anglia.

BREAKFAST AT TESCO'S

Pam Moses

The Book Guild Ltd
Sussex, England

The Book Guild Ltd.
25 High Street
Lewes, Sussex

First published 1997
© Pam Moses, 1997
Set in Baskerville
Typesetting by Poole Typesetting (Wessex) Ltd.

Printed in Great Britain by
Athenaeum Press Ltd, Gateshead

A catalogue record for this book is
available from the British Library

ISBN 1 85776 187 1

1

It was that day, I remember, the day Seth reappeared, when I began to feel appreciably – *older*.

Of course, it had been one of those no-sale-no-fee sort of mornings at Montgomery's. Three seemingly foolproof chains had collapsed, followed by an afternoon that we, in our ill-chosen profession, found so demoralising: frivolous enquiries from people passing through the town who thought it might be enlightening to compare our house prices with those of their own (automatically superior) properties elsewhere. But as a senior negotiator I was inured by now to the thankless world of low reward inhabited by the lesser breed of estate agent.

I was tired by the time I got home. It was an airless evening, threatening thunder, and I felt sticky and irritable. The cat looked dead, stretched out beside the front door. But, as his was a theatrical nature, I knew he was feigning. My bedding plants in the urn alongside, however, actually were dead. Those bloody begonias had been accusing me of neglect for weeks, a neglect echoed by my Victorian monster of a house. I might have ministered to the begonias earlier, had mine been a more caring temperament, but there was nothing I could do about the house.

It could have been a handsome property still, given money, of which I was chronically short. The Georgian overtones were there to be reclaimed, the period features, so beloved of the buying public, were largely in place. But our little town wasn't fashionable, so my run-down semi wasn't valuable, and the cost of the remedial work it now required had begun to overtake any desirability implicit in its potential for refurbishment.

But I brightened as I passed down the dusty hall to the kitchen. At least George, footloose for once, had suggested we share a pub meal tonight. His perpetually ailing wife, Ivy, had taken her psychosomatic illness on a visit to her sister. Indeed, as I had given George a key some months previously, when I had recognised the signs of a promising relationship, I expected to find the back door open, the deckchairs in place on the terrace outside, and a gin and tonic waiting.

Instead, the kitchen was stifling, a clutch of flies were cavorting at strategic points, and my eyes, as if drawn to a dismembered corpse, immediately focused on a large vase filled with gushing red roses. A vase that anchored a large piece of paper. Roses were George's inevitable peace offering. So dinner was off. The note, though, was ominous. George was a man of few words, written words anyway, and the note was lengthy.

Yes, Ivy had returned suddenly and, while George had been in my house making his excuses with the gushing roses, a young man called Seth had turned up with a holdall and gone upstairs to bed. As Seth had claimed to be my stepson, and George recalled I had one idling around somewhere, George hoped he had done the right thing in leaving Seth installed.

My weariness evaporated. I was up the stairs in a second. Oh, how it all came back to me. Seth's daylight sloth, Seth's nocturnal frenzies. The house already felt contaminated.

My bedroom was at the end of a long landing on which stood my only enviable piece of furniture, a tallboy of distinction, the legacy of an aunt who had had no regard for its merit. Gummidge, a bear of battered aspect, lived on top of the tallboy. I grabbed Gummidge, opened my bedroom door and hurled the bear at the mound in my bed. The mound surfaced.

'Oh hullo, Holly.'

'What are you doing here?' I deplored the obvious question, but I needed the answer.

'Well,' said Seth, rising from the tumbled duvet to expose an even thicker figure than I remembered, clad in off-white singlet and underpants, 'it seemed a good time to have a change, if you know what I mean.'

Even if one were uncritical about personal appearances, and I was not, Seth could only be described as an ugly young man. His flesh was of the solidity that no amount of dieting would ever reduce. His was a rotundity that could never be lovable, or even comic, merely repulsive. And with the fat came the grease. He looked as if he always shaved with a blunt razor slithered across an overzealous application of lard.

'You see,' Seth continued, 'Dad thinks he might get married again.'

'So what? Why should you have to turn up here? Isn't my life tough enough already since your father swindled me in the divorce settlement?'

Seth dragged on some spectacularly jagged jeans and crammed his pudgy feet into something thonged from the Costa del Sol, before nauseating me with one of his soulful glances.

'That's another reason why I'm here, Holly. Dad thought I could pay you rent. When I get a job, that is. And Dad really does intend to have a serious go at it this time. He's keen on Philippa.'

'I bet Philippa's not keen on you though, is she? And that's why you've been chucked out. It's typical, really typical. I had to put up with you while I was married to your father −'

'Oh come on, that's not true. I only came back temporarily when Sandra threw me out.'

'But you were always being thrown out by some slag or other. It's your destiny to be rejected. You are anathema to women, Seth.'

'Well, you would think that, wouldn't you? You're so hard to please, Holly.'

Seth had a monotonous voice as well as a maddening imperturbability. Argument became boring in the end. He had by now trundled over to the window seat (a charming feature to the master bedroom) and from there his soulful glances were now cast upon the rest of the room.

'Anyway,' he said, 'This is a much more interesting house than Dad's. I like this period, you know − bit of character. Those suburban places are very bogus.'

Fatigue overtook me again. I went back down to the kitchen. I hadn't had dinner, I hadn't had a drink and I wasn't going to have George. I was hungry, disappointed and thoroughly disturbed. The limpet quality of Seth hit me anew. His removal was going to be difficult. I got out the gin bottle and splashed out a double, but there was to be no slipping into sodden contemplation. Seth was already at the kitchen door.

'We having a takeaway?' he asked hopefully.

'Bugger off.'

Seth opened the refrigerator and grabbed one of George's special brews that I stored for his delectation when opportunity for frolic presented itself. 'Who's George, by the way?' he asked. 'Didn't look like your usual type to me.'

'Mind your own business. I'm entitled to my bit of rough as well as your father.'

'There's nothing rough about Philly. She's a very classy lady. Got a bit of money as well.'

I felt more and more aggrieved. *Money*. My ex-husband was likely to marry a bit of money, was he? While all I had in prospect, currently at any rate, was George, seedy, impoverished and married.

Seth finished the beer and said soulfully, 'Any money for some fish and chips? I really fancy that tonight.'

I pulled open my handbag and threw him a ten-pound note. Anything to get rid of the sod for an hour or so.

'Thanks, Holly. We always did get on really, didn't we. Oh and can you let me have a key to this house? Bit inconvenient otherwise.'

I sighed and prized off the last spare key from the ring. The gin was having a philosophical effect. What use resistance? The lumpish Seth was not likely to take root, not in the undernourished earth I would prepare for his roots anyway. And one day Fate, in her usual blundering manner, would intervene and away he would stumble to blight someone else's life. But I had made a foolish start. That easily gained ten-pound note could give him expectations.

As Seth went out by the front door, he let in the cat, newly arisen from the dead. The only savoury yield from the fridge at

4

the moment was a sausage roll. I crumbled it for my feline friend as I considered recent events. Should I telephone my ex-husband and acquaint him of my innermost feelings at this tender moment in his life? It was very tempting. After all, I might get classy Philly instead and a few home truths from my impeccable source could dent her blissful misconceptions.

My hand bent towards the telephone but the cat, with more inherent dignity than I had, prevented the action. He seized the moment to smother me with lavish affection, the way cats have, purring and pushing and dribbling. I was not impressed. This cat was anybody's for a sausage roll. He was what East Anglians call a cypress cat: long tail and tabby stripes. He wasn't mine either. He had another home with a fussy widow two doors up. He wintered over in her small cottage (a few beams and a half-hearted inglenook made it passably desirable) ensnared by her Rayburn and her titbits. But, in the summertime, he haunted me for the quietude of the jungle conditions in my garden.

I poured another gin: no point in counting calories on a lost night like this. What could be wrong with Immortal Ivy this time? I wondered. What lurid symptoms would be outlined to me tomorrow morning at breakfast with George?

Ah, breakfast, I would have to explain to Seth about breakfast. It was never eaten at home these days; it had become a social highlight. I had discovered breakfast at Tesco's.

The telephone rang and its shrilling startled me. I splashed the gin. The cat took umbrage. It was Mother.

'You got my numbers?'

I had to think. As always, my mother induced an instant paralysis of my mind.

'I want my numbers by Saturday.'

'All right,' I replied testily. 'I'll try and get along to the garage tomorrow.'

'You got that man there?'

'If you mean George, no I haven't. But Seth's come back.'
'Who's Seth?'

'Oh come on, you remember. He's my stepson.'

'How can you have a stepson? You aren't married.'

'I *was* married for ten bloody years.'

5

'Were you? I don't believe you. Your men never marry you.'

My exasperation was mounting; my mother's forgetfulness, in part age, in part evil intent, had recently taken a more capricious licence with her thinning storehouse of facts.

'For God's sake, Mother, you were at the wedding. You were telling everyone that your favourite daughter had died at the age of ten on the operating table. I was only an afterthought and a big mistake.'

'You got my numbers? I want my numbers.'

It always happened. I slammed down the instrument in impotent fury and went to bed. Alone. Which was not at all what I had planned.

As I was crossing the road next morning on my way down to the town, I encountered Mrs Williamson returning from the park. She had been exercising her yap dog, Buster, who was now straining forward on his tartan lead. Buster was soaking and muddied from a skirmish in the lake and the little swine made straight for my ankles and the new sandals George had given me. Not that George was normally generous in the matter of compromising gifts. Roses maybe, gold bracelets never, and anyway I had suspected the sandals were originally Ivy's, pettishly discarded after purchase. Our feet were the same size, a fact I had earlier established; George had a bit of a thing about feet.

Mrs Williamson was panting. It was uphill from the park, but I sensed the crimson in her cheek was caused by displeasure rather than exertion. 'I don't know why you work for that man Montgomery,' she shouted. 'I consider he is extremely rude.'

I could not disagree. Jason was extremely rude, even to clients of some substance such as Mrs Williamson. She had a decent Victorian villa nicely set in mature gardens within walking distance of all the town's amenities. It was just unfortunate that the gardens abutted the car park of the Three Tuns, an hostelry much favoured by the less genteel examples of our mixed community.

'And he's no idea of valuation. When you ask an agent into your home to give you an idea of what it will fetch on the market, you do not expect to be insulted. Get *down*, Buster. Mrs Smith doesn't want you licking her knees.'

'Oh I am so sorry, Mrs Williamson,' I said. 'I do apologise for my employer. You should have asked *me* to come and give you a valuation. I think your house is absolutely charming.'

'One doesn't normally ask the woman in the office to value a house, surely? Although in the case of Montgomery's I doubt if I could have done any worse. And you can tell your employer I shall not be instructing him over my house nor over my land. Come *along*, Buster.'

Every agent in the area knew about Mrs Williamson's land. She had periodically held it above all our heads. The land, a large slab of prime development acreage, lay tantalisingly on the edge of town. It had once been worth a lot of money but Mrs Williamson had let the boom times come and go, playing her game of cat and mouse. It was now worth much less, a fact Mrs Williamson refused to grasp. But, when all was said and done, it was residential land, with outline planning, and ought not to be entirely disregarded. Yet Jason's arrogance could even blot out those marginal shafts of cunning that passed for his business acumen.

Oh dear, was it going to be another of those days? The intake of gin the night before, although reasonably modest by my standards, had done my head no favours. I eased my way gently across the park towards the lake and stood watching the uptipping mallards. The park was empty before nine in the morning, apart from the early dog walkers. The softly lapping lake, spring fed and always filled to capacity, calmed my rising tensions. I yearned to stretch out on the green turf and sleep in the shade of the chestnut tree. But the throbbing life of Tinkerstown awaited me.

I had christened it Tinkerstown some time ago and, among the coterie of small minds that met each morning over breakfast at Tesco's, the sobriquet had caught on as apposite, if not brilliantly amusing. For the little town did attract an inordinate amount of tinkers, or their modern equivalent of unclean nomads. As I went through the alleyway connecting the park to the High Street, one of them was already at his pitch. A dirty rag was placed to catch the coins and a long-suffering mongrel was curled against the shopfront. These mongrels, usually of lurcher origin, were a traditional part of the overall impression of deprivation, although, thankfully, they appeared well fed and free from sores, but not, alas, from fleas. Sometimes tinkers turned up with a horse and cart and parked in front of the post office. It added historic continuity to the market place and was probably construed as a colourful advantage by the tourist arm of the Chamber of Commerce.

Most of our little group were in place in the cafeteria section of the supermarket. We were hardly intellectuals and certainly not the stuff of posterity, merely the odds and sods of humanity not far removed from the breadline but grimly clinging to our jam tomorrow horizons.

George signalled to me to join him at his table. At the sight of his grin and the tufted drifts of white hair tonsuring his skull, my resentment at last night's defection faded. There was a lovable cheekiness to George. In his formative years, back in the Astaire and Rogers era, he must have been taught to keep himself clean and be polite to ladies. He had never failed his youthful formula. He was still pulling ladies and he was always spotless. He worked as a freelance kitchen fitter and no amount of sawdust or sweat ever left its mark on trainer or T-shirt. There he was now, my sprightly bit of rough, positively gleaming above his modest plateful.

Sitting before a portion of buttered toast was Sandy. Sandy had the brain cells the rest of us lacked. He was bookish and superior. He lived, not very impressively, on some handout from a family trust. He had been engaged on a manuscript of immense size and significance for many years. A tome, half fiction, half fact, concerning the vagaries of lesser European royalty. Fame, if not fortune, was his for the grasping, he indicated, should he ever condescend to publish the volume.

At another table Steve and Madge, the archetypal Darby and Joan, were giggling above a newspaper. Madge also beckoned to me, so I shrugged at George and, getting myself a black coffee, sat down beside Steve.

'Holly dear,' Steve began, 'we want you to come and value our house.'

'Why? Not thinking of moving, are you?'

'Yes, Holly, we've decided to have a stab at selling. The garden's been getting away from me lately. And there are other reasons.'

'But you've been there for ever. You can't go. I'd have no bolt-hole.'

I pictured Rose Cottage. It virtually required rebuilding. Certainly rethatching, replastering and even underpinning were imperative. It was a hovel. Its own unkempt meadows surrounded it and these gave it some picturesque point. The one near neighbour, however, was a large, odiferous pig farm. Again not endorsing my idea of a dream instruction. Yet I was fond of the place and frequently sought its dirty kitchen and the comfort of motherly Madge when events (rather than George) got on top of me.

Madge put out an arthritic hand, timidly clutching my arm. 'Don't be silly, Holly dear. We'll see more of you if we can buy the place we're after. It's only just round the corner from here.'

Never having had children of their own, Madge and Steve were childlike themselves. Did they think selling their rural slum would be easy? And what price would they expect to obtain for Rose Cottage? And what sort of dilapidated alternative had prompted this brainstorm? I could see the end of a happy friendship looming – if their cottage did not sell (and what lunatic would buy it?) I would get the blame. The agent always did.

'I think I had better ask Jason to come round and give you a valuation,' I said cautiously. 'I'm not sure that I am the right person for this, being so involved with you both, I mean.'

This threat caused Steve to cry, 'Don't you dare. I won't have that rude young man under our roof.'

I sighed. I knew Jason Montgomery at his most officious would make them nervous. 'All right, darlings,' I said reluctantly. 'But seriously, it's a bad idea for you to move. You'll be lost in a town. And the cats won't be very happy, either.'

But Steve still continued to press me. 'Come and see us this afternoon, *please*. We can talk it over then. Now you'd better go and have a word with George.'

By this time George was wearing his crestfallen expression: he was more adept at assuming a sexual reproach than I was.

9

As I passed Sandy, intent on his masterpiece, he looked up. 'I gather Madge and Steve may be moving, then?'

'Not if I can help it,' I replied.

'Montgomery's usual response. Never sell a house if it can be avoided.'

Sandy was only being peevish. Montgomery's had failed to find a buyer for his featureless modern box (one of nine in an uninspired cul-de-sac), However, I had to admit it had been galling when Ash and Spicer had shifted it within a week (a no chain job too: the blessed rented accommodation applicant we all yearn for). Ash and Spicer were bigger and brighter than we were, of course – they had offices in every local town and sales negotiators up to the ceilings. I despised Ash and Spicer. The buggers at their helm had once refused to give me a job when I had applied for a vacancy. Short-sighted bunch. After all, I had the best legs in town.

I sat down beside George and nudged his ankle with my foot. 'Well, lover?' I asked quietly.

'Don't go on about it. How do you think I felt? I was just in the mood for it too.'

'Ivy's little problem again?'

'I think it may be due to her steroids, they do funny things to the metabolism.'

Throughout our affair George, who enjoyed double standards, had maintained the fantasy that I was a sympathetic friend concerned to be apprised of every detail of Ivy's maladies.

'What's happened about that young man who came round yesterday?' he continued. 'Is he really your stepson?'

''Fraid so, George. And I'm lumbered for a while. Seth's surplus to requirements at the family seat at the moment.'

George raised his eyebrows in consternation. 'What about us then?'

'Don't worry, George. Seth's no startled fawn. Our shagging sessions won't disturb him. He's been married himself, but he's divorced now. I shan't be asking for my key back yet, my sweetheart.'

I could see George rearranging his first impression of Seth. My stepson's marital status had shaken him. George was in his early sixties. To him divorce had never been an option. His was a world of sex on the side.

I was late getting to the office. Alex was already at the instant coffee granules in the tiny back kitchen of the timbered premises we occupied in the High Street. I could never mourn a long-dead sister while I knew Alex: although she was ten years my junior, ours was a compatible friendship. Blissfully married, Alex and her Mark lived in a woebegone semi that had started life as council-owned. Their dream was to move upmarket to have more space in which to swing the babies they had long planned.

Together Alex and I ran Montgomery's. We manipulated Jason as best we could, propping him up there, justifying him here. We recognised he was insensitive and not very cerebral. In fact he was, at times, decidedly moronic. But he was supported by monies from a rich farming background and thus Montgomery's, despite Jason's inadequacies, was solvent enough. And our premises were handsome. Some chamfered beams and a good-quality carpet hinted at a glossy professionalism that our instructions never managed to complement.

'Seth's back,' I announced.

Alex paled. Seth had had one of his 'things' about her when he had lived in Tinkerstown before. 'Why has he come back? I thought he'd prefer living in London with his father — more scope for him there, surely? He isn't going to live with you again, is he?'

'Apparently Seth prefers a period house to somewhere suburban.'

'How will you cope? Can you afford to feed him?'

Seth's appetite was large and legendary.

'He says he's going to get a job and pay me rent. But we all know what a laugh that is.'

'Is he actually qualified?'

'Don't be ridiculous. Seth could even make a cock-up of road sweeping.'

'I know — he could get a job at Ash and Spicer,' suggested Alex. 'They change their personnel every month and their young men are all semi-literate, to judge by the sales details they issue.'

'Oh, Seth wouldn't like it there,' I said adamantly. 'He'd have to wash.'

2

Despite my unwillingness to accept Steve's instructions, I found myself driving the company car out to Garbage Green (another of my puerile nicknames) that afternoon. The heatwave was continuing and the lack of cover in the East Anglian landscape made such combinations lethally hot. Trickles of sweat anointed my forehead, while my designer sunglasses kept slithering down my nose.

I slung the car down the rutted track that led to Madge and Steve's cottage and shuddered as it came into view. It was one thing to visit Rose Cottage for a cosy, if often foetid, hour of camaraderie; it was quite another to contemplate its desirability on a property market that was anything but buoyant. I suspected, too, that this house represented all Madge and Steve's wordly wealth. I was on a heart-sinking mission, definitely the wrong choice of agent for this one. Had I ever had the money I considered Fate should have vouchsafed me, I was decidedly a Colefax and Fowler woman. I liked style. I liked grandeur. The humble – and especially the poor and humble – had no appeal.

But, bless that little couple, to welcome my advent they had put out a wooden table, a parasol struck through its centre, in the small area of grass that Steve now kept mown. The table was laden with the sort of home-made goodies for which Madge was in demand at village fêtes. As I stuffed Victoria sponge, I learned about the house in Tinkerstown that had fired their ambitions. I knew its whereabouts all right, I often passed the bedraggled row of four terraced houses that were wedged between a poodle-clipping parlour and a public car park.

'You'll love it, Holly,' Madge enthused. 'It's quite unspoiled.'

'There's a studio at the bottom of the garden,' said Steve, agog. 'It will be marvellous for exhibitions.'

Exhibitions? They had lost me. Had they been hiding a cache of old masters all these years?

In due course, replete with butter icing and strong tea, I went inside the cottage, where the professional business commenced. Steve and I plodded from dingy room to dingy room, scattering their many family cats as we paraded through the property. There was a general air of discoloration and of something sinister lurking in woodwork and thatch. But, at the end of the day, I had to acknowledge that Rose Cottage might well bring a better price than I had first envisaged. It had the magic ingredient: *potential.*

'All it needs really,' said Steve optimistically, 'is a bit of imagination.'

'It would make a lovely weekend retreat for some young family,' Madge contributed. 'Imagine the peacefulness out here, the freedom, after being cooped up in some London flat all the week.'

'Well,' I said guardedly, 'we might pull something off, if we're lucky. I know a builder who could restore it. Let's have a look at the land, now. What is it – about three acres?'

As we approached the meadow, the long grasses parted, and a girl in a straw hat emerged from the interior. I was not only startled by this apparition, but I loathed it on sight – overcome with an irrational yet intense animosity. The girl had the face of a Madonna, lovely in its youthful way, so uncreased and fresh; yet unnerving in another way due to a certain strange reptillian blankness, unresponsive and cold-blooded. If her face was arresting, her size was even more breathtaking. She was enormous, a giant; Seth was a stick insect by comparison. Big-boned and amply fleshed maybe, but this was no roly-poly fun girl, this was Beauty and the Beast rolled into one deadly parcel.

On balance I found the vision terrifying, but this was not the reaction of Madge and Steve, who engulfed her with screams of rapture.

'Holly,' they trilled, 'We want you to meet our dearest god-daughter, Juliet.'

'She is an artist,' Steve added reverentially.

I saw then that Juliet did indeed have a drawing book under her arm as well as an ostentatious tin of pastel chalks. I saw the need also for the studio at the bottom of the garden. So dear old Madge and Steven were preparing to change their whole way of living for this muscled Miss Muffet, were they? I was put out. Indeed, I abandoned the actual acreage of the meadows to a 'subject to survey' clause, turned on my sandalled heel and strode back to the company car, Steve at my side.

'She's a beautiful girl,' Steve drooled on, 'and so brilliant. She's won ever so many prizes already. We will do everything to help her at this stage in her career and she's going to find a lot of inspiration in the local scenery. She's been telling us about the effect of the great arc of sky and the interplay of light. She's quite a psychic in her way.'

I brushed aside this effusion. 'What are her parents doing to help her? If she's so bloody clever, you'd think they'd be the ones to make the odd sacrifice or two, not you and Madge.'

'They've had to go abroad,' explained Steve. 'Some long-winded contract in one of these God-forsaken climates. The dear girl was grateful when we offered her a home and we didn't want her tempted by a harmful environment. Madgey and I read of such terrible things happening to innocent young girls these days.'

Innocent? Not that one, I thought viciously. But I smiled at Steve, kissed his cheek, and drove away – scattering the resident feline population. Dear Madge could never say no to a supplicant cat or kitten, and over the years at Rose Cottage they had amassed quite a colony.

As I spun along between the wide sweep of sugar beet fields, it occurred to me that when you put Rose Cottage into a less sunlit perspective its chances of securing a purchaser who would know their way around the expensive minefield of restoration were remote; it would have to be offered to my tame builder. And fingers would have to be securely crossed.

My jaundiced mood remained, so to put my ill humour to good use, I made a detour to Mother's bungalow. The old bat lived in a council-run sheltered housing complex of gnome-like dwellings on an arterial road that ploughed through the town. She didn't get out any more, her limited degree of mobility depended on a wheelchair. Instead a spasmodic gang of carers came and went, all bossy and bright-eyed, fuelling Mother's natural aggression with their hearty, well-meant ways. One of these carers was just closing the front door of the bungalow as I marched up the pathway.

'She's a bit upset today, dear. Didn't want her bath. Poor little old girl.' The carer waved light-heartedly, limping away to her car.

The carer had prepared mother's tea and set her wheelchair in front of the television, which, as Mother could never master the complication of the remote control, was either raging or silent. Mercifully, it was subdued in colour and sound at that moment. Mother grimaced up at me. We never exchanged loving greetings, which was, I suppose, a measure of our individual honesty.

'Did you see that? She was limping, wasn't she? Why do they send me cripples? They charge for it too. It's disgraceful. Look at this cup of tea. Gnat's pee.'

'Shall I throw it away then?' I asked wearily.

'Why throw it away? I've paid for it. I've got to drink something, haven't I? I notice you never bring me a bottle of brandy. That's what I'd really enjoy. You done my numbers?'

'You haven't given them to me yet. That's what I've come here for. Where's your pen?'

'Get my handbag.'

I passed her the balding satchel that I had seen her clawing for many years. She rooted about in it and finally produced a ballpoint and a rumpled envelope, on the back of which she wrote six wavering numerals.

'You'll never win, Mother. The odds are too long.'

'Why not? Someone has to. People *do* win things. Mrs Angelicus won a bottle of sherry the other week.'

'That was a raffle. It's not the same thing.'

'Mrs Angelicus has won the Lottery too.' My mother always had to have the last word, even if her last word was irrelevant or downright lunatic. 'It's not fair. She's got plenty of money. Her boyfriend comes from a titled family. He's in a trust.'

15

Mrs Angelicus was the warden of the gnome complex. She was also part of the Tesco breakfasting scene, having a penchant for Sandy, to whom, I supposed, my mother was referring. I had to admire Mrs Angelicus where Mother was concerned. She handled her deftly with the minimum of acrimony.

Mother watched me balefully as I transferred her numbers to my handbag. Most of the time, as now, her expression was petulant, bottom lip pushed out beyond her ill-fitting dentures. Her blue eyes were still miraculously clear and keen but accentuated by lurid eyeshadow. She used lipstick, too, of a fierce red and smeared wide of the mark. Her hair was still thick and the mad mop of white curls was quite natural. She resembled a withered Barbie doll and was just as meretricious. She was still convinced that she was gorgeous and that men lusted after her, and the consequence of such vanity was that she was vitriolic about my liasion with George; even Mrs Angelicus' mild and totally innocent involvement with Sandy aroused her malice.

'What you done with that man?' said my mother.

'What man are you on about?'

'Don't pretend you don't know. You'll be had up one day. It's against the law.'

I deemed my visit at an end. As I opened the front door, Mother's voice shrilled behind me: 'It's disgusting. He's under age. It's disgusting.'

Presumably she thought I was now cohabiting with Seth.

In spite of everything, I retained a vestigial obedience. I drove round to the garage where, religiously since its launch, I had used their Lottery outlet. I filled up at the pump and had the obligatory chat with the girl behind the counter.

'How do you manage in this heat? she asked. 'You must get so hot driving round houses all the time. I bet you wish you could be at the beach. I know I do. These your dear mum's numbers? There you go.'

There I went indeed, straight to Montgomery's. It was now after hours and Alex had gone home. Jason was lurking in the back office munching a chocolate bar.

'Are you there? he called.

16

Jason had several vocal modes of summoning his handmaidens: the snarl, the coldly official and, greatly to be dreaded, the silken. This time it sounded ominous and I feared a heart-to-heart on current market trends with much 'statistically speaking' thrown in. I do not know what it was about Jason that I found so offensive. He was tall, broad and aggressively handsome. His clean-cut appearance suggested an old-fashioned courtesy and a high standard in the conduct of business, while his public school background underlined these fantasies.

'Holly,' Jason began, adjusting his spectacles for the admonition to underling approach, 'Alex tells me you've been out to Rose Cottage this afternoon. Were you serious about taking the place on the books or were you merely having tea with those half-witted old people?'

'Well, believe it or not, Jason, but I think the place *is* saleable. I did have reservations about it —'

'Then you should have held on to your reservations,' Jason interrupted. 'You know we've already discussed the way in which I see Montgomery's developing as an agency. I want us to cultivate the more upmarket instructions. We have got to improve our image. Surely you could have left Rose Cottage to Ash and Spicer? Times are not easy, Holly, and our best bet is to move away from the bottom end and grab our share of the top bracket.'

'I think that's a bit extreme, Jason. There is still money at the bottom end. Anyway, how do we motivate upwards, exactly? Vendors with houses worth real money take their properties to the glossy boys.'

The glossy boys was our flippant way of referring to Glossop's. Now Glossop's did not waste their assets on small-time premises, they went straight to the cities, where their resplendent offices were more like state apartments. The properties they handled were awe-inspiring and offered at never published prices. It had been known for the uninitiated purchaser to enter these marbled halls seeking something decidedly lower-end-of-market and stories were in circulation of such hapless souls having to be revived with tea and sympathy at less exalted agencies. For the glossy boys had a way with them. They were masters of the curled-lip technique and Grade II to their fingertips. But dear old

17

Jason aspired to their sneer tactics and oh how he ached for just one instruction in their league.

'Never mind, Jason,' I said, stretching out my legs, 'there will be another Frost Farmhouse one of these days.'

Frost Farmhouse had been our big moment. We had sold the rambling and, it was rumoured, rat-infested, old farmhouse for a quarter of a million. I always suspected it had been a bit of money laundering. The man who had paid so readily for its rising damp had looked brazenly criminal to me.

'Statistically speaking,' said Jason, 'you are right, of course. But while we are waiting for a decent country house instruction, you might consider abandoning Rose Cottage. We can't afford to take on that sort of place for sentimental reasons.'

I snatched at the first ready lie that came to mind. 'Don't worry, I have someone in mind for Rose Cottage already. And I haven't reduced the commission terms just because Madge and Steve are my friends.'

Jason's expression switched suddenly from interrogating officer to friend of the family. 'I don't know about you, Holly, but I'm ravenous. Hot weather makes me hungry, do you know that?' He left the table and came round to my chair. 'How about having a spot of dinner together? I'm really enjoying this useful exchange of ours. Let's push off to the Suckling Pig.'

Totally unused to invitations to other than an argument with Jason, I was taken off guard and my normal wariness slipped.

'Don't tell me you kitchen fitter is waiting for you back at your grim old mausoleum,' Jason continued, using his dreaded leer. 'Come on, I haven't booked and I don't want to be late.'

A mental picture of my cavernous kitchen back at the mausoleum rose up before me. A straight choice between a greasily expectant Seth and a free pub meal with Jason posed no dilemma. Within minutes Jason and I were speeding towards the Suckling Pig. We were offered a table in the heavily beamed restaurant. It was dark and stuffy on such a hot evening and Jason and I had to share a velvet upholstered bench that serviced the table along a panelled wall. The pub was not renowned for its haute cuisine, but supplied trencherman platefuls of old favourites. The red wine flowed. Jason adjusted his spectacles frequently.

Alex and I often conjectured on Jason's ability to hold on to his driving licence. We were sure most of his evenings were spent quaffing gallons of red, white and pink grape because most of his mornings with us had a hungover tinge to them.

Statistically speaking, I had long expected Jason to make a pass at me. I had the best legs in town and I always endeavoured to dress in a manner that indicated availability. So I was not dismayed when he said, 'You know, you've got the most delectable legs, Holly.'

'Everyone tells me so, Jason. You'll have to be more original than that.'

'You're wasted on that kitchen fitter.'

'Everyone tells me that too. But a girl has to do the best she can when she's down on her luck.'

Jason moved suggestively along the velvet bench. 'This may not be the time,' he said ponderously, 'and this may not be the place, but I've got to confess I keep dreaming of getting your clothes off, you naughty tease.'

'Really, Jason,' I said sternly. 'Although that particular exercise would be very worthwhile – I promise you I'm absolutely stunning in the nude – I think you should remember that I am far removed from your social strata. Someone who hopes for a Glossop's instruction one day should not dally with his negotiator in a public house.'

Jason slowly refilled his glass. 'Stop taking the piss, Mrs Smith.'

Casually, I fluffed out my thick, but heavily assisted, blonde hair. 'Do take your hand away, Mr Montgomery,' I said, 'and remember I am much older than you are.'

'I always fall for older women. I'm mother fixated.'

'I'm not *that* old.'

It was then I observed Mrs Williamson heading for a table across the room. She was attended by an elderly man of some flamboyancy, to judge from his cravat tucked expertly into a white shirt above faultless grey flannels.

I leaned over to Jason, my hair touching his suffused cheek. 'And there's another thing, Mr Montgomery,' I whispered confidentially as Jason gulped and fumbled further up my thigh. 'That formidable lady, Mrs Williamson, has just come into the restaurant.'

19

'Bugger,' said Jason, straightening and distancing himself along the velvet bench. 'Eat up, Holly. We don't want to be in here all night. We'll skip the cheese.'

'Oh but I want some Brie,' I said firmly.

'No you don't. We'll have coffee and push off.'

As the tray of coffee, cream and mints arrived, I stood up.

'Ladies' room?' queried Jason.

'No, I'm going to have a word with Mrs Williamson.'

The old trout had definitely landed herself a lecher. Her companion looked as if he were sizing up my bra cup quite efficiently as I approached their table.

'I hadn't expected to find *you* here, Mrs Smith,' said Mrs Williamson, glaring.

No, Mrs Williamson, I thought, you hadn't expected to find anyone you knew here. But I said, 'It's actually my first visit. The food's not bad. I'm sure you will have a lovely time.'

'It's my first visit too', said Mrs Williamson. 'I don't normally patronise places like this but my cousin assures me it's clean and decent.'

The cousin, if cousin he was, grinned at me. 'It's Dottie's birthday,' he explained. 'Thought I'd give her a treat and show her how the other half lives.'

'Happy birthday,' I cooed.

Mrs Williamson preferred the dismissive. 'Mrs Smith works for some little estate agency in the town,' she snapped.

'Then I must look you up some time,' said the cousin.

I wondered at the cousin's temerity; he must be on very familiar terms with the lady to get away with such a statement. Indeed, as Jason and I left the restaurant, I noticed they were still looking cosily intimate over the seafood pie and carafe of house wine.

'Why the hell,' said Jason as he staggered towards his black coupé, 'did you have to go and speak to that old cow?'

'It's called a public relations exercise. I was trying to restore some goodwill after you upset her the other day. She's not going to give us her house to sell since your rude attitude about its value.'

Jason puts his hands on my shoulders. 'Holly, when will you learn that I do not intend to pursue that kind of property? It's got a pub for a neighbour – and a pub where they dispense drugs, by all accounts.'

'Rumours, Jason, rumours. Anyway, I also thought I had better kill any rumours Mrs Williamson might spread about your having taken me to dinner.'

'What's wrong with that? Jason replied truculently. 'We could have been discussing market trends. But I want you to become much more to me than the woman in the office, Holly. We must start seeing a lot of each other. Know what I mean?'

I steered Jason to the car. 'For goodness' sake, give me the car keys. I'd better do the driving.'

'You are doing the driving. You're driving me mad, you adorable tart.'

'Come on, give me the car keys,' I pleaded.

'Like hell I will. My car and I have a sacred trust.' Jason answered, and turned back towards the Sucking Pig. 'Just going for a pee, sweetheart. Hang on,' he called.

That's it, I thought, as I watched him lurch away. Thank God for George's sandals. At least they're comfortable. I've got a long walk home.

It was then I realised what a furtive little pub the Suckling Pig was, hidden along a remote, lightly hedged lane, at the edge of one of the many nondescript hamlets that infested the East Anglian scene. But my sense of direction and my knowledge of the area were invaluable. I strode out purposefully and with sudden enjoyment. The evening was cool and the light hovering over the fields, the famed East Anglian light, was shading from grey to mauve, outlining the trees in the glory of their high summer foliage.

I felt light-hearted, happy to be a pretty woman with irresistible legs. My euphoria was short-lived. I heard a car behind me in the lane. I would have to suffer drunken Jason laying siege to my knickers after all.

'Hullo, my love. What are you doing here?'

Oh joy. It wasn't Jason, it was George skidding to my rescue in his scratched and dented Ford.

'I'm just robbing birds' nests, darling,' I retorted, thankfully sliding into his passenger seat, where, surfeited with good red wine, I kissed my hero to get him going.

'This is the sort of chance meeting I really enjoy, Holly,' he murmured.

'What are you doing this way, George? I thought you'd be watching telly with Ivy at such an hour.'

'I've been estimating for a kitchen, love. Some young woman who works in the day and doesn't trust anyone with her key. Not like some other young woman I know.'

'Why don't you use your key now, George? I promise not to call the police.'

'That's a very generous offer, Mrs Smith. I'll try and do a good job for you.'

So George and I made the old mausoleum ring that night. Which was not at all what I had planned.

3

I felt rather jaded the next morning. George had slipped out into the early hours of another brilliant morning and I knew Seth was awaiting me in the kitchen, all expectant, like some baby bird with its mouth permanently agape.

Sure enough, he was sitting at the table, a damp towel wrapped around his essentials.

'What a sight for sore eyes you are, Seth,' I said, getting out a plastic container of freshly squeezed orange juice and picking up two cloudy glasses from the draining board. Seth watched me, horrified.

'Is this all there is for breakfast?'

I nodded.

'There wasn't anything for breakfast yesterday. I'm nearly starving. Your ten quid didn't go very far, I can tell you.'

'A touch of malnutrition won't do you any harm.'

'If I don't get enough to eat, something will happen to my sugar levels. I don't like orange juice anyway, so you can stuff that.'

'As it happens, Seth, I don't have breakfast here any more. I go down to Tesco'.

'What – walk all that way first thing in the morning?'

'Why not?' It's very pleasant crossing the park in summertime, very bracing in winter. You'll have worked up an appetite by the time you get to their cafeteria and afterwards be all set up to do a good day's slog in the office of your choice. Found a job yet?'

Seth looked soulful. 'My age is against me.'

'What – at twenty-five?'

'They don't want you after eighteen these days. You become too set in your ways.'

'Oh, I think you might find an employer to stretch a point there, if you look hard enough. Alex suggests you try Ash and Spicer.'

Seth brightened. 'Alex still around, is she? I rather fancied her.'

'It wasn't reciprocated, Seth.'

'That's what she tells you. I was getting all the body language at the time.'

'Well, you can please yourself about Tesco because I'm off there now.'

'I might as well give it a whirl then, if you are paying.'

Having shed his impromptu loincloth and slipped into something stained and smelly, Seth trundled along beside me, breathing heavily. 'You had that old man of yours in with you last night, didn't you? I'm surprised he can stand up to all that activity at his age.'

I had by now made up a bed for Seth in a room at the other end of the landing to where I slept, so I was put out to think that my private movements could be monitored by my prying stepson.

As we neared the supermarket we passed the tinker and his dog.

'I admire people like him,' said Seth. This confession hardly astonished me. 'Salt of the earth, those gypsies,' he added tritely.

'Ever thought of joining them, Seth? You seem to have all the attributes of the open road. You are freedom-loving, bone idle and filthy.'

'You're just full of the prejudices of the home-owning classes. You have to be, I suppose, working in your line. Got to keep the flag boards waving.'

'Talking of flag boards,' I said, remembering Madge and Steve's town house and studio dream, 'I must just pop round the corner here. There's a property I want to check out.'

Seth looked at me in alarm. 'You aren't going to be long, are you? My colon's withering like a balloon for want of fibre.'

As I had suspected, it was Ash and Spicer's flag board advertising that the house was For Sale. Its wooden finger wagged us forward. I stepped gingerly through the nettles of its narrow front garden and peered in at the bay window. Seth surveyed the house from the pavement.

'Not bad,' he said critically. 'Not bad at all. It's got something.'

'You bet,' I muttered as I saw the peeling wallpaper within. 'Dry rot, wet rot and death-watch beetle.'

But would Madge and Steve even *notice*? It was home from home for them. I turned to Seth. 'There's a building of some sort up the garden. Come on.'

Together we smashed through the maze of campion and foxglove, treading where others had recently trodden before, to achieve what had once been a small stable.

Seth appeared to be in his element. 'I like this. You could do anything up here. Restore furniture, practise the drums, knock off your neighbour's wife.'

'You're very inventive all of a sudden.'

'Well, it's got me going, Holly. Dad always said I was a natural-born architect. Or I could have made an interior designer.'

'Always the joker, your father. Anyway, the people who've got their sights on this house intend to make some sort of gallery for exhibitions out of the stable.'

'Not a bad idea that. No, I approve of it.'

'Oh, they will be relieved. You can tell them yourself in a minute. They usually have breakfast at Tesco's.'

'They paint, do they, these friends of yours?'

I thought of poor Rose Cottage, unpainted for years, and bald down to its original exterior wood and said, 'Not often, I'm afraid, not often enough.'

Once at the cafeteria, Seth gave his order: three sausages, two eggs, mushrooms, bacon, tomato and fried bread. 'A man's breakfast,' he breathed.

George wasn't there but Sandy was, and as we passed his table, he said to me, 'Who's the thug with the stubble?'

I made the introduction. 'Sandy, meet my stepson, Seth Smith.'

'Always have enjoyed Norfolk,' said Seth. 'It's got real values.'

This nonplussed Sandy, who returned to his lesser European royalty without further conversation.

25

I looked around for Madge and Steve but they were also absent. Oh what a thrill, I thought, I am breakfasting alone with Seth. He was now wolfing his macho plateful while I took delicate sips of my black coffee. I hoped we made a sufficiently incongruous couple to dispel any suggestion that we were more closely related.

I glanced at my watch and wondered if Jason were already in the office. I had pushed Jason, in his new role as amorous seducer, to the back of my mind. But I now began to be uneasy. What would his reaction be to my flight last night? What attitude would he adopt? Chastened and apologetic – unlikely: thwarted and vicious – more likely. Chilly, perhaps? On balance I thought the aloof approach would be the one. Dignity upheld. On the other hand, would the bastard dismiss me? I liked my job. I needed my job. My salary was imperative. I was on my feet, anxious to discover my fate, when in walked Madge and Steve. And in waddled Juliet.

Madge came gushing up. 'Oh Holly, have you had time yet to think about what price we'll get for Rose Cottage?'

'I'll be writing to you officially today, my darling. Never fear, I'll do my best for you. I've already been round to look at the Chapel Street studio. Seth was impressed.'

I made a quick introduction and left Madge and Steve twittering around an open-mouthed Seth. And, at that moment, Seth was a nauseating vision. He had seen Juliet, blank-faced and silent, dark hair overflowing her stately shoulder, she had sunk voluptuously into the seat I had just vacated. He should be all right there, I thought, providing he changes his shirt and shaves now and then. Juliet had just the right combination of flesh and inscrutability to appeal to that idiot. She was an artist, too. His cup must surely runneth over before long.

I slunk into Montgomery's. 'Anything happening, Alex?'

'Jason's had an accident. His mother has rung to say his head is bandaged from a fall he had last night.'

'Drunk,' I said, with insider knowledge.

'Oh Holly,' Alex remonstrated, 'you would think that. Anyway, his mother has sent for the doctor. It might be serious.'

Seriously embarrassing, I thought gleefully. Aloud I said: 'Jason's mother always overreacts. All mothers do, in one way or another. There's something about giving birth that turns the average female into a soap opera queen.'

Then I realised that had been a harsh comment for Alex, who, I knew, was desperately wishing for a baby. But babies just failed to appear for her and her Mark, despite their giving their all, night after night, to the matter of procreation.

'Well, Jason won't lack for constant nursing attention with Mummy on the job,' I said. 'And it leaves us delightfully free to carry on with our private lives in the meantime. Out with the coffee jar, Alex, and let's make hay.'

'Speak for yourself – I won't be making any hay. Look at all this typing I've got to finish.'

'In that case, I shall pack my picnic hamper and go trekking alone into the wilderness in search of a strolling builder.'

'You want to find Ned? I hear he's working on a pair of cottages out towards the Suckling Pig. You think he might be interested in restoring Rose Cottage, don't you?'

'Alex, I can keep no secrets from you. I have heard on the grapevine that Ned's made a bit of money lately and he's always hankered after becoming a developer in his own right. So here's his chance. Rose Cottage once restored is eminently saleable, even with the pig farm next door. Come to think of it, there always *is* a pig farm somewhere in the vicinity of every house in Suffolk and Norfolk. If not a pig farm, then a chicken farm or a dairy farm. This is muck-spreading territory and we are all here for good deep breaths of old-fashioned country air. Or, as Seth would have it, Norfolk's got real values.'

'What I remember of Seth was that he smelled like a pig farm himself.'

'True, my pet, but I think he may just have met his Waterloo and his days of soap and water have arrived.'

'Don't tell me he's got his eye on some other poor defenceless young girl.'

'Fear not, this specimen is anything but defenceless. It's Seth we'll have to look out for.'

I got as far as the doorway. There, outside on the pavement, stood Mrs Williamson's cousin, winking.

'Dottie didn't properly introduce us last night,' said the cousin, forcing me back into the office. 'She's got the arrogance of wealth, I'm afraid. You know how it is.'

Alas, I did not know how it was to have the arrogance of wealth. I only had the arrogance of poverty, and I found this awful little man with his eager eyes on my legs irksome. 'I'm just popping out to an appointment, I'm afraid.' I said coldly. 'My colleague will assist you.'

'Oh no, it's you I've come to see, Mrs Smith,' he continued. 'My name is Arnold Pearson, but I want you to call me Arnie.' He looked around quickly at the office. 'My cousin has been a little hasty in not giving your obviously excellent establishment her property to sell.'

'Oh, that was a difference of opinion with Mr Montgomery, Arnie. Nothing to do with me. However, she has made it plain that I am too lowly to become involved.'

'She's got me to advise her now, Mrs Smith.' said Arnie. 'And as I can only relate to beautiful women, like yourself, I have told her she must deal with you in future and not those unattractive young men at Ash and Spicer.'

'I'm afraid the instructions must come from Mrs Williamson herself. She is presumably the vendor, not you.'

'She owns the place all right.' There was an avaricious light in Arnie's eye, 'Worth a mint, I shouldn't wonder. Ash and Spicer have down-valued for a quick sale. But they can't fool me. I'm a shrewd cookie.' Arnie let out a cackle. 'I can assess a good property same way I can assess a willing woman.'

Arnie winked again. I was finding this exchange unpalatable. He may have found Dottie Williamson willing, but he would have no joy with me. He barely came up to my waistline.

'I'm sorry but I must dash, Arnie. Tell Mrs Williamson to contact us if she really means to instruct us after all.'

'I look forward to seeing more of you, Mrs Smith,' said Arnie, and pinched my bottom.

I fled for the car park, where the 'company car' was parked in a reserved bay. The company car had been a point of contention between Jason and me. He had his own black coupé, of course, and an inferior second-hand saloon was allocated to the senior negotiator. But I was not permitted to drive it for my own personal pleasure, only on legitimate agency business. Since my husband's departure, I could not afford a car of my own, so the embargo on the company vehicle really hurt.

I decided I would drive back to the mausoleum and change. The heat was becoming intense once more. Shorts and T-shirt would be more comfortable. As I dashed up the stairs I heard Seth in the bathroom. I opened the door a crack and there he was, at extensive ablutions, with my sponge.

'Do you mind,' he said belligerently.

'Don't worry, Seth, I have no intention of violating your body. I am just so surprised to find you being so hygienic, that's all.'

'I tend to perspire in this weather,' said Seth.

'So I've noticed,' I replied, and left him to it. I pulled on my shorts and threw on a plain T-shirt and drove off in search of Ned, the tame builder.

Ned, too, was tending to perspire when I caught up with him, halfway up a ladder with his bucket of mortar. 'Hullo, Mrs Smith,' he called gaily. 'Be down again in a tick.'

'Shall I buy us both an iced lolly from the village shop?' I suggested.

Ned grinned. 'I'd rather have an iced whisky.'

'I've got a flask in the boot of the car,' I said.

'Now you're talking my language.'

We made for the shade of a group of lime trees on the village green. The scent from their green flowers loaded the air. Ned and I lay on our backs and wallowed in the rare beauty of the untenanted sky.

'This beats ridge tiling,' said Ned.

'This beats word processing,' I said.

There was a somnolence to the sunlit moment; I had to achieve my mission before Ned dropped off.

'I have a proposition to put to you, Ned.'

'Blimey,' said Ned. 'It must be my birthday.'

'Come on, Ned, you know what I mean. I hear you've had a windfall and are looking for potential building renovations.'

Ned's expansive attitude tightened. I could already hear the purse strings meshing together. 'You got something in mind, then?'

'How about Rose Cottage?'

'Madge and Steve's place, out by the pig farm?'

I nodded.

'Blimey, Mrs Smith, that'll cost a fortune to do up. Needs underpinning, don't it?'

'Needs damned nearly everything, Ned. But think of the finished house. A neat extension at the back, perhaps, lovely new thatch, couple of en suites, the total works. You've got a grand plot there, remember, and stunning views, if you exclude the pig farm.'

'Not listed, is it? Don't want listed buildings. Too much bloody paperwork.'

'No it's not listed. I checked with the local authority.'

Ned sniffed. 'Could be interested,' he said cautiously. 'Price has got to be keen, though.'

'As mustard, Ned. Trust me.'

Ned leaned over and patted my leg. I allowed his grimy hand to linger. This was business. He chortled amiably.

'I wouldn't trust you, Mrs Smith, as far as I could spit.'

I gave him another swig from the flask. That, and the lure of my legs, seemed to clinch things.

'Well, if we can agree a figure,' he said, 'we might do something. When do I get to look over?'

'Whenever you like. Just call round there and tell Steve I sent you.'

'What's happening to them? Retirement home?'

'Now, can you really see them in that kind of set-up? No, they've got their eyes on a house in Chapel Street.'

Ned whistled. 'Rather them than me. You wouldn't get me living in a town again. And they'll miss all that lovely fresh air.'

I thought of the pervading odour of pigs and wondered at Ned's perception of sweet country air. But, like many a Londoner, he had fallen under the spell of rural life and was only too willing to view it sunny side up.

'I might toddle round there later today,' Ned said, as we rose to our feet. 'And, as you've done me a bit of good, Mrs Smith, I could put something your way.'

It was my turn to be cautious. 'Oh yes?'

'I've been working up at the Old Hall. Big repair job to the conservatory. Now, the chap who lives there wants to go back to town as well. Too quiet round here for him, says he's going off his head. How do you feel about selling it? I could put in a word.'

'It sounds much more a Glossop's type of property. I don't think the vendor would look at us.'

'You don't want to belittle yourself, Mrs Smith. You are a better agent than them snobs at Glossop's. I hate that bunch.'

Ned had obviously fallen foul of the sneer school in his time.

'Not known for their warmth and charm, Ned, but they represent the image of properties like the Old Hall. Still, if you can get us the introduction I am sure Mr Montgomery will be very grateful.'

What luck, I thought, as I drove slowly back towards Tinkerstown. The possibility of such an instruction would certainly demolish any nasty reprisals Jason might be hatching from his sickbed. Along my route a great sweep of barley was being harvested. This was one of those seductive moments in the countryside that offset the muck and the mud and the lowering expanse of dark grey cloud that blighted so many months of the year. I reached the outskirts of town with regret and plunged into the queue of cars that were nudging bumpers along the arterial road. Now for the second half of this exercise...

The offices of Ash and Spicer were double-fronted and their glistening windows bombarded the passer-by with a frenzy of colour blow-ups. The emphasis was on this agency's phenomenal ability to sell, no matter how intrinsically unattractive were the amassed properties that festooned every available window space; some of the houses bore red SOLD stickers underlining the legend of success.

There was an array of desks manned by impersonal young men in similar suits, all briskly interpreting what the management considered was their brand of friendly and efficient service. I flopped on to a seat in front of the nearest desk. There was just the hint from the young man behind it that I was not welcome. He knew who I was, and Montgomery's were, after all, rivals. My legs meant nothing to him.

31

'Can you let me have a set of details of two Chapel Villas?' I asked brightly.

The young man become cagey. 'We can't let you share commission on this, you know.'

'I'm not asking for half commission, am I? I am interested in seeing the particulars because some friends of mine hope to purchase the house.'

'Lot of interest in this house. First time on the market for years.'

'That's no excuse for the lunatic price someone in this office has placed on it.'

'It has been priced to sell, Mrs Smith, so you can tell your *friends* the asking price is not open to negotiation.' My adversary's expression was hardening, 'The stable at the back of the property offers possibilities for commercial use.'

'With the relevant planning permissions, of course. Might be tricky to obtain these.'

'We've already spoken to the local authority. There won't be a problem.'

'Just checking to see if you've done your homework.'

It amused me to needle the young man but I judged I might harm Madge and Steve's position as prospective purchasers if I continued to antagonise him. As it was, he snapped: 'It's not mortgageable, you understand.'

'My friends have cash, of course,' I replied smoothly. It was at this juncture that a door at the rear of the premises opened and a voice, unpleasantly familiar, came floating out.

'I know the area well and I have a great affection for it. I used to live here, you see, and I have always held the opinion that Norfolk and Suffolk have got real values. A true outpost of civilisation.'

A girl carrying two cups came out and closed the door behind her, putting an end to my fascinated eavesdropping. So dumbfounded was I that my mind blanked out. Lost for further intercourse with the young man, I waved the details of two Chapel Villas in farewell and left.

I had a vision of Seth, sweating in singlet and underpants, being interviewed by the manager of Ash and Spicer. Surely an hallucination brought on by the intensity of the heatwave? Seth was not Ash and Spicer material.

I decided to go back home. I could hardly appear in the office in my shorts, and George might have left a message for me at the mausoleum. I was in the mood for nooky.

The cypress cat was still playing dead beside the urn, but the postman had called. I turned the envelope over and, with awakening joy, recognised the handwriting. It was a letter from Grover. At last. At last. A letter from Grover. Clasping the envelope dramatically to my heart, I took it into the back garden and, sitting on the low brick wall that fronted the terrace steps, I held it tightly for several minutes.

I had always been imbecilic over Grover. The love of my life, the boy next door. I had only to see his handwriting, spiky and neurotic, to be reduced to a sickening sloppiness. I was reluctant to open the letter. Might it not contain news that I would find unendurable? Grover returning to his wife, for instance. Worse than that somewhat implausible situation, Grover finding a replacement wife? The only purport of his letter that would save my sanity was that Grover was coming back to England, unattached and ready to accept that I was the only girl for him.

Grover really had been the boy next door. In our teens we had exchanged sly kisses in my father's garden shed. I was the willing object of Grover's first fumbles and more, much more, in the months before his first disappearance into a distant county to attend university. I remained in the parental home, corresponding in a slushy fashion, thinking myself pledged to him. But while he was at university, the evil Fates had distorted my dreams in the shape (quite shapely, I had to admit) of Grover's wife. They were married while still students, with distressing speed and in some secrecy, so that when Grover finally came back to the house next door, he was accompanied. Later I got married too. Then I got divorced. And Grover got divorced. But instead of hurtling to my outstretched arms, he went abroad to work. He wrote spasmodically and, now and then, in traditional bad penny manner, he would turn up and spend days – and nights – with me.

Eventually I opened the letter. It was all right. Grover was still a free man and was coming to see me again. '*Change the sheets, Holly,*' he wrote, '*I'm on my way.*'

33

The cypress cat wandered out to me, suffused with full-throttled emotion. I snatched him up and cradled his throbbing tabby body. He shared the happy anticipation of that golden moment. The miracle had happened. Grover was coming for me.

Miracles in fact were bursting around me like fireworks. Seth appeared wearing a suit, a new suit. Seth was shaven and he was fragrant with deodorant.

'Good God, Seth,' I said, 'I wouldn't have recognised you.'

'A trite response,' he rejoined. 'Want a gin and tonic?'

'Sod the gin and tonic. This is a champagne evening. Nip along to the off-licence and buy a couple of bottles of the divine bubbly. I'll treat you, even if I have to extend my bank loan.'

'No, Holly, *I'll* pay. Dad's lodged a bit of cash with the bank in the High Street for me today. And he's promised another dollop if I get a job. And,' Seth concluded proudly, 'I have got a job with Ash and Spicer. No trouble about my age or education, although I did lead them to believe I was a graduate. They swallowed it all easily. I look the executive type, of course.'

'Well, I've got to hand it to you. You are quite the little quick-change artist. Empathising with tinkers this morning, every inch the thrusting young executive tonight. Well done, Seth. Now give me back my ten quid you conned out of me the other evening.'

'I intended to pay you back, Holly. I am a man of integrity. And I'll pay you rent as I promised I would.'

'In that case, we'll have a takeaway with the champers.'

We supped in harmony that evening, the cypress cat, Seth and I. And, when we finally went to our several beds, all three of us were in a haze of dizzy contentment. I put Grover's letter under my pillow. I wanted to dream of him. But I didn't. I had a nightmare and awoke at three in the morning with indigestion. Seeking the bathroom, I found Seth being sick in there.

4

The impetus of Grover's letter had faded when, a month later, there was still no sign of his arrival (and I had changed the sheets, too). He was an unreliable bastard. Why should he expect, with such arrogant confidence, that I would be so willing and so thrilled at the prospect of his taste of honey? But I was and he would have known it. I was pathetic.

In my state of suspended eagerness, I fell back on good old George. At least George was inexhaustible. The clean sheets were now well rumpled. Immortal Ivy had had a prolonged bout of diarrhoea so he had made almost nightly visitations.

Seth, the new improved Seth, was earnestly toddling off to Ash and Spicer's each morning. The management were giving him a training course, inculcating their friendly and efficient service practices – or brainwashing, as I called it. After his period of initiation, he was going to be given a company car which would also be for his personal use. This aspect of his appointment stung me. I considered it sexist.

Of course I had realised the underlying reason for Seth's metamorphosis. *Juliet.* They were inseparable at the moment, like two slugs on a cabbage leaf. Seth was besotted with Juliet. She had the poor sod transfixed. Still, I had to acknowledge a debt to the girl. Seth was now almost normal. At his instigation, he and I were sauntering across the park together that Sunday afternoon on our way to visit Mother. Even Seth's leisurewear had undergone upmarket revision. But no amount of washing and after-shaving could quite erase the congenital greasiness.

The heatwave still held. Now there were daily announcements on local and national news bulletins concerning water shortages and dropping levels. There was a hosepipe ban in operation and the normally luxuriant summer undergrowth in my back garden had fallen victim to the drought, with ugly, barren consequences.

As we came to the gnome complex, I said, 'Now, don't expect any sense out of the old bat. She's still strong on snide comment and argument, though.'

'I don't think Granny's condition will be as advanced as you suggest,' Seth replied. 'You will have failed to home in on the geriatric wavelength, that's all.'

He was prone to make pseudo-intellectual remarks since coming under the spell of Ash and Spicer, not to mention the crash course in artistic appreciation handed out by Juliet.

Mother was attired in baby-doll get-up and appeared to be in some agitation. Mrs Angelicus was alongside the wheelchair. 'Oh Mrs Smith, I'm so glad you've come. Now perhaps between the three of us we'll be able to calm your mother down. She's under a slight misapprehension about her numbers.'

Mother looked at Seth with rapture. 'Oh here's the man with the money.' she cried.

'Hullo, Granny dear. You remember me, don't you? I'm Seth.'

'You're not Seth. You don't look like Seth. You're far too clean. Come on, let's get on with it. Give me my cheque and then I can get out of this cell block and live in a proper house again.'

'She thinks she's won the Lottery,' explained Mrs Angelicus. 'I keep telling her she's only got two numbers right.'

'No, Granny, I'm not the man from Camelot. I'm Seth. I'm sure you remember me, you're just teasing.' Seth leaned over and kissed my mother.

Mother sank her nail-polished claws into his open-necked shirt. 'Don't mess me about. Just give me my cheque. And I don't want any publicity. I'm not having an army of cadgers after my money. I know my rights. She'll expect some, for a start.' Mother turned on me her glare of dislike. 'She's always hard up. All the men she sleeps with, and she doesn't know how to get a penny out of them.'

I shrugged my shoulders at Mrs Angelicus, 'I don't know how you cope. I'd take a hatchet to the lot of them.'

'I don't mind,' said Mrs Angelicus. 'It's really a very interesting job.'

Seth disengaged Mother's grasp. 'It's lovely to see you again, Granny. And looking so young and pretty as well.'

'I'll look a damned sight prettier when I get that cheque. Don't beat about the bush.'

'She's determined to have a cheque, Seth,' said Mrs Angelicus. 'The easiest way is just to write her one. The amount need not be too generous. Think of it as a donation to your favourite charity.'

'I haven't got a favourite charity,' bawled Seth. 'This is bloody blackmail.'

'Write her a cheque, Seth,' I said between clenched teeth. 'I'll pay you back sometime. And let this be a lesson to you. I told you not to bother with the old cow.'

The cheque pacified Mother. Smilingly, she put it into the balding satchel. She beamed up at Seth. 'You insurance men are all the same. Always after the premiums but never want to pay out.'

'Thank you so much,' said Mrs Angelicus, with feeling, as the three of us hovered at the door. 'Your mother's a very determined lady, Mrs Smith, but very noble in her way. You'll miss her when she goes.'

'Like I'd miss a ruptured spleen,' I said bitterly.

Mother waved a claw. 'Cheerio,' she called. 'Good to see you again, Seth. Come again soon, there's a love.'

'You are right about her condition, Holly,' said Seth, as we tramped along the scalding pavement. 'She's absolutely barking.'

As Chapel Street was a short cut back to the mausoleum, and as number two Chapel Villas currently held a lot of promise to both of us, we made our way to it now.

'I think we'll pull this one off, partner,' said Seth, donning his Ash and Spicer cap and referring to the sale now in progress. The fact that Madge and Steve were actually in a position to proceed on the villa after Ned had rashly made them an offer for Rose Cottage was a plus for Seth's new career, while on my side Jason was mollified over Montgomery's pending commission.

Juliet was sitting on the low brick wall of the villa, a sketching pad on her knee. How she was able to capture an image with her crayon while her huge appendages hung across the page, I could not imagine. At the sight of her, Seth started to quiver. He sat down on the wall, his flesh meeting Juliet's flesh, and peering into the depths of her bosom, he exclaimed, 'Look, Holly, Juliet's got the house opposite in just a few vigorous strokes.'

I wondered just how vigorously Seth stroked Juliet when they were alone together, but he pushed the sketching pad under my nose and much was expected of my reaction. All I could decipher were some irregular black lines and a few smudges. 'It's no use asking my opinion,' I said crossly. 'I am the total Philistine.'

'You miss so much, Holly,' said Seth soulfully, 'not being able to enter the world of Juliet's conceptual realisation.'

That was my cue to go in search of Madge or Steve. At the back of the villa I found Steve, workmanlike in dungarees and brandishing a spirit level. Further down the now much trampled garden, Madge was in the stable pouring strong tea from a thermos, while a pair of familiar legs were in motion descending backwards from the worn wooden treads of the loft ladder.

'Hullo, George,' I said. 'How you do turn up.'

'George is giving this place the once-over,' Steve explained, joining us for the tea ceremony. 'He's going to fit up this stable ready for Juliet's exhibitions when we've finally bought this place.'

'I can get some velux windows into the roof space,' George expanded, 'and put in a stainless steel sink unit and some cupboards over there, see, then were can dispense wine to the people who come to the exhibitions. It'll be just like a real art gallery.'

'This *will* be a real gallery,' protested Madge. 'Juliet is a real artist.'

'Juliet is a very lucky girl,' I said dryly, wondering anew at the dear old couples' unselfishness, their naivety.

Madge handed me a mug of tea and while I sipped this daintily, the three of them chorused around me outlining their unrealistic scenario. The public (hordes by the coachload, to judge from their description) would surge along the narrow side path between number two Chapel Villas and the fence that screened off the car park from the house. The car park would, naturally, provide the parking. The car park was council-owned, so the fence, council-owned also, was the only part of the property in really good repair. The fence was eight feet high and close boarded, and no previous owner of the villa had ever tried to entice a creeper to invade its panels with softening tendrils.

'This sort of enterprise can be expensive,' I warned them.

'We shall register as a charity,' Steve said proudly.

'That's smart thinking,' said George. 'Charities can be very helpful with advertising and promotional things.'

'But of course Juliet isn't interested in making money,' Steve continued. 'She just wants to make a name for herself.'

'I suspect she'll do that all right,' I said acidly.

After several other aspects of the proposal had been tossed about a bit, George turned to me. 'Can I give you a lift home, Holly?'

I kissed Madge and Steve, and George and I went round to the car park, passing Juliet and Seth, who were now pressed together like dried flowers and presumably exploring another facet of Juliet's conceptual realisation.

'Ah,' George gushed fondly, 'nice to see young lovers, isn't it? They do seem keen on each other, don't they?'

The sight of those entwined slugs had put George in the mood; once inside his car, he let his hand stray knowledgeably around my erogenous zones.

'You rushing home to Ivy?' I asked.

'I did promise I'd take her to the cinema tonight – she's mad on that actor, whatsisname. But –' George glanced at his watch – 'I'm not pushed for an hour or two.'

So, an hour or two later, I said, 'I'm rather glad we formed this habit, Geroge.'

'As a matter of fact,' said George in a surge of serious affection, 'I'm growing rather too fond of you for my own comfort.'

'Oh, I can understand that. After all, I don't have diarrhoea.'

'Don't be mean. Poor old Ive's prone to bowel disturbance.'

'Whereas the only disturbance I'm prone to is you, George. But weren't you supposed to take her to a cinema tonight?'

'Sod the cinema,' said George.

'I think,' I told Alex the next morning as we drank our coffee, 'George is coming up to the boil.'

'What exactly does that mean?'

'I'm not sure. It's just that he's getting pretty heavy lately. Last night he actually put our carnal interests before Ivy's obsession with whatsisname, the actor. It's a milestone in our relationship.'

'I won't ask you what you were doing to his feet.'

'It wasn't his feet. It was much more conventional stuff. I wonder what it would be like to marry George.'

'I think you are crossing a bridge too far there, Holly.'

Trust Alex to quench my vibrant fantasies.

'After all,' she went on coolly, 'you must not underrate the power of Ivy's bowels, and if they are running out of steam she can always fall back on a hundred and one other little maladies to tempt the errant George back into her medicine cabinet. Anyway, you don't really want to marry old George. Why don't you widen your horizons? Give Jason a chance.'

'How *can* you? The man's grotesque.'

'No's he not. He's very dishy. He can be positively heart-stopping when he smiles. And he hasn't come out of the ark, like your poor old kitchen fitter.'

'Anyone would think you fancied Jason.'

'I'm just making sensible suggestions. I have your welfare at heart.'

Ten minutes later Jason crashed through the office, calling over his shoulder, 'Are you there?'

Alex, her fingers rattling across the computer keys, muttered, 'Go on, let him have his wicked way with you now. It'll make both our lives easier.'

'Sit down, please, Mrs Smith.' Jason looked at me over his glasses. The bruising to his forehead had faded at last. The actual cause of this temporary disfigurement he had never disclosed, although I was certain the urinals at the Suckling Pig had been responsible.

'Well, I think you've got the message at last,' he said.

'Message, Jason?' I echoed.

'I'm talking about our better class of instruction. We've been asked to go out to the Old Hall and give them a valuation. They

40

are a natural for Glossop's in the ordinary way, but I gather you used your influence with some contact of the vendor's. Anyway, they are prepared to give us a chance first.'

Light dawned. 'Oh, it's the people Ned knows.'

'Who's Ned?'

'He's the developer who's buying Rose Cottage. Another sale, may I remind you, Jason, that I made by accepting instructions that you were originally opposed to.'

'Yes, I am aware of that fact, Mrs Smith.Well done. Now, as we've got to be out at the Old Hall by two o'clock, I suggest we grab a bite somewhere on the way.'

My heart sank. 'I'm very busy, Jason. I really think you ought to handle this big one on your own.'

'Oh no, you'll have to come with me,' Jason insisted. 'Always gives a better impression if two people arrive at a property. Anyway, you can write down the necessary details. You always see more cupboards than I do. Women are into the minutiae of nest-building.'

An hour later the black car was rocketing along the lane towards the Suckling Pig. The day was overcast, the humidity intense. The weather forecasters had blithely predicted thunderstorms. I was wearing cotton slacks, so I hoped my legs would not produce the usual dire effect on Jason's libido. The spectacles were not slipping, even slightly, and his profile was positively austere.

Despite the threatening thunder, the Suckling Pig was doing grand business. The tables, their striped parasols flapping merrily in the gathering breeze, were almost filled. We found one eventually, Jason viewing the spilled beer on its surface with distaste.

'Sorry about this, Mrs Smith. Didn't expect the bloody place to be so crowded.'

'I'm surprised you've come here after the other evening,' I said daringly.

'What other evening? I'm here a lot. Landlord's a friend of mine. Sandwich do for you? Cheese?'

'Fine.'

'I'm having a beer. You want a gin and tonic, I suppose?'

41

'That would be nice.'

After three pints, Jason said 'I'm bloody thirsty. You want another?'

'One is enough for me, thank you,' I said primly. 'I think we should try to appear sober when we meet the vendor of the Old Hall.'

Jason drank deeply. 'I'm lucky in that respect. I can hold my liquor. So there's no need for you to adopt that schoolmarmish attitude with me. As a matter of fact, I'm going to have another.'

As we were leaving the forecourt, we almost collided with Mrs Williamson and Arnie. Staggering to the car, Jason said, 'Wasn't that old Williamson again? And still with that gruesome midget. What's he up to, do you suppose? She wants to be careful, silly old moo.'

On our drive to the Old Hall, the car was given to sudden swerves which set my capped teeth on edge. But, apart from startling an ambling pheasant or two, we arrived unscathed and on time.

The Old Hall was breathtaking. Every inch a Glossop's glossy brochure. It stood at the end of a long avenue of oak trees. These gave a slightly raffish air to the drive as the dead branches, gnarled grey and misshapen, stuck out at right angles to the main members who still wore their full summer regalia. The house was moated, of course. We drove across the bridge and parked in front of the impressive doorway. I glimpsed the cluster of rounded brick chimney pots and the ironwork of the Gothic windows. A riot of climbing roses, yellow and white, clung to the timbering in the walls. They hurled their petals towards us like a cloud of confetti, released by the frenzied wind.

Jason clasped my hand in a clammy, desperate grip. 'Oh Holly,' he said. 'This is it. This is the Big One.'

The door opened and a tall man with a paunch, wearing a straw hat and smoking a cigar, leered at us. 'Hi,' he said, using a phoney mid-Atlantic accent, 'I'm Bernard Maddison-Savage. Glad you could make it, kids.'

Jason's grip on my hand tightened, and I gripped back. We both knew Mr Maddison-Savage did not complement the image of his house. He jarred. But, as our unlikely vendor led us around, the ambience of the place soothed our troubled spirits. Each and every room was gracious, no liberties had been taken with its period detailing. The Aga in the kitchen was dark green, I noticed enviously, the bespoke units were painted with subtlety and the bathrooms were exquisite, no brashness anywhere, no eccentric touches. The conservatory, containing Ned's remedial handiwork, was more basically designed, and it was large to the point of absurdity.

'My orangery,' said Bernard Maddison-Savage. 'Like it?' He made for a table, a completely glass table, on which stood a wine cooler and glasses. 'Time I gave you kids a drink. Thirsty weather, this.'

I accepted gratefully, and considering it pointless to make a secret of my admiration, asked, 'Why do you want a leave a dream home like this, Mr Maddison-Savage?'

'The country makes me sick.' replied our host. 'I've been bored out of my pants ever since I came to live here. What is there to do in this goddamned dump? All I can see from the windows here are miles and miles of bugger all.'

'As good a reason as any for moving,' said Jason.

'Glad you're on my wavelength, fellah. Well, before we get down to the bottom line of what you think this old pile's worth, and I can tell you it's worth plenty, have another drink.'

'Gladly,' said Jason, extending his glass.

'Cigar?'

'Actually, I don't smoke,' said Jason awkwardly. I could tell he was praying that this sissy fact would not cause Bernard Maddison-Savage to retract his good opinion of our credentials.

'Oh well, have another drink. Every man needs some damned vice.'

As part of our genial vendor's conjuring repertoire, more and more bottles of wine kept appearing from the discreet cabinet let into the brick wall of the house.

'Bloody hot,' agreed Jason, his spectacles slipping.

'Feel like a swim, you kids?'

'In the moat?' I asked incredulously.

Bernard Maddison-Savage reacted as if I had a made the joke of the century. 'Gee, isn't she a peach?'

43

'Yes, she's a peach,' said Jason dreamily, 'Oh Holly, I love you.'

'Thought I could detect the old chemistry,' said Bernard Maddison-Savage. 'Come on, you sweethearts, the pool's through here.'

They each grabbed a cheek of my bottom and propelled me through the conservatory and out on to a terrace towards the inevitable sunken swimming pool. There, stretched full length on some Mediterranean contraption, lay a young girl. Her hair was in two plaits, no doubt to heighten this under-age effect, and tied with striped ribbon. The ribbons were all she wore. Her vital parts were well displayed, but as she was whip-thin, there was little seduction in her appearance. She waved gaily.

'Oh goodie,' she cried. 'I wondered when old Bernie was going to get around to the business.'

'I prefer things au naturel,' said Bernard, rather stating the obvious. 'I find bikinis to be a bit of an obscenity. Don't you agree, Jason? It is Jason, isn't it?'

Jason burped. I began to be uneasy.

'No point in concealing what we know we've all got', continued Bernie breezily. 'So come on, you two. Rip it off, and let's get stuck into some real fun.'

I looked towards Jason in horror. Surely he was man enough to tell Bernie we were professional agents on professional business and that nude bathing was not within our terms of reference? I could not see Glossop's representative stripping off under similar circumstances.

At that moment there was a fearsome flash of lightening. Little Lolita gave a squeal and in one bound she had jumped on to Jason, arms around his neck, legs around his middle.

'That's as good an invitation as I've seen today, fellah,' said the odious Bernard. 'So I'll take your popsy for a swim instead.'

'Oh no you won't, you bugger,' I yelled, throwing our coveted instructions to the wind.

The thunder roared out and the rain, not content with sedate drops, tipped out like a demented waterfall. In seconds, I was drenched.

'I told you to get your clothes off,' said Bernard. 'Rain is sensational on bare buttocks.'

I dashed for the conservatory. I wanted a weapon, any weapon, and if it were a priceless artefact, so much the better. Bernie was hard on my heels, his breath hotter than the storm. 'You may as well give in and strip, girlie.' he called.

All that came to my eager hand was a large crystal vase of some size and splendour and filled with tarty-looking orchids. I smacked this, orchids and all, down on Bernie's straw-hatted head. I did not care what damage I might inflict on his skull, and I certainly squashed his straw hat. My outrage had given me maniacal strength. Bernie crumpled and dropped to the Italian marble flooring (ordered direct from the factory in Milan at astronomical cost, we had been assured).

'I hope I've killed you, you rotten sod,' I added.

Then I heard Jason's faint wailing and, slithering my way through the puddles that had formed outside, came back to my beleaguered employer, who was looking very sick, very bewildered and very drunk.

'Oh God, Holly, don't leave me,' he entreated.

'What's with your fellah?' cried Lolita. 'What a wimp.' To underline her disgust, she pushed Jason angrily. His foot slipped and he toppled into the pool.

'You silly little cow,' I screamed, 'The poor sod can't swim.'

What with the beer, the wine and the unusual turn of events, Jason had sunk to the bottom of the pool. The nymph and I managed to drag his submerged bulk back to safety while I bestrode his unconscious form, pumping at his chest.

'Do you think he needs the kiss of life?' asked the girl. 'Because if so, you can do it. I don't fancy him that much.'

Nor, of course, did I, especially as, at that moment, Jason stirred, sat up and began retching. His spectacles, not surprisingly, were missing so I was slow to come into focus. But when I did he burbled, like some latterday Horatio Nelson, 'Holly, darling, kiss me,' and then vomited copiously into the turbulent waters of the swimming pool.

'Just get up, Jason,' I said furiously, 'and let's get out of this knocking shop.'

45

Bernie, holding his head with an encouragingly bloodstained handkerchief, came into view. 'You're a spunky little lady,' he said to me, 'and God, I like a woman with spunk. It's been real fun, but I guess you'll be hearing from my lawyers.'

'And you'll be hearing from my mother,' said Jason.

'Incidentally, Mr Maddison-Savage,' I said coldly, 'you can stuff your instructions, I would try Glossop's if I were you. They could do with this kind of experience. Liven up their act no end.'

Once outside, I pushed Jason into the soaking passenger seat of the black car. 'As for you, you drunken clod, you can give me the car keys and no more sacred trusts. I am taking you back to Mummy.'

'Oh Holly darling,' breathed Jason, 'I think you've been a little hasty just now. We'll never get the chance of another instruction like that again. And a bit of nude nooky wouldn't have been too bad, you know.'

5

Entering the office, Alex told me Jason's mother had been on the telephone. Jason was in bed with a chill and would I care to come round and take some dictation from him?

My shorthand was rusty. No one had asked for it for years. I was a negotiator, not a secretary, and I leaned firmly on the distinction. But I guessed this request had been issued to appease Mother Montgomery's curiosity, so I found a notebook and set off for the farmhouse. The sky was grey now, the thunderstorm had temporarily swept summer away. It was colder, too, so I had put on a suitably secretarial cardigan and some jeans.

The farmhouse was typical: colour-washed elevations under a pantiled roof. A sprawling, wandering house, updated in the 1930s and again in the 1950s, so the inglenooks were hidden (no draughts) and the doors were flushed over (no dust). The ceilings were low and sagging, undoubtedly concealing the earlier beams. The usual collection of farm buildings, some now redundant, straggled the yard.

As soon as I parked the company car, a Jack Russell of fiery temperament came barking up. Mother Montgomery came hurrying out, admonishing the dog and giving me a guarded smile. She was an elegant little woman, dressed to kill at all times of the day.

'I gather you are the heroine of the hour,' she said to me as we started walking together to the house. 'My poor boy might easily have drowned if it hadn't been for your prompt action. My dear, I am eternally in your debt.'

47

Could I capitalise on a mother's gratitude? Was she prepared to write me a sizeable cheque, perhaps?

'Such terrible people,' she continued, leading me through the kitchen to the front hall. 'What hazards you professional people face these days.'

I followed her up the stairs and along the galleried landing. Just what details had Jason disclosed about our visit to the Old Hall? Surely Mother Montgomery had been spared the full frontal account?

'He's looking peeky this morning, poor boy, and no wonder. What a soaking. And being so sick. He's ruined his suit.'

'It didn't do my clothes much good, either,' I said, still wondering if some monetary compensation was in the air.

'Are you insured, my dear? I'd look up your policy if I were you.' Mother Montgomery tapped on a door. 'Are you respectable, darling? Mrs Smith is here.'

Jason was sitting up in a large bed. A noble mahogany headboard set off his halo of golden curls. He was wearing silk pyjamas. The silly sod looked like some bygone Pears' soap poster.

Mother Montgomery closed the door behind her, but I felt certain she was keeping watch nearby. Despite my cardigan, I was a threat.

Jason patted the old quilted coverlet. 'Sit on the bed, Holly. I want you near me.'

'Am I here to visit the sick, Jason, or do you really want to dictate something important?'

'After what we went through together yesterday, Holly, I think our relationship has ripened into something rather more than an employer—employee interface, don't you?'

'No. And that's statistically speaking.'

'You are an obstinate woman, but you can't go on resisting me for ever,' said Jason complacently. 'You treated me tenderly yesterday, Mrs Smith, you were as gentle as a mother. Psychologically, you gave the game away.'

'Jason, if you've really no dictation for me, then I'm off. I want to see that rat Ned and ask him a few searching questions about Mr Bernard Maddison-Savage and the sale of his house. If it *is* his house to sell.'

Jason grabbed my hand. 'Darling, we even think alike now. I've spent most of the night probing that situation. There's something wrong with that set-up. That gentleman does not belong in that house.'

'He would be happier living in a nudist colony, that's for sure. Either he is a tenant or, if he is the true vendor, then he's into the bank for the lot and no longer cares. Yesterday was just his idea of a spot of real fun and we were just the gullible stooges. I am sorry to disappoint you, Jason, but that sort of instruction would always, always, go to Glossop's. You can't beat them, you know.'

Jason sighed. 'You had better have a word with your Ned. But go carefully, we don't want to rock the sale of Rose Cottage.'

'I'll watch it. But if I do find Ned's in league with that monster at the Old Hall, I'll screw the little rat on his next development.'

'I'm not really angry with either Ned or Bernie,' Jason said equably. 'They have been Fate's tool for bringing us together like this.' Jason leaned across the bed eagerly. 'Why not hop in beside me now, Holly, and try out a real man for once?'

On cue, Mother Montgomery entered the room, cafetiére and cups on a tea tray, all tastefully arranged underneath an embroidered tray cloth. 'I'm sure you can do with some refreshment,' she said brightly. 'And are you really going to insist this poor woman goes back to the office, Jason? Because I think she should be given the day off, she's looking so tired.' Mother Montgomery put a sisterly arm around my neck. 'I know what these ordeals do to the older woman, my dear.'

'Not a bad idea to take the day off, Mrs Smith,' Jason agreed. 'Feel free. But leave the company car at the office, mind.'

Day off indeed. I had scores to settle.

I buzzed along the lane where I had been told by the obliging landlord of the Suckling Pig, I might find Ned at work on an old barn. Following directions, I discovered the group of barns and saw that they were sufficiently derelict to tempt a small-time developer. Sure enough, I found Ned astride a wooden box, involved with his elevenses.

'Hullo, Mrs Smith. Come to chase me up, have you?'

'I've come to pick a bone with you.'

'No need to panic. My solicitor tells me we shall be exchanging on Rose Cottage by the end of this week. I'm not going to pull out.'

'I'm very glad to hear that. However, I have something else on my mind just now.'

Truculently Ned put down his sandwich box. 'What's all this about then? I don't like being messed around.'

'Nor do Mr Montgomery and I.'

'What you getting at?'

'Mr Maddison-Savage. That's what I'm getting at.'

'Oh him. Don't talk to me about him. He's not a favourite of mine.'

'Really? I thought he had come highly recommended by you.'

'Now look here, if you didn't hit it off with him, it's not my fault, is it? I've only done some work for him. Not that he's ever paid me for it, the bloody crook.'

'No, and frankly I don't suppose he ever will pay you for it. Didn't he strike you at the time as being, well, not quite the right sort. if you follow me?'

'I thought he was all right. Drank like the proverbial fish, of course, but that suited me. I can put a few away, you know.'

'Did he ever ask you to take your clothes off?'

'What are you trying to say? I'm no sodding pervert.'

I felt this confidential chat was getting out of hand. 'I know you're not, Ned,' I said hastily. 'It's just that Mr Montgomery and I had a most peculiar session with the man yesterday. He seemed to have nooky on the brain and his girlfriend was in her birthday suit. Rather put us off our stroke, to be honest.'

'Oh her. Never took much notice of her. All these young people are the same if you ask me. My own daughter goes round the garden topless in the summer. Thinks nothing of it.'

'Did it ever cross your mind that Mr Maddison-Savage might not actually own the Old Hall?'

Ned was silent for a few minutes while his grey cells grappled with these unwelcome tidings. 'You mean his mortgage is bigger than what his bank balance is?'

'Maybe. Or else he's a tenant and, if so, is probably in extensive arrears. In other words, I think he's just a common or garden con man.'

50

'Blimey. Well, I just take people at face value, Mrs Smith. I haven't got your knowledge of the world. If someone asks me to work for them and the trappings looks tasty, then I'm in there. I know I get a bit of hassle from farmers now and then – they never wants to pay up without an argument – but I thought Bernie would be a push-over. I even stuck a bit extra on my bill because I thought money was no object to a man like him. Eccentric millionaire, I had him down for.'

'I hope I'm wrong, Ned, and anyway, keep this under wraps, please. We don't want an action for libel.'

'Why don't we just go round there together, Mrs Smith, and have it out with him?'

'Oh, I'm not sure about that,' I said uncertainly, recalling the injuries I had bestowed upon the lascivious old ram the day before; but Ned was not to be deflected.

'I'm not going to be buggered about. I want my money.'

So we climbed into Ned's van and sped off to the Old Hall. There was no doubt about it – the house was majestic. It looked serene and untouchable. Owners would come and owners would go, but the house would command respect from them all. Ned got out and hammered on the great front door. There was no answer. 'I'll go round the back,' he called. 'Must be in that bloody swimming pool again.'

I sat on in the passenger seat, lulled by the tranquillity, the aura of riches. The Old Hall was the embodiment of the fairy-tale castle of a childhood dream. The stuff of charity open days when you paid your money and gawped for an hour or two. For one unbidden moment I felt bitter, the Colefax and Fowler part of me thwarted by circumstance. It would be quite a shock to find that Bernie was, despite conflicting evidence, the master of all he surveyed at that fine house.

Ned came scampering back. 'Something very funny going on, Mrs Smith. Come and have a look.'

At the rear of a house, inside the conservatory, was a large placard. It was a real fun announcement. Written in red were the words: SOD OFF ALL YE WHO ENTER HERE.

Ned's voice was hushed. 'What do you make of that?'

'A confirmation,' I said.

51

'It's not written in *blood* is it?'

'Don't be so melodramatic. It's just Bernie's way of giving everyone the two-fingers sign.'

'You reckon Bernie's done a moonlight – and I'm not getting my money?'

'You've got it, Ned. He's buggered off.'

'The rotten swine. Shall we tell the police?'

'You can tell the police, Ned, and do it quickly, but leave Montgomery's out of it. We don't want to become involved in a mess like this.'

Before going home I returned the company car dutifully and popped into the office.

'Alex, sweet child, I've been given the day off.'

'Sorry to disappoint you, Holly, but Mrs Williamson and Mr Pearson are waiting for you in the back office.'

Mrs Williamson, Buster at her heel, was struggling to assume a friendly expression. Arnie, on the other hand, had no such emotional reservations.

'Ah – the lovely Mrs Smith,' he cried.

At that moment Buster roared into action and came snapping and snarling across the room.

'Don't be alarmed, Mrs Smith, he's harmless. He wants to play with you, I expect. And,' Arnie added roguishly, 'I can't say I blame him. I'd be glad of a game with you any time.' He chortled wildly. Mrs Williamson winced but said nothing to deter his fatuous exuberance. I was puzzled. She must be inordinately fond of her cousin.

'Well, how can I help you?' I asked briskly.

Dottie Williamson took a deep breath. 'My cousin and I have a confession to make to you.'

I was intrigued. I slipped into Jason's leather chair behind Jason's rent table (an antique legacy from a farming relative). I decided to do some exploratory teasing. It was my day off, after all.

'A confession? What have you both been up to then? Something naughty?'

Arnie responded in kind. 'Only some very old tricks, Mrs Smith. If you get my drift.'

52

Mrs Williamson's cheeks turned her very own shade of crimson. 'Arnold, really. What must Mrs Smith be thinking of us? No, I have to confess that, in the end, I am very disappointed in Ash and Spicer's performance since they have been representing my beautiful house.'

'Dottie's house is worth a packet,' Arnie said, with fervour. 'It needs some exclusive coverage. These rogues up the road don't know how to market the place. They are out for a quick sale at a low figure. Dottie's house is in another league altogether. Know what I'm saying?'

'Of course,' I said, 'I have always considered Smallwood House to be a gem in its way and because of its character I think we can be a little saucy with the asking price.'

Arnie turned triumphantly to his cousin. 'There, Dottie. Didn't I tell you Mrs Smith would have the right approach?'

I was determined to gain these instructions and therefore I knew I would have to come up with a higher price than that of Ash and Spicer – and their price was fractionally higher than could be justified on a sluggish market. It was an awkward moment and I felt trapped. If I failed to get them a good offer, or, worse, make a sale within a reasonable period, or finally, commit the most dastardly sin of all in a vendor's black book of agents' transgressions – suggest *reducing* the price later on – then I would have justified Mrs Williamson's original dismissal. As it was, I was always going to remain, in her eyes, 'the woman in the office'. Her change of attitude had been occasioned by randy Arnie. He had pushed me into a situation of potential peril whereby my own professional instincts were sublimated. But I said, recklessly, 'Nothing ventured, nothing gained. So let's up the price by twenty thousand. That should give room for manoeuvre.'

They both looked so astonished that I immediately cursed my tactics. Had I only increased the figure by ten thousand they would have been satisfied. As it was, they would now cling to that inflated price tag and want to achieve it without adjustment. I also realised that I had never actually stepped over the threshold of Smallwood House and was merely following my silly instinct again. I had always supposed the interior of that house to be

Colefax and Fowlered rather than decorated by courtesy of the High Street DIY store. What if I were wrong?

I arranged to call the following morning, with my agents' paraphernalia. I could see Mrs Williamson still harboured misgivings about my credibility. But Arnie was fairly drooling.

I walked home up the hill (one of the few in Norfolk, thus a standing joke). As I passed Ash and Spicer's, Seth emerged, with a colleague. He was looking self-important and gave me only a cursory grunt. The Ash and Spicer's method acting school had cast its spell. Seth was more receptive than I had realised. He had assimilated the part of tense and single-minded negotiator in a few easy lessons.

The cypress cat was sitting up and taking notice at the front gate. Gathering him into my arms, I chided him for taking a life-threatening position at the kerbside. He purred mightily as I marched him to the front door. We entered the dark hall and proceeded to the equally mournful kitchen. I switched on the light.

I was never sure that I enjoyed a day off. Days off were unplanned spaces in my life, lacking motivation and conducive to depression. Idly, I got down the biscuit tin and nibbled my way through a digestive. The cat looked hurt. So I got out the remains of the chicken and dumped the carcass in front of him. I was rewarded by full cat homage, and the purring and the bone-scrunching continued for a long time.

I deliberated on the unfilled hours ahead. I could do some dusting. Or some baking. Or get out the vacuum cleaner. I sighed. I loved that old mausoleum of mine. It was something tangible left behind from the ruins of my marriage, my settlement from the court proceedings. Yet I lived in it like a lodger. The compulsion to clean it, to maintain it, to cherish it in any way, was missing. Was I just a lazy, promiscuous bitch?

In the end, I decided the garden would be less depressing than the house. The weeds, after the rain, would be easier to lift. I might even get out the Flymo. The old cypress moggie could sit and watch me. I know he ached for a touch a human company during his long listless days. It was flattering to think he preferred me, with my cavalier disregard for his welfare, to the fussy widow two doors up. I changed into something soiled and unattractive and got on my knees wielding my trowel.

I had been concentrating on these unaccustomed labours for some time and was well begrimed when I became aware of someone else in the front garden with me. In some irritation, I looked up expecting to find one of my do-gooding neighbours rattling a collecting box in my direction.

But it was Grover.

And I hadn't changed the sheets.

6

I met Seth on the landing as I was making for the bathroom.
'Can I hear Grover's voice? he asked as he passed.

'He's staying here for a few days,' I explained.

'You're a pushover for thin men, aren't you?' Seth said
disparagingly.

'And you're a pushover for fat slags,' I retorted blithely.

'Juliet and I are going to eat in an amusing little vegetarian place
tonight,' Seth said, 'so you can have your long-lost lover in peace.'

Alone in the bathroom I contemplated my reflection in the
mirror; relaxed, full-lipped, immeasurably content, hair snarled
and rumpled from an afternoon's joyous romping. This had been
a day off to remember. Grover and I had dispensed with the
trivia normal to meeting up with an old friend after a hiatus.
None of this 'How have you been?' and 'What was the journey
like?' stuff for us. Our reunion was much more basic. Upstairs,
clothes off and straight to it on top of the unchanged sheets.
Grover had always been an inconsiderate and single-minded
lover. He hadn't changed over the years. And I wanted him for
this very selfishness, this greedy exploitation of my long-standing
adoration. Every time he reappeared in my bed it provided a
continuity that consoled. Nothing was really altering in the world;
the boy next door was having his wicked way with me again. All
would be well. He would marry me in the end.

When I returned to the bedroom he was sitting in the window
seat, looking down critically on my front garden. 'You're letting
this place go to pot, do you know that?' he said.

'Oh, Grover, don't start,' I pleaded.

'Look at that front garden. It's a bloody eyesore. Surely now you've got that lout living under the same roof the two of you could start licking it back into shape. This old house and garden are the only assets you've got, Holly. You should remember that and treat them with respect. You're not getting any younger.'

'Oh, Grover,' I bleated stupidly, 'don't tell me you think I'm looking older.'

'You haven't changed,' he said grudgingly. 'Take that silly wrap off and let me look at you properly.'

Gladly I pranced before him; I knew I looked winsome with nothing on.

Grover smiled. 'There's always been something of a bordello girl about you, Holly. And now you are approaching middle age perhaps you should think seriously of turning this house to its best advantage. You'd make a first class madam. Few more mirrors around, swags of green velvet here and there. Get the local talent into suspenders, and all the old solicitors would beat a path to your door. Make a packet, Holly, make a packet.'

'Don't be so nasty,' I said sullenly. 'So nasty and so ridiculous.' I snatched a dress out of my wardrobe and slid it on. I had forgotten how easily Grover enraged me.

'Don't be cross now, you silly girl. What I'm saying is said as your friend. It's good fun for you now, Mrs Smith, but the future lies in wait for us all. And one day, my pretty temptress, money is going to be far more important to you than sex. Just make sure you've got some.'

I hated Grover in his financial moods. I knew of old how he could harp on about money. I could have had him make love to me endlessly, but I think he could have taken as much pleasure in a tangle with a calculator.

'You sound as if you're trying to sell me a pension, Grover.' I pushed my feet into some mules and flounced down to the kitchen. I supposed he'd want something to eat now. Of late, Seth had been stocking the fridge with some ready-made meals. I searched through the packages and found a lasagne. Grover had followed me downstairs and now watched me indolently, sprawled in a kitchen chair.

57

'This all right for you?' I asked.

Grover shrugged. 'You're the hostess,' he replied, urbanely.

I wondered if this were a further innuendo about bordellos. 'Hostess' smacked of call-girls and nightclubs.

'So, what's old Seth up to these days?' Grover asked. 'Seems cleaner somehow than when I last saw him. And what's the latest on the ex-husband?'

'The ex-husband is threatening to get married again so Seth's been slung out and sent to the provinces to spoil my life, although,' I conceded, slapping Seth's lasagne into the microwave, 'he's not all bad. Got himself a girlfriend, too. She's been a refining influence.'

Grover whistled. 'A girl of strong character, evidently.'

'And the biggest boobs you've ever seen.'

'Oh, very refined.'

The microwave pinged. I set out two plates while Grover uncorked a bottle of wine.

'Nice, this, Holly. Two old friends together again. Very civilised.'

'Boy and girl next door, don't forget.'

'As if I could. You remind me of that quaint old-fashioned fact every time we meet up.'

'Which isn't often, Grover.' My voice sounded plaintive. He had the knack of reducing me to a whining teenager.

'It's my job, Holly. I can't get away as often as I'd like. And unlike most men of my age group, I've still got a job. I'm lucky. And I intend to stay that way – lucky and ultimately rich.'

I had to ask; I didn't want to, but I had to ask: 'Anyone special in your life now, Grover?'

'No, I'm surprisingly celibate.'

'You're still in good practice for a celibate.'

'Well, Mrs Smith, anyone special in your life?'

I'd better come clean about George, I thought. After all, the dear old boy could come toddling into the house at any moment. 'Well, there's George. But he's not serious, Grover. He's over sixty, with not much hair and not all of his own teeth. And he's married to an immortal wife.'

58

'What makes her more immortal than other wives, pray?'

'A string of life-threatening illnesses that leave her as fit as a flea.'

'Oh, a hypochondriac, you mean. Well, there's a lot of it around. Does she know about you and good old George?'

'I don't think so. No, I'm sure she doesn't. George is pretty careful.'

'It's a small town, Holly, and it's full of small minds. You watch it.'

I pondered on Tinkerstown for a moment. On the whole, I suspected the minds of its inhabitants were much broader than Grover could ever envisage.

'And George is my only rival then?'

My heart started a silly pounding. Was he teasing, only teasing, or did this particular visit have a deeper significance?

'There's my boss, of course,' I admitted. 'He gets a bit fruity now and then. But he's only a mother's boy with a crush. It'll pass.'

'Got money, though, hasn't he?' Grover mused. 'Worth cultivating, Holly. Farmer's son, surely? Must be loaded, those Montgomery's. Parcels of land all over the place.'

'Grover — Jason's at least ten years younger than I am. Strange as it may seem to you, I am scrupulous about cradle-snatching.'

'Yes, it does seem strange to me, actually. I've never had you marked down as a girl with scruples. And you're fourteen years older than Jason by my reckoning. There is the toyboy phenomenon these days, remember. You should be flattered you can pull a young man. And a wealthy young man, too. He must have all the nubile farmers' daughters thirsting for him.'

'Grover you're becoming a money freak. Anyway, Jason's halfway towards being a lush.'

'Ever thought he might be drinking out of sexual frustration? Go on, take him to bed, Holly. Give the guy a break.'

This was not the turn in the conversation for which I yearned and Grover, the rotten sod, knew it perfectly well. Angrily, I splashed the dishes into the sink. Grover came up behind me, putting his long arms around my waist.

'You always did have a bit of a paddy, didn't you? And you are developing a bit of a tummy, girl.'

59

'I'm not getting fat,' I retorted swiftly.

'Did I say you were fat? Just gently rounded. Lovely. My word, good old George doesn't deserve you.'

I dredged up what resolution I could muster and pushed Grover off. 'You won't get round me this way,' I said breathlessly, knowing quite well that he would.

And he did, of course. Which was exactly as I had planned.

Around seven the next morning, I made coffee. I carried the mugs upstairs, accompanied by the cypress cat. It seemed more of a family affair with a pet in tow. I could wallow in the pretence we were an old married couple. Grover was sitting up in the bed, his hands behind his head.

Now that I came to look at him, in comparative calm, I thought he had grown older. He had certainly grown thinner. Always angular, spiked of nose and mean of lip. He was more of a fragile daddy-long-legs than ever he had been years ago.

Struck by foolhardy inspiration, I said abruptly 'Why don't I give a dinner party tonight?'

'Good idea. You can invite George and his immortal wife and young Montgomery and his mummy, then we can all have a laugh, especially if you're doing the cooking.'

'Don't be unfair. I prepared gourmet meals when I was first married.'

'All young wives experiment. It's the novelty. But look at you now, my dear − queen of the microwave. God knows what there will be for breakfast.'

'Don't you worry about breakfast,' I answered, 'I've got that licked these days.'

Once at Tesco, Grover fell easily into animated discussion with Sandy. There was no sign of George, for which, for once, I was grateful; and no sign of Juliet, for which, as always, Seth was demolished. These days Seth had cut down on his full English breakfasts. On the plate in front of him was a piece of toast, unbuttered, and one small green apple.

'The love of a good woman is having its effect, I see,' I said, gaily tucking into sausages and egg.

'Your appetite's improved,' Seth said, moodily eyeing my intake.

'I've got to get my strength back,' I said coquettishly, 'I'm giving a dinner party tonight.'

I had decided on a guest list: Seth and Juliet, Madge and Steve, and Alex and her Mark. For good measure I had included Sandy in the shindig. Poor Sandy always looked skeletal and in great need of nourishment. The family trust allowance wasn't generous.

'Don't forget Juliet's entirely organic,' prompted Seth.

'No flesh, fish or fowl?'

'She will take a little fish sometimes,' Seth said seriously, 'but nothing coarse-textured.'

'Of course not,' I agreed. 'The most delicate of palates, I'm sure. I wonder what makes her so bloody gross then.'

Seth frowned. 'Juliet is not overweight, Holly. She's statuesque. But gross would be your uncouth reaction to a perfection of form you can never hope to attain.'

'You take my breath away sometimes, Seth. Go on, have one of my sausages, you poor sod.'

'Well, I won't refuse,' Seth said hastily, grabbing the banger with relish. 'I've explained to Juliet that it might actually be harmful to my psyche to withdraw too much sustenance too soon. But she insists I reform my diet in order that we may achieve a mutual cleansing before our eventual consummation.'

'Rubbish, Seth. You're already consummating like crazy, if I know you.' I slid the last section of egg into my mouth and, draining my coffee cup, I stood up. 'Must be off. I have an appointment at Smallwood House first thing.'

Seth became agitated. 'Smallwood House – you mean Mrs Williamson's, the one with the iron railings next to the Three Tuns?'

'Yes, I'm taking it on this morning.'

'Is she going multiple?'

'No, I believe she intends to cancel her contract with Ash and Spicer and let us handle the sale.'

'That's not fair. What have you lot at Montgomery's been up to? She doesn't like Jason's approach, she told us so.'

61

'There's nothing underhand going on. She's being advised by her cousin now and he isn't impressed by Ash and Spicer, I'm afraid.'

'She wants to check her contract with us very carefully.' Seth said in a flurry of executive spleen. 'Anyway, it won't do Montgomery's any good to have that house. It's vastly overpriced.'

'Thank you for your informed opinion, Seth. How long have you been in the estate agency business – a month?'

'I've learned a lot,' retorted Seth. A spirit of unhealthy rivalry had already shaken him by the throat. Was it the influence of the Ash and Spicer method school, or Juliet, or traces of both? I had known Seth as a man of sloth, but never of hostility.

I was lost in undermining doubt as I walked across the town; no point in taking the company car to Smallwood House, sitting, as it was, in yellow line territory. Overpriced, and its interior a question mark; had I put my sexy feet in it this time? Yet there it stood, four-square and beckoning; primly imposing behind its protective railings. It looked reassuringly middle class and of distinct appeal to an up-and-coming orthodontist, perhaps, or someone with aspirations towards an acceptably fringe occupation – aromatherapy, reflexology? In my mind I could see the brass plate affixed beside the green-glossed front door whose knocker I now lifted with a lighter heart.

At the sound of my imperious rapping there came a crescendo of barking from Buster. Mrs Williamson, flustered, opened the door to me, bent double over her yap dog and hanging on to his (tartan) collar with one bejewelled hand.

'Scotties are so boisterous,' she panted. 'But such good little guard dogs. Go on into the sitting room, Mrs Smith – there on your left. I'll put Buster into the conservatory for a few minutes. He's got his toys in there.'

I had seen enough in the hallway to quell my incipient misgivings; it was going to be Colefax and Fowler all the way. The sitting room was divided by an arch and I wandered through towards the bay window at the end, which provided a view of the rear walled garden. It was true from this window one caught a hint of Mrs Williamson's neighbour but, again, the Three Tuns had been given a facelift from the brewery in recent months and looked quite wholesome with its florid hanging baskets. I wondered if its more bizarre clientele had been persuaded to move elsewhere for their ulterior trafficking.

'The public house isn't the problem people think it is,' said Mrs Williamson defensively. She had come into the room and now stood beside me. 'In any case, my garden has been landscaped to distract the eye from any possible crudities next door.'

'Oh jolly good,' I said. 'But the old pub doesn't look bad to me.'

'I could be living next to something far worse on the other side of that wall,' agreed Mrs Williamson. 'One has to put up with a cheek-by-jowl existence in a town. Take my nice piece of land, for instance. One day that open space will be covered with little houses, so I can't resent a town environment too much, can I? And at least I don't have to watch other people's washing dangling about on a line. The pub uses a laundry service, of course.'

'I hadn't thought of that aspect.' I said absently, wondering whether the famous land was about to fall towards Montgomery's as well. Jason will be offering me a partnership at this rate, I thought, and if I possessed any ambition at all it was to be publicly acknowledged as more than just 'the woman in the office', more than just a hand hired for her leg appeal. But I guessed I had Arnie to thank for this potential plum so my legs had already played their part. So where was Arnie?

'Is Mr Pearson going to join us?' I asked.

'My cousin has gone up to London for the day,' Mrs Williamson said, reddening at his name. 'He has so many business interests, such a busy man. Now do let me show you around, and perhaps you might care to stay for coffee?'

I was enchanted by the house. Even given money and a free hand I could not have made so apt a choice of decoration. I kept exclaiming and cooing as we tripped about, and my 'I love this fabric' or 'what fabulous wallpaper' kept Mrs Williamson smiling throughout the tour.

We came finally to the kitchen, and from the bespoke domed cabinets, painted by a little man she knew of, to the marble worktops to the dark green Aga, I lusted after that kitchen. It

63

may have dawned on me then that Grover's obsession with money wasn't an idiosyncrasy, wasn't an attitude with which to ignite my temper. Grover was right. Before I could stop myself I had turned to Mrs Williamson and cried out like a prophet who has seen a holy vision: 'Money *is* more worthwhile than sex.'

This electrified Mrs Williamson. 'Oh no it's not. Give me sex any day.' Her voice was raised in protest. 'I've had money all my life and I know which I prefer.' Then, beetroot to all exposed parts, she took my arm. 'Mrs Smith, I wonder if – I mean you seem the sort of woman –'

I put her out of her misery. 'Do you want to tell me about Arnie?'

'I'll make coffee first,' she volunteered. 'And if we're to get to know each other for a discourse of such intimacy, you'd better call me Dottie. And I shall call you Holly, of course. But only when there's no one else present, you understand.'

As I watched Dottie dapping about her divine kitchen, warming her scones in the top oven of that dark green Aga (the second I had seen that week: was my nose to be rubbed in dark green Agas wherever I went?) and filling the cafetière from the dark green kettle. I decided to revise the impression I had always loosely held of the lady. She was trim, conventionally but expensively dressed and well jewelled. Her white hair was not the usual Women's Institute topping – all puff and no substance – but was coiled, sleek as a model's, around a head of elegant shape above a neck that had not suffered the ravages normal to ladies of uncertain age. Now that I had taken the trouble to make this in-depth appraisal, I saw that Mrs Willamson was not to be dismissed as well preserved but menopausally on the shelf and that she had much more to offer than a decently baked scone.

'Let's stay in the kitchen, shall we, Holly? More conducive to girls' talk. Oh and do you mind if I let Buster back in? He does so love to share elevenses with his mummy.'

Buster tore into the room snarling at my unconfined toes.

'He'll settle down in a minute,' said Dottie, unconcerned about where his molars might rest. 'Milk and sugar?'

'Black, please. And Dottie, tell me the truth. Arnie isn't really your cousin, is he?'

'Oh good heavens no. I got him out of a newspaper.'

'Not the personal columns? Massage and fun-loving and all that?'

'Of course. All the best class of daily carry these advertisements now. It's quite above board. So sensible too, I think, although you have to sift through a lot of twiddle about people being country loving and theatregoers. I made it quite clear to Arnold from the beginning that I wasn't prepared to go on long nature rambles even with Buster, that plays made me fidgety and that I thought opera was lunatic. No point in preambles or niceties when you're knocking on. So I got on to my back within fifteen minutes of our introduction, and if he hadn't performed I'd have shown him the door. Do have another scone.'

Without considering my rounding stomach, I accepted.

'So comforting for me to talk to a woman friend like this,' Dottie went on. 'I knew I wouldn't shock you, Holly. I expect you're always on top of that rent table with Mr Montgomery. That's quite a valuable old piece, by the way. Family heirloom, I suppose? I admired its patina the other day.'

'You are quite wrong, Dottie. There's nothing going on between Jason and myself. I only work for the man.'

'Oh but I quite thought that your appearance at the Suckling Pig betrayed a deeper involvement. That hostelry has a reputation as a trysting place for lovers with urgent requirements, you know. The management is very broad-minded. And Mr Montgomery, is obviously enamoured of you. But if you wish to play hard to get I'm sure you know what you're doing. The man's a definite catch, my dear. And if money does mean more than sex to you, then I admire your single-mindedness. The man looks an absolute stud to me even if he is a jackass and incredibly rude. But if you can get him to the altar you'll have all the money you desire and plenty of sex too. What a prospect. I do admire your skill.'

'I don't aspire to Jason, Dottie, believe me. He gives me the horrors.'

Dottie gazed at me with approbation. 'Clever, clever. Keep everyone guessing and Mr Montgomery at fever pitch. That's the way to get your cake and eat it. I married for money at around your age, you know. It was a late marriage, of course, and there were never any children. Just as well as there was never any sex either, moribund little man Alfred Williamson. I was *thrilled* when I was widowed.'

If Dottie's reminiscences were the route to the land with outline planning permission for 60 detached dwellings, then I was happy to encourage our newly founded friendship. Other agents had failed before me but they had never turned the simple key of nooky.

'I'm so delighted we've had this opportunity to get to know one another better, Dottie,' I said. 'It makes all the difference putting a friendly hat on to our clients.'

'And it's a positive relief for me to discuss my current situation with a chum who's sexually active herself. I can't talk to my contemporaries any more. They'd think I was deranged. They are all obsessional grannies, you see.' Dottie leaned across the kitchen table and clutched my hand. 'You wouldn't happen to know any extra *tricks* would you? To keep Arnold amused. He's got a roving eye – even I can sense that.'

'I'm not a circus seal, Dottie. I don't think I know any actual tricks. But I would be grateful for your advice.'

Dottie tensed in expectation. I knew I was going to disappoint her. There she was all eager to unfurl her umbrella of bedroom experience and all I wanted was some culinary counselling.

'I've got a dinner party tonight and I'm out of touch on appetising dishes. When my marriage ended I chucked out my cookery books and bought a microwave.'

'Oh, my dear, a great mistake. Men can't do their stuff on empty stomachs.' Dottie rose and went across to a drawer. 'I'll lend you my old Fanny Craddock,' she said, 'and my fish kettle, too. Do a whole salmon – so easy. Serve it cold with a salad or two but get the dressings right. As for dessert, well, I wouldn't attempt anything elaborate yourself. Much better to buy something ready-made from Tesco'.

After this exchange it transpired that our sexual disclosures were at an end. Dottie became Mrs Williamson once more and property matters took over. I measured, I photographed, I discussed contracts. In the end I persuaded her to keep on Ash and Spicer as well but to tell them to put the price up to meet that of my valuation. A house could not be offered at two different prices. The constantly changing legislation had reduced what had once been a gentlemanly arrangement between vendor and agent into a minefield over which seller, purchaser and agent had to pass. No wonder the exercise brought so many innocents to breaking point.

When I left Smallwood House nothing further had been said about the parcel of land, but if I could keep Dottie content on unseemly tittle-tattle, then those prime instructions were within my reach. But for now, like Dottie herself, I would have to put sex first. Grover was still with me.

Grover had put his orderly regime to the test that day. When I got back from Montgomery's that evening – released early for what lay ahead – I found he had applied a scorched-earth policy to the garden, which looked cropped; and a sanitising programme to the house, which looked pristine.

'Oh Grover,' I cried, kissing him in delight. 'You're a wizard. Marry me immediately and let's live happily ever after in a nice clean house in a nice neat garden.'

I had forgotten how gruelling polite entertaining could be. There was suddenly so much to do and and to be done in so many directions at once. Timing was crucial. Just laying the table brought me out in a sweat of anxiety. I found one of my grandmother's white damask tablecloths and spread it across the gateleg in the dining room. This room was not often entered, let alone used formally. It smelled musty, confirming my suspicions about rampant rising damp. I discovered then that my best silver cutlery (a wedding present that rarely saw the light of day) was tarnished with verdigris to the point where it was imperative to remove it, so I ran into the scullery and started frenziedly polishing the place settings.

It was then that the salmon bubbled over in its kettle, sending the scaly water swooshing about on the cooker top. The kitchen already looked like a battlefield anyway; packets fully opened here and packets nearly opened there, the sink overflowing with unwashed lettuces of several varieties alongside a gathering collection of dirty crocks.

Through it all Grover remained aggravatingly efficient and I feared his disapproval at my trail of chaos.

Seth's advent could have been a blessing if he hadn't dropped the saucepan of newly scraped potatoes all over the kitchen floor tiles. But by far the most agonizing catastrophe was that I had decanted a defrosted package of king-size pawns into a glass dish and forgotten to put the dish into the fridge; Seth then surprised the cypress cat feasting blissfully on this unexpected crustacean windfall.

'Oh God – what can I give them for starters now?' I screamed.

'Don't panic so, Holly,' Grover said calmly. 'I'll run down to Tesco and buy some melons.'

'But melon is so *boring.* I wanted prawn cocktails. My dinner party has got to be sophisticated.'

'Prawn cocktails are naff, Holly, not sophisticated. You've spent too much time in the Suckling Pig. I fear. It's warped your sense of the adventurous.'

'There's nothing adventurous about a melon,' I snapped.

'Depends on what you do with the melon, I guess.' For a minute Grover had me wondering if melon had assumed some aphrodisiac recreational status of which I was unaware. Dottie would have known for sure if it had, but I was in the dark.

'Don't look so worried, Holly.' Grover pecked my cheek. 'It's all going to be splendid. Keep faith. None of us is expecting a miracle from you. It's the company that's the fascination, not the food. For instance, I can't wait to meet Juliet.'

Seth glowered at me when Grover had gone whistling down the passage. 'What did he mean by that?'

'How should I know,' I answered crossly.

'If he thinks he's going to get into Juliet's knickers this evening, he's in for a shock,' Seth said darkly.

'Don't be such an oaf, Seth. It's not going to be that sort of a party. And I want you to keep your hands off Juliet for once. You're like a bloody pair of Siamese twins whenever you're together.'

To my relief Seth ambled off upstairs, presumably to continue the executive-about-town routine and change for dinner.

By the time the guests were due I was on the edge of collapse. In the bedroom I put on something floating, short on length and with a very low cleavage. My newly blonded hair I pushed behind into a large clip. 'How do I look?' I asked Grover.

'Bare, but enticing,' he answered. He was standing in front of the cheval mirror brushing his thick brown hair, not yet sullied by the greying strands of age. As always he was freshly scrubbed, his wand-like body at that moment completely unclothed, taunting me yet again with his boy-next-door appeal, an appeal that refused to be exorcised through the years.

Downstairs Alex and her Mark had arrived and Seth was pouring out wine for them on the terrace, where Grover had placed my few tatty deckchairs and an old wooden table, bedizened for the occasion by a bright gingham cloth. Seth looked at me glumly.

'The cat's sicked up those prawns all over the dinner table. Bit of a mess.'

'Who left the dining room door open?' I cried wildly.

'You did,' said Seth.

Wearily I stripped the dining table, divesting it of tablecloth, napkins, silver and cursing the culprit in the most disgusting epithets at my command.

'Gosh Holly,' said Sandy materialising in the doorway, 'does this mean the party's off?'

'Bloody cat,' I yelled. 'Just fouled up my place settings.'

'Nice little fellow, though. I've been stroking him.'

'You should have kicked him under a passing bus not made a fuss of the little bugger,' I said viciously. 'He's not even my cat.'

Back in the kitchen another appalling possibility struck home. 'Oh God. I think I've forgotten to defrost the raspberry pavlova.'

'It's all right', said Grover comfortingly, 'I defrosted your pavlova. Now buck up, darling, and go and talk to Alex. I've got everything in hand – just leave it to me.'

I had had, by this point in the fraught preparations, recourse to the gin bottle several times and all the action was now pleasantly fuzzy. Grateful for kitchen parole at last, I flopped beside Alex in the cool shade that was dappling the terrace.

'Have I got things to tell you,' I began. Not having had an opportunity to gossip with my surrogate sister during the day, I was now bursting to amaze her. 'Dottie got Arnie out of a classified ad.'

'You mean he's not a kosher cousin?'

I shook my head. 'And she turns out to be sex-mad at sixty-something. We had already guessed that Arnie had bonking on the brain but I got a shock when I learned that the respectable widow Williamson can't get enough of it.'

'Holly – stop telling me such fibs. You know geriatrics can't manage it any more. It's all in Dottie's mind, must be. The only male she'll be taking to bed with her is Buster.

At that moment Juliet, mountainous Juliet, came heaving forward, her acolytes, Madge and Steve, in devoted attendance. This procession must have impressed even Grover, for there he was hovering like a daddy-long-legs in the background, having briefly forsaken his kitchen duties. As for Seth, poor besotted sod, his passions aroused, his wine pouring had become so erratic that most of the golden liquid was spilling and pooling outside the glasses.

I had to bestow full marks on Juliet for impact. She was dressed in a cream-coloured muslin outfit, Indian in concept but scant on beading and embroidery. She wore Balouchi-style pantaloons and over this a voluminous tent the neck of which she must have cut out and adapted herself to rivet all attention upon the preponderance of bosom. Her long dark hair she had twisted into some form of top-heavy bun, and this bounced gently in rhythm with the inordinate swell of loosely confined breasts. The effect was to distract and titillate; an unfair advantage, I thought, as most eyes were mesmerised by these giants for the remainder of the evening. Conversations were disjointed and there were pauses and stoppages in mid-sentence to accompany Juliet's slightest movements.

At the dinner table Alex was reduced to intermittent giggling; Steve was embarrassed and uneasy; Sandy, on the other hand, was the only guest who was impervious to Juliet's etceteras and he held forth frequently on the topic so dear to his literary heart. But it was Grover's pulse I endeavoured to put my finger on. His eyes twinkled a lot, I noticed, and he put himself about a little too assiduously for my liking. This may have been to infuriate Seth, of course. Seth, at my insistence, was sitting as far away from the girl of his dreams as the table would allow. It was not

Seth's evening so far. Juliet was unquestionably taken by Grover. Grover, slimline Grover in his jaunty bow tie, was at his sexiest. I could have killed the bastard.

In the excitement Juliet had not forgotten to be organic, however. Faced with the salmon, she had asked, huskily, 'Not farmed, I hope?' I think that was the very first time I had ever heard the bitch speak.

'No, no it's wild,' I invented. 'Straight from the tumbling waters of the Spey.'

'That's right, Juliet,' Grover said, backing up my deceit. 'I have a friend who owns the fishing rights on the left bank. He chartered a plane to get it here to us today. Post-haste.'

Sandy raised his fork happily. 'I am reminded of Queen Victoria when someone mentions Scotland. Did you know she was illegitimate, by the way? Had no right to the throne at all.'

'I gather you're a budding Picasso, Juliet,' said Grover. 'Some mayonnaise for your salmon? I made it myself. Sunflower oil, naturally.'

Juliet corrected him with Madonna sweetness. 'I owe nothing to Pablo. My style is strictly my own, Grover. You must come up to my studio when I'm finally in there. I would love you to evaluate my canvases.'

'Queen Victoria used to sketch,' Sandy announced. 'Some of her water-colours are really quite appealing. Pity about her antecedents, though. Rather makes the House of Windsor a bit of a sham, don't you think?

'I love the dear Queen Mum, Sandy,' said Madge loyally. 'I won't have a word said against her, mind.'

'Alas, Juliet,' said Grover with mock sorrow, 'much as I would like to see more of your work, I don't live here. I'm off again on my travels in a day or two.'

'Then I must contrive a viewing before you go.' said Juliet.

'A preview? I am honoured.'

'More like a private view,' I chipped in acidly.

Seth choked. At that moment the telephone shrilled from the kitchen.

'Oh hell,' I cried. 'Mother and her bloody numbers, I suppose.'

'I'll go,' said Seth, lumbering to his feet.

71

'Wasn't Queen Victoria's son Jack the Ripper?' asked Steve.

'I always thought Queen Victoria was Jack the Ripper,' said Grover flippantly.

'I use oils a lot,' Juliet continued undeflected. 'My method is to rub with my fingers to get the right effect.'

Feeling it was time he made a contribution, Alex's Mark said, 'Didn't Queen Victoria go down on the *Titanic*?'

'No, Jack the Ripper went down on the *Titanic*,' explained Grover. 'He was actually an American serial killer.'

'It wasn't the *Titanic* that sank, you know,' Sandy said. 'It was her sister ship. The whole thing was an insurance scam.'

Seth returned to the room and announced rapturously, 'It wasn't Granny on the phone. It was Dad. He and Philly are getting married next week and I'm invited. And Dad says –' here Seth's gaze fell adoringly on to Juliet – 'that I can bring my beloved Juliet along as well. It'll be a super affair. Morning suits, of course, marquee, a sit-down job not a lousy buffet. Philly's parents are loaded.'

The Madonna features offered a response of faint boredom, but Madge piped, 'Oh it'll be lovely for you, Juliet dear. And think of the publicity being seen in the right places. You could get your photograph in *Hello*.'

'That's right', said Seth. 'Up-and-coming young painter attends famous musician's reception on the occasion of his third marriage.'

I could not let that one pass. 'Famous musician?' I snarled. 'He's a drunken freelance saxophonist who's been chucked out of every orchestra in Europe for his bum notes.'

'Philly's taken Dad's drink problem in hand,' Seth said coldly. 'And it was probably living with you that caused his boozing in the first place.'

'Didn't Queen Victoria have a drink problem?' Steve asked.

'No, it was Jack the Ripper,' said Alex's Mark. 'How else could he have disembowelled all those floozies if he hadn't been stoned out of his skull?'

'Poor young girls, cutting them up like that,' said Madge.

'They weren't young girls, Madge,' said Sandy patiently. 'They were middle-aged and of loose morality.'

'Just like Holly,' said Seth.

'I wish I hadn't given this bloody party,' I screamed.

Afterwards, when the guests had repaired to their lairs replete with wine, raspberry pavlova and bloodthirsty relevations, Grover and I were at last alone – in the kitchen, with the wreckage. Seth had insisted on seeing Juliet, heavily chaperoned by Madge and Steve, back to Rose Cottage.

'That's the last time I ever entertain.' I said, trembling with fatigue and fury, 'It was a shambles from start to finish.'

'Don't exaggerate,' said Grover. 'it was an enormous success, really it was. I, for one, found it all riveting, especially Seth's fat friend. What a gal.'

'I could see you were smitten. And so could Seth.'

'Holly – please get your facts right. Juliet was smitten with *me*, not I with her. She's far too prominent a citizen for my retiring nature. Did you know she made a pass at me on the landing after dinner?'

'What were you doing with her on the landing?'

'I wasn't doing anything with her,' protested Grover with dignity. 'I'd gone up for a very necessary pee and when I came out of the lavatory that mammoth mantrap was lying in wait for me.'

'You aren't winding me up, are you, Grover?'

'Cross my heart. There the damsel stood, leaning nonchalantly against your tallboy. She shook poor old Gummidge to his furry soul and she seriously impaired my blood pressure. She had doffed that curious garment of hers and those fabled boobs were indecently exposed. God, they are a lethal pair, Holly.'

I felt faint. 'What happened? Oh nothing did happen, did it, Grover?'

'Holly, I may not be a perfect gentleman, but I do try to be a perfect house guest. Would I insult your hospitality with other than your charming self by indulging in a quick bang in the upstairs corridor? My refusal was blunt and to the point: put it all away, darling, I said, it doesn't turn me on. My God, she was angry. She cast unsavoury aspersions on my masculinity, I can tell you. It was very hurtful and, of course, totally untrue. But,' Grover continued rather more seriously, 'she's a dangerous

73

nympho, Holly. I hope Seth can appreciate he's merely a sacrificial lamb to her slaughter. Her advent in this town will end in tears. Mark the words of the Prophet Grover.'

'Oh, I don't care about Seth. He's a silly fool. He'll have to look after himself. I'm worried about Madge and Steve. She's taking them for a ride, Grover. All this nonsense about her being an artist. You should see her awful daubs.'

'I can imagine. But if she wields her paintbrush like she wields her boobs, then the results might well be formidable, so she might make some money. You can actually fool most of the people most of the time. If the patter's good enough, the product doesn't matter that much.' Grover looked beyond me into his own cash-absorbed distance. 'Yes, on balance, I fear that over-endowed young woman is going to make a pile along the way.'

'Back to money again, Grover. You really are a walking piggy bank.'

'Don't scoff, Holly. Incidentally, your tallboy is worth a mint, even on the depressed antiques market. Cash in, girl. It's not doing you any favours standing on your landing.'

I reached up and kissed my boy next door. 'I'm very relieved to know you didn't do Juliet any favours on the landing,' I whispered. 'So how about doing me one now?'

'I thought you were too exhausted?'

'Try me.'

So he did.

7

Grover was packing his bag. Grover was leaving. The week he had just spent in the mausoleum with me had been a comfortable one, a contented one. He loved me, at times with a rapt concentration that seemed as desperate as avarice.

I sat on the edge of the bed like a discarded piece of clothing and watched him fill his holdall, neatly, methodically, until all trace of his presence was zipped away inside the canvas bag, the anonymous canvas bag. And very soon, I supposed, Grover would merge into the London crowds at the other end of the railway line and become an anonymous man.

He glanced at me quizzically. 'No need to be so tragic, Holly. I'll be back again one of these days. I promise you, I'll never disappear without an explanation.'

'You don't even leave me an address,' I said plaintively. 'I'd give anything to write to you now and then. You always seem so *obliterated* the minute you are out of my sight. Why can't you tell me where to contact you? Anyone would think you were going straight from here into a cell in a top-security prison.'

Grover laughed. 'Don't tell anyone, Holly, but I'm the man from MI5.'

'You are just as stupidly cloak-and-dagger. I can't understand it. We've known each other all these years.' I felt cheated and cheapened suddenly. 'I feel such a fool when people ask me how you are. *Where* you are.'

'I am not the pawn of nosy people, Holly. Anyway, the answer is simple. I am travelling. A roving commission, as they say. I like to be unencumbered. And it's not as if I forget you, you silly girl. I think of you a lot when I'm by myself in some strange town in some strange country.'

He put his holdall over his shoulder and made for the bedroom door. I followed him, pattering along the landing like some faithful pet spaniel. Gummidge, from his vantage point on top of the tallboy, gazed on impassively. He had seen Grover come and go on many occasions. At the top of the stairs Grover turned, fingering the mahogany handrail. 'Now Holly, think about what I've been saying to you. I know you feel I place too much emphasis on getting money, but you really ought to give more attention to your financial future.'

I could have murdered him. I wanted to hear words of endearment, words of passion, not another homily on fiscal security. Was he so insensitive to the intensity of my adulation where he was concerned?

He went on down the stairs, light and lithe and casual. I ran barefoot after him, crying, 'It'll serve you right if you come here one day and find I've gone and married someone else.'

He bent over and kissed me. 'If you marry a man with a substantial background, like your Jason, then I will be delighted for you. Indeed,' Grover continued, opening the front door and stepping out to the gravelled pathway. 'the more I consider your position the more I fancy a farming connection for you. Old money, Holly, believe me, you can't beat it. Goodbye, my darling. Take care.'

I ran after him, the gravel digging into the bare soles of my feet, but I didn't heed it. 'Sod off,' I yelled. 'Sod off and don't ever come back again.'

Grover turned, his eyes merry. 'Dearest one,' he said softly, 'you can be had up for standing in your front garden stark naked on a Sabbath afternoon. Bad example for the Sunday school kids. For shame, Mrs Smith. Go indoors this minute and recover your equilibrium.'

I ran back, slamming the front door behind me, whereupon a large piece of ornamental plaster dropped off the cornice. I sat down on the bottom stair, hugging my knees. Tears were very close, but they refused to fall. The cypress cat appeared alongside, mewing for attention. So we sat together until the afternoon sun had ceased to filter through the stained-glass fanlight. I imagined Grover striding across Tinkerstown on his way to the railway station (he had not hired a car on this visit as he sometimes did). There on the down platform he would board an InterCity connection en route to somewhere I knew not of, and at this moment cared not about.

I was glad of the company of the cypress cat. Without Grover I felt strangely vulnerable, full of presentiment and lost illusions. Seth was out, naturally, doing some consummating with Juliet. Rose Cottage was completing the next day, and Madge and Steve were spending their last hours at Garbage Green alone together, mulling over 20 years of sentimental memories.

I was just considering whether to dress or just get into bed with the gin bottle when the key rattled in the front door and my bit of rough stepped inside. Seeing my winsome nudity, he raised his eyebrows and grinned in ill-concealed anticipation.

It was not usual for George to be available at the weekend and I had heard on the breakfast grapevine that Immortal Ivy's sister was staying with them. I therefore assumed drives out to coastal cafés for cream teas were taking precedence over George's more rudimental inclinations.

'Oh George,' I cried, falling into his ready embrace, 'it's so lovely to see you again.'

'It's lovely to see *you* again,' he said gloatingly. 'All of you, too.'

'I have missed you,' I lied, and burst into the long-overdue tears.

'Georgie Porgie Pudden and Pie,' crooned George in my ear, 'kissed the girls and made 'em cry. Have I made you cry, Holly? Or is it some other fellow?'

I didn't reply. I knew George was aware of Grover's visit. I knew also that Grover had met George one morning at Tesco when I had left the cafeteria for the office, because Grover had told me. Told me, additionally, that he didn't think George was quite my sort. I had had no idea that Grover fostered any unfashionable snobbery of that kind.

'Were you just on your way to bed?' asked George hopefully.

'I thought I'd take the gin bottle with me. Couldn't think of anything else to do on a dull Sunday evening.'

'I can think of something else to do,' said George.

At breakfast at Tesco's next morning, Sandy said: 'I gather it's all hands to the deck up at Chapel Street today.'

I had joined him and Mrs Angelicus at the table they were sharing. Seth had taken the day off to assist with the removal; likewise George had promised to lend assistance with his tool kit. Selfishly, I was determined to keep myself distanced from the uproar. Moving days were stressful anyway without the involvement of Madge's seven cats dispossessed of their rabbit-filled meadow.

'Your mother,' said Mrs Angelicus to me, 'is very anxious about her Lottery numbers, dear. She tells me she tried to ring you last night but got no reply.'

George and I had been too absorbed to answer the telephone.

'My mother's paranoid about those numbers but the old fool will never win anything.'

Mrs Angelicus smiled. Was she a genuinely saintly woman, I wondered, or just a smug Goody Two-Shoes? I could never make up my mind.

'Oh, come now, dear. You know you love your mother very much.'

'No, I do not love my mother, Mrs Angelicus. It's not compulsory to do so, you know.'

'Many mothers are monsters, of course,' Sandy mused. 'Take Queen Victoria, for example. The hand that rocks the cradle and all that. Had no concept of child psychology at all. And being born under Gemini didn't help. Think of Marilyn Monroe – another ill-starred child of the Twins.'

'I am born under Gemini,' I said, aggrieved.

'I am pretty certain in my own mind,' Sandy continued, 'that Queen Victoria did enjoy a lewd relationship with the ghillie John Brown in her later years.'

Mrs Angelicus admonished Sandy gently. 'Queen Victoria and Marilyn Monroe are a rather far-fetched connection, dear, but if you put them together in a book I am sure it would be a best-seller.'

'I didn't claim an actual connection,' answered Sandy, 'but I might study the relevant family trees more closely. It's amazing what links such a source can reveal. And these Americans all carry genetic threads from Europe. I'll start on the wrong side of the blanket – that's usually a rewarding path.' He looked thoughtfully at his buttered toast. 'Best-seller, eh?'

'Well, as long as one of the breakfast gang makes some money in the end, any rewarding path will do,' I said, my mind still full of Grover's propaganda.

'Talking of money,' said Mrs Angelicus, 'did you hear that George's wife Ivy has had a little bit of luck?'

'Don't tell me *she's* won the Lottery,' I said furiously.

'No, dear,' replied Mrs Angelicus. 'Her uncle left her a small house in Romford. A modest enough legacy but so useful in these straitened times.'

Crafty George hadn't disclosed that to me last night, but, then, modest legacies had not been on his mind at the time. Had Grover finally sown a financial seed in my subconscious? What with my ex-husband marrying loaded Philly, and now Immortal Ivy inheriting the proceeds of a small house in Romford, not to mention builder Ned's ability to purchase Rose Cottage from some nefarious source, was mine the only face to be ground when all around me were up to their necks in gratuitously acquired banknotes? My poverty insulted me again. I stood up.

Mrs Angelicus' steely righteousness struck: 'Don't forget your dear mother, now.'

'If only I could,' I replied tartly.

I turned to leave the cafeteria, but Mrs Angelicus, showing sublime faith in my ultimate conversion to mother-worship, called sweetly, 'You don't mean that, Holly. You'll be devastated when she goes.'

'I wish,' I said bitterly to Alex as I stalked into the office, 'that people would stop ramming the sacred cow of motherhood down my throat.'

'You're in a bad mood,' observed Alex, intent upon her word processing.

'I'm fed up.'

'I won't ask about Grover, and I won't ask about George.'

'Good. If there's nothing special happening here then I'm going over to the park to unwind.'

'Push off then,' said Alex. 'You're far from indispensable, Mrs Smith.'

It was August, humid August, and a midpoint in that marathon summer of drought and despairing water boards. The grass was brown and balding, the leaves listless and stilled. These were indeed dog days. Moving house was the last thing on anyone's mind. No one paused to gaze either longingly or derisorily at the properties in our windows: the telephone was silent; instructions, like most of the ponds in the area, had dried up altogether.

Jason was away on holiday — with Mummy. They had gone to somewhere exotic, to judge from the palm trees on the one postcard I had received, a postcard couched in sexually disgusting terms.

I flopped down on the cracking turf beneath a chestnut tree. Around me children played fitfully on the swings, the slides, the roundabouts, their squealing becoming fainter as I suspended my consciousness. Gradually my tetchiness dissolved and, later on, in that long, lost Monday morning, I sauntered across to an ice cream vendor and bought myself something sickly in a cone. After this I felt capable of facing the confusion reigning at number two Chapel Villas and wandered off there to investigate.

The removal vans were still parked in the road outside the house and Seth was squatting, begrimed and weary, on the stone wall of the front garden. He groaned as I approached. 'Do you think I could get a heart attack at twenty-five?'

'You look awful,' I assured him gaily and, stepping over the stacked cardboard cases in the hall, thrust my way as far as the kitchen at the rear of the villa. Here I found Steve, in similar disarray, sleeves rolled up, sweating dismally. I could see deflation had set in. He and Madge had been so buoyant, so confident, about what they had undertaken, but there was nothing like an actual moving day to bring home to new house-owners just exactly what they had let themselves in for.

'I only hope,' said Steve, 'that this has been worth the effort. We've only done it for Juliet's sake.'

'I know that,' I said grimly. 'Where is my dear old Madgey?'

'Upstairs. She's fine though, Holly. Ever so happy.'

I struggled up the stairs, pushing between a couple of removal men. I found Madge sitting on the edge of a bed that had just been reassembled. But she was not ever so happy. She was crying. I sat down beside her and pulled her into my arms.

'It's all right, Holly. I'm only tired, that's all.'

'Moving days are always a strain,' I said lamely. 'You begin to wonder why ever you left the house you had. But this house will seem like home before long, don't worry.'

'I want to go back to Rose Cottage,' Madge bawled. 'I don't want to live here. And neither do the cats.'

I felt suddenly ineffectual. My platitudes would be to no avail. I, too, wished they had never left Rose Cottage; that crumbing old hovel fitted them to perfection. I was even beginning to miss the stench of pigs that had become my invariable association with the couple. I stroked Madge's grey head, but I was no good coping with grief like hers. Presently she raised her poor, puffy little face.

'It *will* work won't it, Holly?' she pleaded. 'The exhibitions, I mean?'

'Oh, I'm sure it will. Grover thinks Juliet will make a fortune once she gets going.'

'That's all that matters then,' Madge said. 'It's Juliet's happiness that counts. The old should always make sacrifices for the young. It's only fair.'

'Where is the lovely Juliet now? I asked, my dislike for the fat slag mounting.

'She's checking her canvases in her studio. We told her not to tire herself out – and of course she has to protect her hands.'

'Why? What's so special about her hands?'

'Well, they are very sensitive and she uses them in unusual ways. Her oil technique, she calls it.'

I had my own ideas about Juliet's oil techniques. Leaving weepy Madge, I decided to thrash my way to the stable studio. An overspill of packing cases was now evident in the garden, while a recumbent removal man was taking a nap against the fence. The stable was empty but from the loft above came the unmistakable sounds of consummation. Were Seth and Juliet at it amid all the chaos? Although by nature a participant, not a

81

voyeur, I climbed halfway up the loft ladder until I caught a glimpse of the action. It was Juliet all right, but not partnered by Seth. She was riding some hapless male like an avenging Valkyrie. I supposed such chores were all in a day's work to a removal man.

I realised retreat was politic – the sight of the artist at work, although uplifting in the strictly technical sense, was not instructive in any other way, and it occurred to me that Madge should be protected from Juliet's zealous antics. I sought Steve urgently. He was now unwrapping the kitchen utensils.

'Steve,' I said quickly, 'Juliet doesn't wish to be disturbed for a bit. Just in case Madgey thinks she ought to give her a hand.'

'Oh thanks, Holly. I know Juliet is a funny, solitary sort of girl. Artistic temperament, I suppose. She's always shutting herself away from us. I think she shuns human contact, sometimes.'

'That's not good for her, though,' I said impishly. 'I think you should send Seth up to the studio at once. Bring her out of her reverie.'

'Poor old Seth's knackered, I'm afraid.' said Steve. 'He can hardly help himself at this moment. He was up in the studio with Juliet all the morning and came back looking done in. Some of her canvases are really heavy to shift, you know.'

8

A couple of evenings later I had the classic opportunity of a tête-à-tête with Seth. He was in the bath and could not easily escape my interrogation.

'I wish you wouldn't barge in on me like this,' he complained, as I settled on the bathroom stool. 'You getting frustrated since Grover went off?'

'I want nothing more from you, Seth, believe, me, than a little light conversation. And a conversation that will be dear to your heart.'

'That means you're going to say something bloody-minded about Juliet. You are so jealous of her that it's positively sick. Yours is the typical reaction of the ageing woman. Do you know that?'

'I am sure you are right, Seth,' I said gravely. 'You've matured so much since joining Ash and Spicer. And, when you take your beauteous Juliet to my ex's nuptials on Saturday, everyone will be amazed at the transformation in you.'

'Cut the crap. What are you after?'

'I'm after giving you a word of a stepmotherly advice, that's all.'

'Anyone wanting your advice would have to be senile. Now leave me alone. I want to wash my privates.

'My advice could well concern those parts of your anatomy that are forever out of bounds to me.'

Seth started splashing wildly. 'If it's about me and Juliet, you can mind your own bloody business. She's over age and we've got an understanding. I know Madge and Steve want to keep her virginity under lock and key, but she's only human and times have changed and those old idiots don't seem to have caught on to that fact. I'm not taking any risks, if that's what you're getting at, you filthy-minded old cow.'

'It's not your extramural activities with the blessed damsel that's worrying me,' I said blandly. 'What about all the other men she practises her oil techniques with?'

Seth was almost apoplectic. 'When women get to your age they should be locked up,' he yelled.

'It's when women get to my mother's age that they lock them up,' I replied imperturbably. 'I am forty-four, not eighty-four. And I know nooky when I see it and hear it. Add I heard and saw nooky in that massage parlour Juliet calls her studio the day she moved in.'

Seth rose from the water like an outsize Neptune. To be fair to him, he delicately concealed his hardwear department with his flannel. We now stood eye to eye. It was war.

'Just keep watch on her at the wedding, Seth. Knocking off wedding guests was one of your father's specialities, as I remember.'

'You have to degrade everything, don't you,' said Seth. 'But I know what my father is capable of and it is Juliet's misfortune that she sends every man who sees her crazed with desire. Look at your Grover the other night,' he taunted. 'Mad for her, he was.'

I refused to rise to the bait so Seth continued, crisply, 'I intend to make other arrangements very soon, Holly. I want Juliet to share in every minute of my life. I shall look for a flat for us where we can be together without any grubby interference from you or from her godparents.'

I knew I had handled the stepmotherly scene badly. I fretted about that confrontation over the next few days. Seth, understandably, cold-shouldered me even to the point of providing himself with a bleak breakfast in the kitchen rather than accompanying me to Tesco. I was also left wondering whether Seth knew already about Juliet's knicker-dropping tendencies and condoned her generosity. Perhaps I was being old-fashioned. Was I really too old to understand their generation? Yet somehow I could not visualise Seth, for all his Ash and Spicer coolness, passing Juliet around the town with a casual 'help yourself tonight, pal' attitude. Seth had always been a possessive lad and almost intentionally naive. His soulful poses possibly did him credit. So, in the end, I came to the conclusion that Seth truly thought I was a warped woman who ached for Juliet's youth and talents and, this being so, I was prepared to invent any salacious story to discredit her virtue.

But the 'getting a flat for them to share' angle bothered me. I would miss the rent, on which I now relied; I would miss the additions to our groceries; indeed, I would even miss Seth. He was thoughtful about feeding the cypress cat, too. As for Madge and Steve, they would be desolate if Seth were to take their beloved god-daughter away from them – when they had sacrificed Rose Cottage for the girl's future. In other words, I had put my sexy foot in it. Nevertheless, Grover and I were right about Juliet. She was insatiable, she was trouble.

I was on my own in the office on that Saturday morning, the morning that Seth and Juliet, in their preposterous finery, drove off from Chapel Street to attend my ex's third wedding. I closed the office briefly in order to join Madge and Steve at the kerbside, in thrall to the occasion.

'Don't they look a lovely young couple?' breathed Madge. 'Isn't Juliet a picture?

For Madge's sake I was circumspect in my comments. 'Lovely, absolutely lovely.'

'You disappointed you aren't going to the wedding as well?' asked Madge.

'Madgey,' Steve reproved her, 'Holly isn't Cinderella and she was married to the man, remember. It wouldn't be fitting.'

'Oh, I'm sorry, Holly. I didn't mean to be tactless. Only nowadays everyone is so modern about marriages and though people get divorced they still remain friends. I had forgotten you don't like your ex very much, though, do you?'

'I hate the bastard,' I answered. 'I wouldn't be throwing confetti at him and his classy Philly, I'd be throwing a bomb.'

As I left them, I overheard Madge saying to Steve, 'I wonder if our darling Juliet and dear Seth will make it up the aisle one of these days? I do so love a wedding.'

It was an appalling thought. For one surrealist second, I saw Juliet, in purest white satin, heaving towards the altar, surrounded – not by simpering bridesmaids – but by an assortment of men, all of whom had known her intimately.

Half an hour later, as I was selecting some recently developed photographs of Smallwood House for our window display, Steve sidled into the office. He looked conspiratorial, so I feared a discussion about the lovely Juliet and her little habits could well be on the agenda.

I was right. 'Can I have a word, sort of private, Holly?' said Steve.

I ushered him into Jason's office and took up my position behind the rent table.

'It's about Juliet.'

'I thought it might be,' I replied smoothly 'Pregnant is she?'

Steve clutched the table edge for support. Always a pasty-faced man, he looked at that minute like some old cracked enamel bowl, chalky and lifeless. 'Oh my God, not that – it would kill Madgey. You don't really think – you haven't heard …?'

'It's all right, Steve, don't look so horrified. I only thought that's what had brought you round to see me in this secretive fashion.'

The poor old boy was quite shaken. 'We don't understand young people,' he said. 'Perhaps we shouldn't have had Juliet to live with us in the first place. I've got to admit I had my doubts about it at the time. But Madge, well, she wanted children of her own so much and Juliet was like an answer to her prayers, if you follow me. It was too late in the day for us, really, but that made it seem all the more wonderful to Madgey. And then there's our obligation to a god-daughter. But now I'm worried to death.'

I could gladly have strangled Juliet at that moment. What right had she to so distress my dear old friends? Steve looked so wretched that I began to consider the possibility that Juliet had made a pass at *him*.

'Come on Steve, don't be shy, you can talk to me about anything. I'm born under Gemini.'

'If I can be blunt, then, Holly, it's about Seth. I'm afraid he's gone too far with our dear girl. I actually found them,' Steve swallowed, '*doing* it yesterday. I was so shocked I nearly passed out. I realise all young people do it before marriage nowadays, and Seth, of course, has been married already so I guess he knows his way about. Do you think Juliet minds him taking these liberties?'

I gaped. '*Minds?*'

'She's such a sweet girl, Holly, she wouldn't want to upset anyone. But I want to know what Seth's intentions are. He can't trifle with something so rare and precious and then walk away having slaked his lusts.'

'In these modern days, Steve, it's not a question of lust-slaking, as you so quaintly put it. Juliet could well have taken the initiative in this case. Seth's not a baddie, you know. He's a simpleton, really. And if it puts your mind at rest, I'm sure Seth will hope to marry her one of these days.'

But not, I thought to myself, if I can help it.

Mollified, Steve replied, 'I'm glad to hear he's prepared to be honourable in the end. But you are wrong about Juliet. She's not at all *physical*, she lives on a completely spiritual plane.'

Steve looked all in. What with the upheaval of the move, the humidity of the season, and the sight of Seth and Juliet in the raw, it was enough to put him into the grave.

'I'm sorry I'm such a old fuddy-duddy, Holly,' he said apologetically. 'I can't help it. I shall be eighty-two next year and I wasn't brought up to accept all this free-and-easy stuff. I'll never get used to the way the world is now. While Madge and I lived at Rose Cottage we could shut all the changes out, but now we're in the town it's all around us. We don't like what we see.'

I was just closing the office, an hour later, when George appeared. 'Can I have a word?' he asked.

'Why not, darling? Everyone else is having one with me this morning. Come into the back office.'

It passed through my mind that I might try out the rent table, if George was in the mood. Liven up a dull Saturday.

I took up my senior negotiator's pitch from Jason's chair. 'Anyway, I have a bone to pick with you, George.'

'Oh, really?' George swiftly rearranged his expression into total innocence, a trick at which he was adept, due to his double life with Ivy.

'You haven't told me about Ivy's little inheritance.'

'Oh, *that*. Well, I was going to get around to it, Holly, but we're always so busy doing the other when we get together – not much time for chit-chat.'

'Well, chit and chat now then, George. What's all this about a small house in Romford?'

'Ivy was always her uncle's favourite niece – she rather took after him, as a matter of fact. He had a dreadful time with his colon, too. Had to have it irrigated in the end.'

'Stick to the point. How much was this small house in Romford worth then?'

'Close on a hundred thousand. Not a bad little dab in the hand. Then there's his little bits and bobs, they was worth a tidy sum, and there was this little offshore account as well.'

'And Ivy's come in for it all?'

'Yes, she quite perked up. Actually, she's talking about getting a new house. She's never taken to the village we're in. Ivy don't make friends easily, not with her poor health.'

George's glance fell upon the blow-ups of Smallwood House that I had left scattered about the rent table.

'Now, here's something she'd like. I know this place, don't I? Up by the Three Tuns?'

'That's it. Right next door. I don't think Ivy would like a pub for a neighbour, though, would she?'

'She'd love it. Her dad ran a pub for years.'

The estate agent in me smelled blood. 'Well, George, there it is on the market and up for grabs. But it will cost you. Not much room for bargaining with that particular vendor.'

'How much then?' asked George cautiously.

I told him.

George whistled. 'Is it really worth all that?'

I smiled complacently, holding my breath. 'I valued it, George dear.'

'Then it must be. Well I never. But you're nobody's fool when it comes to prices.'

'I'm glad someone believes in me.'

'I'll get Ivy to have a look at it. Are the rooms nice?'

'Beautiful,' I said wistfully. 'I'd swap my old dump for it any day.'

'Your house is a bit grim,' George agreed, a little too readily for my liking. 'But I'm willing to stretch a point and keep my key.'

Still with the rent table in mind, I asked, 'Are you having lunch with Ivy today?'

'No. She's gone off with her sister shopping in Norwich.' George slid his hands under my blouse. 'If you've no objection I fancy doing something else this lunchtime.'

'I shan't put up a fight, George. Shall we stay here?'

'Oh, not in the office. Jason might get to hear of it. You're getting as bad as Juliet, you are.'

I froze, pushing George away fiercely. 'What do you mean, you bastard?' Don't tell me you've had her as well.'

'No I haven't,' said George indignantly. 'That's why I wanted a word with you. Me and Ivy think there something wrong with Juliet's glands. They don't just work overtime, they never even go into neutral. She's getting too much for Madge and Steve, she's running wild and I'm sorry for poor old Seth. He's got himself involved with a very demanding young woman.'

'Grover said something like that too. A dangerous nymphomaniac, he called her, but that was after she'd exposed herself to him on my landing.'

'What did he do?' George asked eagerly.

'He told me he repulsed her advances,' I said primly. 'And I believed him.'

'I hope you won't repulse my advances,' said George. 'Come on, Holly. It's Saturday afternoon and your Grover's over the hills and far away and my Ivy's gone shopping. There's only one way to fill in our time really.'

'I am not in the mood,' I said. 'Juliet's come between us.' But I was yielding to George's familiar persuasions. 'Anyway,' I said presently, 'I thought you'd put an embargo on doing this sort of thing in the office.'

89

'I've just lifted the embargo,' George murmured. 'How about that?'

It was late in the afternoon when I eventually left the office and strolled back up the deserted High Street. George had driven off to meet Immortal Ivy at the bus stop. I passed a lone tinker outside the church gates. He was playing *Are You Going to Strawberry Fair?* and the languid notes saddened the sultry evening. I thought of George's words – Grover was over the hills and far away now. And I doubted he would ever come back and marry me.

The cypress cat was looking out for me on the pavement. It was well past feeding time and desperation tinged his welcoming mews. I opened a tin of tuna flakes in aspic (one of his favourites, stocked up by Seth). The cat smacked and suckled and purred over the saucerful, making me realise I had eaten nothing all day. Seth's contributions to the freezer had been diminishing since our scene in the bathroom, but I unearthed a plaice mornay and poured a gin and tonic. I would have to make amends with Seth somehow. This gulf in the victualling was a blow. I carried my gin out onto the terrace and contemplated the garden: its collapsing fences, the skinny border of moth-eaten roses crying out for dead-heading and the one vibrant shrub, a lavatera, the now compulsory weed in the soils of rich and poor alike. Grover's ministrations had helped the layout; at least I could see to the end of the oblong patch at last. Here, at its furthest point, stood a crumbling greenhouse, disused since the First World War. Not many panes of glass were now intact and an ivy was well established through the rotted woodwork of the roof structure. I noted dismally that the ivy was the healthiest form of growth in the entire garden.

So the house and the garden were the only assets I possessed, were they? I sighed. Well, my assets were on the blink, then. All I had still that were not showing signs of age or neglect were my legs. But I wasn't a bad-looking woman. Assisted blonde hair, thickly growing; my capped teeth, despite resembling tombstones, would be good for years; my figure had not attracted cellulite; and my breasts, although not show-stoppers like Juliet's, were distinctly well set up. I had sex appeal, that was undeniable. Even Dottie, whose opinion on these matters I now had to take seriously had recognised it.

As if to confirm my glowing statistics, my front door bell pealed out and, when I opened the door in response, there swaying on my doorstep stood Jason. A Jason in mufti, safari shorts and a T-shirt emblazoned with the legend DO SEX NOT TIME. He was also wearing a sunhat of the style used by small boys on the beaches of the 1930s; it had probably belonged to his father. I found him more repulsive than ever. If Jason was to prove my road away from ruin, I was going to have a tough time retrieving my fortunes.

'Mummy and I got back a day early, sweetheart,' he said. 'So I've come straight over to see you. I couldn't wait.'

There was the slurring normal to Jason in his cups and my heart sank. Before I could remonstrate, he had pushed on into my hall and was wandering through to the kitchen.

'I've brought you a present, my darling,' he continued, leering through his spectacles. Delving into the pocket of his shorts, he brought forth a small, very small, packet, its gift wrapping somewhat crumpled. 'Come and get it, you adorable tart.'

'Just put it on the table, Jason. And I warn you, don't try anything on.'

'Stop teasing me, Holly,' Jason said lumbering forward. 'You know you want it as much as I do.'

'I'll send for the police,' I cried, stepping backwards. A loud hissing and growling accompanied my action. 'Oh God, now I've stepped on the cat.'

Instinctively I bent over to look at my feline friend, who, eyes blazing at my disrespect, struck out with a claw and landed a gash on my forearm. I screamed. Jason grabbed me. The cat leapt out of the back door.

'Now look what's happened,' I said furiously, extending my injured arm.

'I'll kiss it better,' said Jason, slobbering, over the gash as I wrestled fruitlessly.

'Jason,' I yelled, trying to stamp on his sandalled foot. 'There are laws these days about sexual harassment. Don't forget I'm an employee of yours.'

'But we're not in the office now, sweetheart.' said Jason, wrenching my blouse off.

'That doesn't make any difference. I intend seeing a solicitor in the morning. This time, Jason, you've gone too far.'

'What has your kitchen fitter got that I haven't? From the look of the weedy old creep, I am far better equipped – if only you'd give me the chance to show you.'

'Get off me, you clod. Can't you appreciate I'm not interested? Anyway, I love George.'

I was astonished at my statement. Love George – did I? No, of course I didn't, I loved Grover. But I was flustered. Jason's probing hands were not that unwelcome. Indeed, as he pulled away from me I felt unaccountably eager for the situation to unfold.

'You know, Holly, you are just one hell of an exclusion clause,' said Jason angrily.

I might, just might, have been on the point of capitulation, but at that absorbing moment the telephone rang. I picked it up.

'I've won,' screamed my mother. 'I've won and you never put my numbers in. You wicked, wicked trollop. Too busy with all your men to think of a poor old woman like me.'

I was livid at the interruption. 'You won't have won, you old fool. Ask Mrs Angelicus to check.'

There was the sound of muffled yelping combined with soothing remonstration at the end of the line. Then Mrs Angelicus came on. 'It's all right, Holly, I'm with your dear mother. A little mix-up with numbers here. If it wouldn't inconvenience you, perhaps you'd better come over right away.'

I glanced across at Jason, who was simmering on the kitchen table, irritably polishing his spectacles, his Southwold sun hat askew.

'What was all that about?' he muttered when I rang off.

'My mother's upset. I've got to go round to her bungalow now. She gets muddled up about things these days.'

Jason's belligerence vanished. The magic word mother had ignited his benevolence. 'Poor old girl. I'll drive you over, Holly. You don't want to go walking round the town late at night.'

'Well, thank you Jason, that's kind of you,' I said. And I meant it. 'Perhaps you'd let me have my blouse back first, though.'

'Sorry,' Jason gazed longingly at what was barely covered by my skimpy bra. 'Pity, Holly, you have missed a great experience, believe me.'

'Shall I drive?' I asked as we walked down the front path together.

'If you like, I feel more like going to sleep now. I had rather hoped to sleep with you tonight, too.'

'Jason, you are incorrigible. Do you never give up on your quarry?'

'I won't stalk you for ever, Mrs Smith, so be warned. Take me soon or count the cost of your loss.'

At the gnome complex, I insisted Jason come into the bungalow with me, to provide another slant on his mother fixation. It promised to be an amusing little episode.

Mrs Angelicus was in full saintly throttle as she met us at the door. 'The poor dear has been almost paralytic. It's understandable. I did ask you to see to her numbers the other morning, didn't I? But I suppose you have been very busy with Mr Montgomery away.' She turned to Jason. 'Did you have a good holiday?'

'Marvellous. Terrific scenery and great drinking.'

'You young people, must have your little tipple.'

Mother was sitting in her wheelchair, a dressing gown of torrid pattern dragged about a madly frilled baby-doll nightdress. Her head of white curls was jerking like a demented dish mop, the benign tremor of old age intensified by her agitation.

'For God's sake, Mother, calm down,' I said curtly. 'Now, will someone tell me just what money has been won, or not won, with these stupid numbers?'

'Millions. I've lost millions,' screamed my mother. She turned glaring blue eyes to Jason. 'She's robbed me. That bitch has robbed me.'

'She would have won ten pounds,' Mrs Angelicus explained. 'She's got three numbers right.' She bent over my snarling mother and, raising her voice the obligatory notch or two used to address the elderly deaf, said. 'All you had was three numbers right, dear, not the vital six numbers. You should have won ten pounds.'

'Don't you tell me what was coming to me. I know it was millions. Just because I'm old I'm not mad. I know it was millions. I would have had all that money if it hadn't been for my cruel daughter.'

'I can't seem to get through to her,' said Mrs Angelicus wearily. 'I'm supposed to be playing bridge with Sandy tonight but I can't leave your mother in this state, can I?'

'Don't worry,' said Jason cheerfully. 'You cut along. Holly and I will cope from now on.'

'It's my job to be here. My old ladies and gentlemen are my special charges. It's rather like being in holy orders to be a warden, you know.'

'I don't want you here,' shouted my mother. 'You're always winning things. It's all right for you. You haven't been robbed blind by your nearest and dearest.'

I could see Mrs Angelicus was wavering. Sandy was a temptation, even to those in holy orders.

'Well dear, if you really don't mind. Anyway, there's always Mrs Hackett to call. She's the deputy warden.'

After Mrs Angelicus left us, Jason stepped forward and took hold of my mother's hand. 'Buck up, old love,' he said consolingly. 'I'll give you your ten pounds. You shan't lose out.'

'Make it twenty,' said my mother.

'Right,' said Jason, getting out his wallet.

'What's a nice handsome young man like you doing with that soiled baggage over there? You watch out for her. She'll have your trousers off.'

'I wish she would,' said Jason, grinning.

Mother hung on to Jason's hand. 'Oh, if only I was thirty years younger. I'd get the trousers off you, all right.'

'I bet you would too,' said Jason waggishly.

My exasperation was increasing. 'Oh, come on,' I said. 'Stop playing silly games with her.'

Jason leaned over the dish mop head and planted a kiss on Mother's cheek. 'Goodbye, you gorgeous old tart,' he said.

'Come and see me again, luvvie,' she cried. 'But don't bring her with you. Find yourself a nice young woman. There's no knowing where she's been. She started by chasing the boy who lived next door to us. But he was much too intelligent for her. Went off to university. She can't get a man once he's been to university.'

Jason was chuckling as we left the bungalow.

'Stop that silly giggling,' I said, hitting him with my handbag. 'And don't believe a word that evil old crone says.'

'I only wish half of it were true. Would I be having this tussle with your chastity now, if your mother was right about your moral history?' Jason grabbed me again, holding me tightly. My resistance was flagging. And he sensed this. 'When, Holly, when?' he whispered.

'Very soon,' I said weakly.

He seemed satisfied at last and drove me home without further fumbling.

'Better cut off now, sweetheart,' he said, stopping at my front gate. 'Mummy will be getting anxious. See you good and early on Monday morning, Mrs Smith.'

'Of course. I've got a lot to discuss with you. Oh, and thank you for being so generous to my mother. She didn't deserve twenty pounds, you know.'

'I agree. Cunning old vixen,' Jason chuckled again. 'But don't worry, Holly. I'll stop that twenty pounds out of your commission next month.'

The black car swished away from the kerb and roared off up the hill.

'Typical bloody farmer's son,' I screamed, shaking my fist in the car's direction.

Seth and the cat were both looking disconsolate in the kitchen.

'Had a good wedding, Seth?' I enquired sweetly.

'Don't ask,' said Seth.

Tactfully, I withdrew upstairs. But I started singing as I ran my bath. Had Seth's disenchantment with Juliet set in? Possibly. Was my initial revulsion at Jason ebbing? Definitely.

I went to bed. Alone. But I had begun to rearrange my future plans.

9

'I think I'm changing my mind about Jason,' I told Alex first thing on Monday morning.

'Oh, so you've come round to him at last. I'd wondered when he'd get his turn. What has he done to bring you to this decision?'

'He was kind to my mother,' I answered piously.

'Kind to your *mother*? I'd have thought that would have finished his chances for ever. Now, if he'd threatened her with a carving knife, I could understand it.'

Just then Jason's voice came floating out of the back office. 'Are you there?'

I had dressed with greater care that morning. I intended to make myself alluring and, with a low-cut neckline to my floral dress, I had even left off my bra to facilitate greater wobble.

'How do I look?' I whispered to Alex as I undulated towards Jason's door.

'Edible,' she said. 'Take care he doesn't strip you on the spot. There's evidently not much to take off.'

Jason, however, hardly looked up as I took the seat opposite his rent table and put my legs on tempting display.

'Good morning, Mr Montgomery,' I said pertly.

Jason grunted. 'Now tell me, where are we at with Smallwood House? Any movement at all since you thought fit to place it on the market at that absurd price?'

I was piqued. My entire thigh was on show to the point where it met my lacy black briefs. 'As a matter of fact, Jason, I've got a bite already.'

'You can't have.' Jason said evenly, 'Selling that dump Rose Cottage so quickly has given you ideas beyond your capabilities.'

'My friends George and Ivy are interested.'

'What, that old kitchen fitter and his half-dead wife? Don't make me laugh. They haven't got the price of a mobile home.'

'Just because you despise the working classes, Jason, doesn't mean you can write them all off as paupers. Ivy's just inherited from her uncle. An offshore account has been mentioned.'

'Rubbish.'

'No it's not. George wouldn't tell a lie to an intimate friend like me.'

'Statistically speaking,' said Jason, 'we are unlikely to make another sale so easily and at such a good price. You know what a tough game this is, Mrs Smith. You've been at it long enough.'

Was this an oblique reference to my *age*? Things were not going as I had planned. 'Yes, you're right. I have been at it long enough – long enough to smell a sale when one's in the air. And, incidentally, if we can pull this off then I am sure that parcel of development land is ours for the taking.'

Jason hooted. 'You mean that land of Alf Williamson's? My dear girl, that planning permission has been dangling about since I was in my pram. The old moo's had to renew the permission three times. Don't imagine you can get round her.'

'Mrs Williamson and I have reached an unusual degree of understanding,' I said loftily.

At that moment Jason glanced across at my legs. He adjusted his spectacles. 'If you intend seeing your solicitor this morning dressed like that, Mrs Smith, then you'll loose all credibility as a plaintiff.'

'Oh no,' I said hastily. 'I was only kidding about that, Jason.'

'So I've not been sexually harassing you, then?'

'Well, not exactly. Anyway, I am prepared to forget the other evening. After all, I recognise that you are an attractive man and I'm given to a little flirtation now and then.' I uncrossed my legs, giving Jason the benefit of a further flash of black briefs and, for good measure, I added, 'By the way, thank you so much for bringing me that little bottle of scent. I'm wearing it this morning actually – just here.' I demurely indicated my plunging neckline.

97

'I thought I could smell something. Perfume always brings on my hay fever, so keep your distance, Mrs Smith. Has your kitchen fitter been round to view Smallwood House yet?'

'He has an appointment there this morning, I believe.'

'Good. Then we might be getting somewhere. I must congratulate you on the photographs. They look great in the window, quite up to the Glossop's mark. The more upmarket we can go, the more likelihood we have of bucking the current market trends. Now, about this land. What sort of understanding have you achieved with the old moo? Because if you really do think there's an opportunity for us there, then I've got just the man to develop the site.'

'Have you ever heard of geriatric sex?'

'Don't be disgusting.'

'I'm not being disgusting. It's a fact. Mrs Williamson likes to discuss her natural inclinations with me. She still needs a man. Now, you can't have a greater understanding with a vendor than that, can you?'

'Rubbish. The only man Mrs Williamson's likely to need is a funeral director.'

'Mr Pearson isn't a funeral director.'

'That bandy midget she goes around with? You mean he's some sort of boyfriend?'

'I gather he gives satisfaction.'

'Bloody hell,' said Jason, obviously shaken. Perhaps the notion that his own mother, being of Dottie's generation, might still hanker for sexual solace was disquieting. For whatever reason, he signalled abruptly to me to leave the room.

'I need strong coffee,' I said to Alex. 'I must be losing my touch.'

I had a further setback a few minutes later, when Jason emerged from the back office and strode out with only a: 'Won't be back today, girls.'

Feeling I was going to require matronly assistance, I rang Dottie.

'Oh, Mrs Smith,' she responded brightly. 'Do come and have some tea with me this afternoon. I'd like a chat about the couple who viewed this morning. They are tremendously keen. Most gratifying.'

'Well,' I said to Alex as I rang off, 'at least I can still sell houses, even if I can't get Jason to take the hint any more.'

'Jason will come round,' Alex said soothingly. 'You know he's moody in the morning. I expect Mummy gets him to wash behind his ears before he leaves for the office. Anyway, you've given him a hard time for so long now, I don't expect he knows how to take you. Even I can't follow your violent swings of affection. Why do you want Jason so much all of a sudden?'

'He's got money. I crave his farming subsidies. Grover says I must look to my future.'

'Oh, I might have guessed Grover was at the back of this. But I thought you loved George? You were talking about marrying him eventually. Really, Holly, I don't think you will ever marry again. You like your fun too much, you like sleeping around. You're not like me. You've never wanted a baby. It's breaking my heart that I can't conceive.'

'Sometimes, Alex,' I said waspishly, 'your girlish confidences make me sick.'

'Sorry I spoke,' said Alex, attacking her word processor.

'Do have some chocolate cake,' urged Dottie. We were sitting in her garden under the cherry tree. 'I make them all the time now. Arnold loves a slice. He says the rich mixture puts him in the mood. Something to do with cocoa being a potency stimulant. I keep a tin of chocolate cake beside the bed at night these days and sometimes he's nibbling on and off until breakfast.'

'Is Mr Pearson in London again?' I had seen no sign of the little man, unlike Buster, who was busy worrying around my ankles; sometimes I wondered if Dottie banished Arnie deliberately when she knew I was calling.

'Yes, I let him go up now and then. He recharges his batteries in the City and comes steaming back to me full of energy, bless him.'

'So, Dottie. Tell me about George and Ivy. What were their reactions to all this?'

'Well, they seemed on the verge of making an offer. I was rather surprised. I hadn't expected that sort of person to be appreciative of my taste and I suppose if they do buy my house then they'll fit it up with all kinds of vulgar ornaments from various coastal resorts. One good thing, they didn't object to the Three Tuns. I gather Ivy's father was a publican at one time, so the woman may want my house out of sentiment. Who knows? By the way, Holly, how do they intend to fund this purchase? I don't want to spend money needlessly on abortive solicitors' bills if they can't manage to meet my price at the end of the day and then pull out. I know people have daydreams, especially that sort of person, and it may be just wishful thinking that they could actually afford a house like mine. I'm sure they are too old to start taking out mortgages.'

'Don't worry on that score. Didn't George explain about Ivy's inheritance?'

'Inheritance? Really? Well, the most extraordinary people seem to have money these days.'

'What did you think of George?' I asked slyly.

'Pleasant enough man, I suppose. Yes, I think he was rather nice. Admired my feet.'

'*Did* he?'

'But I do have elegant feet, of course.'

'Did he strike you as being sexy?'

'Well, now you mention it, he did have a certain gleam in his eye. It's all to do with eyes, you know, and that colour of his, sludgy blue, usually denotes the owner's ready for it. Still, he's utterly devoted to that sick wife of his. Such suffering. The poor dear had to use my bathroom twice.'

'Probably just checking to see if your flush was working. I don't think her condition is as bad as she makes out.'

'Now, Holly, I'm dying to hear the latest on your assault on Mr Montgomery.'

'I'm going wrong somewhere, Dottie. I thought I'd got him hooked this weekend. He even came round to my house uninvited. Couldn't keep away, he said.'

Dottie got to the edge of her canvas chair. 'I'm all ears, dear. Don't leave out one detail.'

'There's nothing to tell. It was my fault. I pushed him away. And now he's not taking any notice of me.'

'Oh dear. Never put off tonight what may not be offered tomorrow, silly child.'

100

'What can I do?'

'In the circumstances, you'll just have to throw yourself at him. Subtlety never works with these farming types. They've got knickers humour, dear. So get yours off straight away and he should get the message – although I do agree he's rather thick in the upper storey, but his lower storey will be worth all the effort.'

'I practically disrobed this morning. I'm not sure that outright nudity would pull him round now. I think I've blown it.'

'Blatancy can't fail with his sort. But do choose your moment. There's a time and place for everything. One has to maintain the social standards, you know.' Dottie rose and showed me to the green-glossed door. 'I do enjoy these meetings, Holly. I'm growing quite fond of you – and so is dear Buster.'

On the spur of this proffered fondness, I said: 'Can I take it, Dottie, that if we successfully conclude a sale on your house you'll consider selling your land at last?'

Dottie smiled enigmatically. 'You never know, Mrs Smith, you never know.'

George was waiting for me when I got back home that evening. He had placed a bunch of gushing red roses in a vase on the kitchen table and he handed me a gin and tonic. Dear faithful George – why on earth, I wondered, was I going to such extremes over Jason, when I already had such a steady, good-natured lover? Then I remembered Immortal Ivy and the Common Agricultural Policy. Still, no point in not exploiting the moment.

'Oh darling,' I said gratefully, 'you are sweet. Such heavenly roses.'

There was no need to be blatant or cryptic with George. His hand was already straying nimbly into the area where I had earlier tipped the entire contents of Jason's very small gift-wrapped package.

'You smell lovely, Holly,' he said, unzipping my dress.

'Tell me,' I murmured in his ear, 'what's the verdict on Smallwood House?'

'Well,' replied George, 'Ivy's mad on the place, doesn't even mind the horrible decoration, and I can always emulsion over the worst of it. Course, I'll have to change the kitchen round a bit –'

101

I stopped kissing him in outrage. 'Change that kitchen, you bloody vandal. You'll do that over my dead body.'

'I'm only winding you up. It's not a bad kitchen, really. The carpenter certainly knew what he was doing. Ivy's a bit scared of that Aga, though, but she loved the toilet, said the seat was very comfortable.'

'So – are you going to make me an offer then?' I wriggled my dress to the floor.

'Course I am. I'm even willing to make an offer for Smallwood House as well.'

'Oh George, where would I be without you?' I was guilty again about my aberrant infatuation for Jason. 'Come upstairs now, I want to show you my gratitude.'

'I can't stop very long,' George warned, deftly removing my briefs. 'I only came round to tell you we're going to make an offer for that house first thing tomorrow after Ivy's seen the bank manager.' He grinned his slow suggestive smile which showed his crooked teeth, while his giveaway sludgy blue eyes took in my winsome figure. 'I never tire of being shown your gratitude, Holly,' he said picking me up and carrying me to the bedroom.

We spent a blissful two hours sharing mutual gratitude. Then George pulled away from me and reached out for his T-shirt. I put my arms around his waist and restrained him. 'Don't go, don't go,' I whimpered.

'Got to, Holly. Old Ivy'll start fretting if I'm not home soon.'

'Does she never suspect what you get up to?'

'I don't think she bothers to think about it. She just takes it for granted that I've been out on the job. Anyway, she doesn't really want to make unpleasant discoveries about her old man.'

'I don't see why she should get to live in that pretty house,' I said petulantly, stroking George's thighs, 'and have a husband who keeps such regular hours.'

'You've got a point there,' said George, resuming his former position. 'And there's no sense in wasting good gratitude, is there?'

'Absolutely not, sweetheart,' I agreed, showing him some more.

10

The breakfast gang were putting their heads together at Tesco that morning. Seth, Steve and I were at one table, Sandy and Mrs Angelicus at another.

No details had ever been vouchsafed to me by Seth of the wedding of my ex and Classy Philly. Somehow, tacitly, the wall of silence had been observed. But Seth had not, so far, sought a flat of his own and, thankfully, his contributions towards bed and board at the mausoleum had continued. However, his addiction to the dreadful Juliet was still unshaken. And, from Steve's strained attitude towards Seth, consummation must be as frequently performed as ever. Without confirmation, therefore, I was left with my suspicions: that Juliet had besmirched the celebrations by going the rounds of the available male guests. Certainly a sourness had seeped into Seth's relationship with his father. No 'having a good time' postcards had arrived for him from the honeymooning couple. No subsequent telephone calls or letters since their return. As for me, I hadn't even rated a piece of wedding cake.

On balance, I felt a kindred sympathy, of sorts, for Classy Philly. But at least she had her money to console her growing awareness that my ex would be beyond her crusading salvation.

On all our horizons at the moment, of course, was the looming horror of Juliet's exhibition. It had been decided to have a trial opening of a limited collection of her paintings. There was going to be a private view, naturally, and it was this occasion that was under acrimonious debate.

103

'Everyone know my views,' said Steve. 'I think it is too soon to hold an exhibition. Juliet's soul is a very tender thing. She must not be rushed into baring it like this.'

'It's not her soul she'll be baring, if I know her,' I muttered.

Seth scowled. 'Why will no one give Juliet credit for knowing herself when she's ready to bare her soul.'

'What's her soul got to do with it?' asked Mrs Angelicus, who knew more about the soul than most of us. 'Surely she's only done a few nice little paintings that she hopes to sell.'

'These aren't just *paintings*' Steve explained, 'they are part of her whole being. She's shedding something vital of herself every time she puts brush to canvas. It exhausts the poor child, and there's Seth forcing this public display on her before she's quite ready.'

I took a gulp of my black coffee. 'I would have said she was always ready for public display.'

Sandy, the ever factual, closed his manuscript to give the discussion his full attention. 'Let's get this straight. I thought the whole object of your moving from that lovely little country place you had to Chapel Villas was to enable Juliet to exhibit her wares. The sooner she gets on with it, then the sooner she's justified your faith in her.'

'Sandy's right,' Mrs Angelicus said, always wishing to side with her literary hero.

'Yes, I know,' Steve said, crushed. 'I suppose Madgey and I are just worried now that it's actually happening. It seems so ambitious all of a sudden. And what will the cats think of strange people wandering about their territory?' He looked, as he often did these days, as if about to break into sobbing.

'Don't bring the cats into it,' Seth said impatiently. 'They'll have to be shut into the house on the night of the private view.'

'Oh, I don't know,' I said. 'I think a few cats around the studio should make for a more authentic artistic atmosphere, especially if they pee on a painting or two.'

'Don't be facetious, Holly,' admonished Sandy. 'If we are all to take this business seriously, then we must get the atmosphere absolutely in tune to the occasion – and talking of tunes, what background music does Juliet propose to use?'

104

'Music?' cried Steve, alarmed. 'What music? Madgey and I don't know anything about music. There won't be room for a band in the stable.'

'Of course there will be music,' Seth said. 'I'm fixing up the stereo equipment.'

'Beethoven,' Sandy said.

'Scott Joplin,' Mrs Angelicus suggested.

Seth frowned. 'Beethoven's too heavy and Scott Joplin's too trivial. Juliet and I think Vivaldi offers the right sound for middle-class classical recognition.'

'I must point out,' Sandy interjected, 'that we all belong to the emergent working classes around these tables, so I wouldn't lean too strongly on middle-class ethos. Why, in Victorian times not one of us would have had the money for a decent breakfast.'

'Hackneyed,' I said. 'Vivaldi's hackneyed and precious. Put some fire into the proceedings. Use flamenco.'

Sandy and Mrs Angelicus approved. 'Great thought, Holly,' said Sandy, while Mrs Angelicus enthused. 'It'll make everyone feel like dancing.' Obviously Mrs Angelicus' holy proclivities erred on the side of the evangelical movement.

'Wait a minute,' said Steve. 'Isn't that that Spanish muck, all yelling and stamping? We don't want that sort of thing going on in the stable. Juliet requires something more peaceful so that people can drink in the meaning of her paintings without disturbance.'

'Vivaldi it is,' shouted Seth. 'And no more argument.'

'Well, I hope there's some booze, anyway,' said Sandy.

'We aren't inviting people to some sort of knees-up,' said Steve sternly.

'Juliet doesn't approve of wine,' Seth announced. 'Fruit juice from the health store will be provided and maybe some sesame-seed crackers.'

Sandy looked across at me and raised his eyebrows. 'Sounds like a fun evening.'

'Who is paying for this bash?' I asked, knowing already the answer was obvious – who else but that dear selfless old couple.

Steve confirmed this, adding, 'Seth's chipping in, as well.'

105

'I'm sorry,' said Mrs Angelicus, 'I don't presume to criticise, but sesame-seed crackers alone don't sound sufficiently tempting. They wouldn't be enough to satisfy my old people, let alone folk without infirmities.'

'Madgey has suggested making some of her lovely fruit cakes,' said Steve.

'I could do some savouries, if that would help,' Mrs Angelicus offered.

Seth was displeased. 'Juliet doesn't want this affair degenerating into some village hall bun fight.'

Mrs Angelicus bridled. 'My savouries are highly thought of, Seth. They've been in circulation at the vicar's drinks parties for years.'

Unable to resist it, Sandy said, 'Then they must be somewhat stale by now.'

I always enjoyed jokes of puerility and I giggled immoderately, while Sandy added more jovial fuel by suggesting, 'Why not print that old standby at the bottom of your invitations – bring a bottle?'

We chortled together. Seth's fury increased. 'If you think,' he said angrily, 'that the debut of a brilliant young artist is merely to provide an opportunity for people to have a free guzzle and a good snigger at her expense, then I don't think any of you need attend this function at all.'

'For once I agree with you, Seth,' said Steve. Both men rose to their feet preparing for indignant departure.

'Oh, go on,' I said. 'You'll need all the support you can get, otherwise you'll be sitting around that stable like stuffed donkeys and that won't look too good in the local newspaper, will it? Unfortunate lack of response to artist's exhibition. Boycott by general public.'

'We promise to behave,' said Sandy. 'It'll be all right on the night.'

'I've had enough of your jeering,' snarled Seth, waddling away.

When Seth and Steve had merged into the mainstream of the supermarket, Sandy asked me, 'Do you think it's going to be a fiasco? Are Juliet's paintings any good?'

'Don't ask me, Sandy. I think they're trashy. But I hope for Madge and Steve's sake that the whole thing is going to be a

106

success. We'll have to show up on the night, whatever we really feel, and bring friends with us.' I proposed to bring Jason, even if I had to shackle him to my wrist.

Mrs Angelicus put her hand over mine, 'Oh, we'll come of course. I only wish my charges were not so decrepit. I suppose there is no provision for wheelchairs?'

'Count me in too,' said Sandy. 'I wouldn't miss it for anything. More amusing than a book launch, any day. Pity about the booze, though.'

'What, no bloody wine?' was also Jason's response.

I had been constantly setting and resetting my snares to trap Jason into another amorous tangle with me. He was naturally obtuse, of course, but I feared Mother Montgomery might be plotting against my ascendancy. I knew I was up against a steely skinflint in Mummy. A marriage of land holdings would be her goal for her only son and heir to the farming fortune. My snares had been further upset by Jason's absence from the office for a fortnight due to a prang in the black monster. Again, details had been censored. We in the ranks had been told nothing of how this had occurred, or how serious might be the repercussions.

However, Jason was now back with us, but driving a Range Rover instead. The low-slung black car was gone for ever. Jason had dismissed it as a 'bit of a boy's toy, that old banger'.

My hopes were now orbiting on Jason's coming with me to Juliet's private view. Even with the absence of alcoholic stimulation at the event, I considered myself sufficiently experienced to persuade him to take me on afterwards to the broad-minded atmosphere of the Suckling Pig, where, influenced with a little liquid refreshment of more inhibition-releasing propensity than fruit juice, Jason and I might indulge in satisfying consummation.

The guests were mustering. Alex and her Mark were coming. Dottie had agreed to bring Arnie. Immortal Ivy would accompany George, bowels permitting. And, of course, there was the full complement of the breakfast fellowship plus local art lovers and a sprinkling of nosy neighbours, along with Madge's friends from the Save a Kitten Society. An off-duty nursing sister had also been enlisted.

107

It was expected that the carefully placed posters advertising the evening might yield further peripheral loonies. So, all in all, a goodly crush was anticipated. Thus Mrs Angelicus' savouries had been required. Even so, all those apprised of the paucity of tasty nibbles were eating beforehand. Jason was dining with Mummy back at the farmhouse. Seth and I were having a microwave back at the mausoleum.

When the happening finally came round, it was an autumnally grey day with a keen wind from the north-east. My intention of wearing something flimsy gave way to a skinny-rib sweater and my obscenely short skirt. I left off my bra to ensure no restriction on my upstanding nipples and, with those twin sirens sending out their unequivocal invitation, I was confident of attracting attention.

Bunting had been tacked to the two spindly silver birches that graced what there was of the Chapel Villa rear garden. These flags of impoverished gaiety flapped and flopped overhead as the privileged viewers wound up the pathway towards the stable. All necessary carpentry and wiring had been accomplished therein by this time. A quick emulsion job (at cut price) had been undertaken by George, who had also kitted out the makeshift kitchen.

The ladder leading to the loft area was now remade into an open-tread version and the inclusion of roof lights into the pantiled roof had provided Juliet with a studio workshop which contained, sinisterly, I thought, a closed-off cubicle. The door to the cubicle bore a cheaply printed notice from Woolworth's stating that what lay beyond was STRICTLY PRIVATE. This, I knew, was no modest washroom. Toilet facilities were, indeed, provided by an erstwhile lean-to-outside privy, now updated with a low flush WC and a small spittoon-style wash-hand basin.

Juliet's paintings were hung and lit quite expertly. And there was room for an overspill in the loft section. In the latter area Juliet had displayed further evidence of her talent – her sculptured forms. These were all squat and round with very suggestive excrescences and indentations. To my practised eye they looked like a collection of bums and genitals. They had already attracted a profusion of red stickers.

The stable was filling up. A heartening number of guests mooched about to the accompaniment of blaring Vivaldi. The artist herself was in prominent form. Long phallic earrings hung from the Madonna lobes, while the Madonna hairstyle had been let flow in freedom. This gave rise to a great deal of lock-tossing and every time a swatch of hair was shunted from shoulder to back, it caused volcanic mammary wobble.

Immortal Ivy, trim in black grosgrain, was in conversation with Dottie, sultry at sixty-something. My poor Madge, on the other hand, was still pinafored from kitchen chores. She darted about, harassed and hot, in pursuit of four of her cats, escapologists from the villa, who were bent on feline mayhem.

Seth, juggling the emotions of pride and apprehension, had been commissioned to oversee the fruit juice supplies. These were contained in two enormous ceramic pots – presumably planters plugged at the base for the occasion. Juliet, I was told, had insisted on filling these Aladdin's casks herself, and Seth was distributing the contents, via a dipped jug, into the massed rows of hired wineglasses.

The fruit juice was proving popular. 'This isn't bad stuff,' Jason commented, draining his third glassful. 'Unusually stimulating.'

'I'm finding it rather heady,' admitted Mrs Angelicus, squinting a little.

Sandy winked at me. 'I think it could well be lethal,' he murmured. 'Watch this space.'

'Quite agree, old boy,' said a very tall man with a biblical beard who had been pointed out to me by an awed Steve as being the president of the local art society. 'I lived for years in Borneo,' continued the president, 'and it reminds me of the liquor the natives brewed for their fertility rites.'

Jason's face lit up. 'Let's get some more of it down then, before supplies run dry.'

We pressed forward towards the improvised bar. As I squeezed past Dottie, she beamed at me approvingly. 'I see you are laying siege, Holly. Lucky girl, you are in for a tempestuous night.'

'I hope so,' I whispered.

'Is the old cow drunk?' asked Jason.

'On fruit juice?' I replied.

109

'She's in a funny mood, then.' Jason grabbed another glassful and confided, 'I reckon her pint-sized paramour is up to something. He's been following Juliet everywhere and now he's gone up the stairs to her boudoir, or whatever it is behind the closed door. Does she tell fortunes up there – or what?'

'I've been wondering what goes on there too,' said Alex's Mark, edging up to us. 'Men keep going in. Does she take handprints?'

'Could be,' said the president. He was displaying a flattering preference for my company and was, at that moment, letting his hand stray tentatively across my buttocks. 'Compiling her next exhibition, perhaps – "Lines of Humanity", a splendid title. She is an amazingly talented creature, of course, and full of animal passion. What do you think of this example, for instance?' The president steered me to one of Juliet's more obscure canvases. 'It's called *Beehives at Dawn*. Artful composition, isn't it?'

I peered at the picture. 'What are those nasty white blobs in the middle?'

'Those are the beehives, my dear. Juliet's encapsulated them into the shifting seasons of the wild.'

'Bloody hell,' said Jason, baffled.

The president's hand had graduated from my bottom to the underside of my obscenely short skirt and, as Jason's glasses had started to slip, I was beginning to feel the evening would lead to a rewarding climax.

'I would value your reaction to this painting also,' said the president. 'It's called simply *Nettles and Nightshade*. Gloriously evocative of primordial fear.'

'It makes me shudder to look at it,' I said truthfully.

'I knew you were sensitive, my dear. You must let me have your address.'

It was really becoming a fascinating occasion. It was even turning out to be unexpectedly dramatic. There was a cry from the loft area and Arnie toppled down the open-tread stairs, his bow tie at an angle and a tell-tale untidiness to his shirt. He came to rest, lopsidedly, at the foot of the flight and lay there, smiling insensibly.

'Arnie darling,' Dottie's voice screamed above the hubub. 'Let me through, please, he's my cousin.'

110

'It's all right. I'm fully medically trained,' cried the spare nursing sister, surging to the rescue.

'The midget's copped it,' said Jason. 'Heart attack, I suppose.'

To further enhance the scene of casualty, there was a searing flash of light and thunder cracked above the roof, momentarily overwhelming Vivaldi. One of East Anglia's famed electrical storms was again upon us.

Arnie sat up. 'If I've got to go,' said the incorrigible gnome, 'then this is the way. Whoopee.'

'What exactly do you mean whoopee, you little sod?' Dottie's voice had assumed a cutting edge.

At that propitious moment the lights went out. I heard Steve wail, 'That's all we need. A power cut.'

'That's all I need,' muttered the president, his competent hand now in my briefs.

That was my signal for action. 'Come on, Jason,' I said. 'Let's go.'

Disengaging myself from the practised president, I forced an exit through the viewers and, once outside, Jason and I dashed for the Range Rover. We were soaked by the time we had gained its interior. Across Tinkerstown, all the lights were out and the storm went on ripping up the heavens in ugly, angry slashes. With his usual reckless lack of consideration for either his own vehicle or those parked nearby, Jason backed out the Range Rover and raced it through the town towards the encircling countryside. My excitement increased with the speed.

'Where are we going?' I gasped.

'Barty's Field.'

'I'm no wiser.'

'You will be, sweetheart.'

All was darkness, except for the bobbing headlamps. In intermittent flashes the awesome light from the storm lit up an unrecognisable landscape, freezing bucolic images into split-second compositions. I was aware of cows clustered, terrified, beneath an oak tree as Jason swung into a field and, thundering up the track, skidded to a stop beside a copse of wildly swaying alders.

'Barty's Field,' he announced proudly. 'Belonged to my grandfather when I was a little boy, but it's mine now, of course.

111

I used to come here fishing – there is a tributary runs the other side of these trees. No fish in it any more, though. Too much pollution. Sad, really.'

Undoubtedly the Montgomery's farming practices had been responsible for the pollution, but I let it pass. Not the most auspicious moment to cast such slurs on the connections of the man I urgently wanted to make love to me.

Jason took off his spectacles. At last. Any minute now I should be on my back. However, Jason hesitated. I held my breath.

'I want to get this straight, Mrs Smith. How many more exclusion clauses are you going to invent?

I shook my head. 'It's all right. I've rewritten the policy.'

'Sure?'

'Very sure.' I was so sure, in fact, that I didn't think I would have to lie back and think of the Common Agricultural Policy at all.

'You adorable tart,' said Jason. 'The setting could have been more glamorous, I suppose, but at least the back of the Range Rover and old dog blanket come cheap, not like some bloody motel room.'

'I don't care where we do it, or even if we have to do it on a bed of red-hot nails. But let's get on with it, Jason.'

'This sounds like sexual harassment to me,' chuckled Jason. 'Don't be in such a hurry, sweetheart. I'm worth waiting for.'

And he was.

The storm had blown itself out by the time Jason drove me back to the mausoleum. It was two o'clock in the morning. I was curled up, still undressed, in the passenger seat, the dog blanket covering my erogenous zones. Jason lurched the car onto the pavement outside my front gate.

'I'll carry you across the threshold, sweetheart,' he offered. 'The lights are on in your hall so I guess Seth's still up. Perhaps he can give me the recipe for that marvellous fruit cup.' He scooped me into his arms, strode up the pathway and rang the bell. I hoped it would not be George who answered the summons. I acknowledged that George might be yesterday's lover (although I would let him keep my key; it was always as well to have a lover up one's sleeve). But magnificent Jason was top of the list. I would accept others from now on only as second-best. I adored Jason. Even mercenary Grover, the boy next door and hitherto love of my love, was consigned to the dustbin of spent passion.

It was Seth who opened the door. He cast a soulful eye upon my winsome nudity. 'Oh, it's you, Holly. Forgotten your key?'

Jason carried me on to the kitchen before setting me down. 'Any coffee going?' he asked.

Seth pushed the cafetière towards us. 'Help yourself.'

We positioned ourselves around the table while the cypress cat did the rounds, purring.

'Bloody good thrash, Seth,' Jason said. 'Congratulations.'

'Thanks, Jason. Yes, I think we can truly say Juliet has made her mark on the art community of this town.'

'I don't think I would buy any of her gruesome paintings,' confessed Jason, 'but she certainly knows how to serve up a drastic fruit juice.'

'Ah. The fruit juice,' Seth replied. 'Apparently, Juliet's idea was to use it as an integral extension to her theme of rural life. She intended it should awaken dormant Bacchanalian instincts. She wanted to blend the fruitfulness of Mother Nature as depicted in her canvases with the fecundity of *Homo sapiens* when the social taboos are lifted.'

'Sound like a lot of crap to me,' said Jason, while I cried, 'I knew it. The bitch had spiked the drink. What was it? Vodka?'

Seth nodded. 'Most people missed the point, of course. No subtlety or appreciation to the general public as a rule.'

'I bet most people passed out; not a lot of subtlety to drunks,' I said.

'One or two couldn't handle the situation,' Seth agreed. 'And things weren't helped by George's wife barricading herself in the toilet. I'm afraid a lot of people were taken short and had to use the car park. Lucky there was so much rain, really.'

11

I did not go to breakfast at Tesco's that morning. I ambled across the park, gazed dreamily upon the quarrelling mallard, and lounged on a bench for five minutes, smirking inanely at anyone strolling by.

I was happy, aimlessly, joyfully happy. My sense of purpose was blunted. The real world – apart from looking roseate even down to some smelly tinkers at the edge of the lake – was evading my attention. Instead I roved my imagination across a range of amorous daydreaming.

There was nothing – but nothing – like being in love. From the amazing physical feats that beckoned, there were other lures. A moated farmhouse of my own, golden-beamed, green-Agaed, a shaggy dog, a cypress cat. No more worries about meeting bills, no more anxieties about rising damp and rotting joists. My future was suddenly assured, underwritten by the Common Agricultural Policy. For Jason, devoted Jason, would look after everything. I could handle Jason. I sighed with languorous pleasure. Handling Jason would present no onerous duty. In fact, I would go round to the office now and start handling him again.

I mooched around the corner – and bumped straight into George.

'Oh, Holly, I'm glad I've seen you. We've got trouble.'

The real world grabbed me by the throat once more. 'Yes, I heard that Ivy had had a bad time in the loo last night.'

114

'Oh, that was nothing. Ivy always feels better for a good clear-out. No, its Smallwood House. Dottie isn't going to sell it to us after all.'

My commission bit the dust. 'Oh sod. I thought everything was going too well. What's the matter with the bloody woman? We've got her her price.'

'I don't know, Holly. She just rang up Ivy and said it was all off. No explanation, nothing. I'vy's in a terrible state. She'd set her heart on the place – and so had I. It's everything we've ever worked for. It was a dream come true. Oh Holly, get Dottie to change her mind, for God's sake.'

'Don't worry, my darling, I think I can get round Dottie. We've got a special relationship.' It occurred to me that an unexpurgated account of my night of uncontrolled lust with Jason on the dog blanket should rearrange Dottie's current tantrum. 'I'll go and see her today, George. But it's not unusual for a vendor to get cold feet like this.'

'And she's got lovely feet.' said George thoughtfully.

I squeezed George's arm. 'I'll ring you later. Cheer up, my sweetheart. Good old Holly's on the job.'

I went into the office. Alex looked at me. 'You don't have to say anything, Holly. It's as if you and Jason are wearing placards.'

'What do you mean?'

'It's written all over you. You spent the night together.'

'Oh, Alex – how could I have been so blind for so long? Jason is fantastic.'

'Don't go mushy on me, please. I couldn't stand it. So spare me the details,' Alex said with feeling. 'I'm still weak from last night's bash at Juliet's exhibition. What on earth was wrong with the fruit juice?'

'Did it make you ill? Juliet had laced it with vodka.'

'Oh, so that accounts for it. No, it didn't make us ill, rather the reverse. Mark got quite lively.'

'Spare me the details,' I retorted crisply. 'Is Jason here?'

'Has been,' Alex said briefly. 'Dashed in, left you a note, and dashed out again.' Alex handed me an envelope.

I wrenched it open and read his jagged scrawl in excitment. Jason was nothing if not graphic. I liked a man without inhibitions.

Alex held up a hand. 'Don't read it out.'

'I couldn't, it's positively pornographic.'

'I may be ten years younger than you, Holly, but you make me feel as old as your mother sometimes.'

'He wants me to meet him at the Suckling Pig for lunch,' I said.

'I'll be glad when this affair of yours cools down, Mrs Smith. If it doesn't, I shall wind up running Montgomery's single-handed.'

'Don't be mean, Alex. I'm madly in love for the very first time.'

'I thought Grover was the love of your life?'

'I can't help it if I'm fickle. Stop looking so peevish. I'll make you some coffee.'

I slapped instant granules and half-boiled water into a mug and twirled it all feverishly with a teaspoon.

'Here, drink this odious brew, it'll make you feel better. I'm off to Smallwood House now. Dottie wants to pull out on George and Ivy.'

'I'm not surprised after last night. I think Arnie blotted his copybook.'

Until that moment I had forgotten the randy dwarf and the episode on the staircase. 'I don't see what Arnie's got to do with it. She forgives him anything once he takes his trousers off.'

'I think he took his trousers off once too often.' Alex said cryptically.

At Smallwood House there was no initial response to my knocking. For one maddening moment I feared Dottie was not going to answer the door. I was sure she was at home because Buster certainly was, as from the other side of the green-glossed door came the most savage snapping and snarling. Eventually, there were shuffling footsteps in the hall and the door opened a chink, Buster safely harnessed by the bejwelled hand.

'It's Holly, Dottie. Please let me in. I need to talk to you.'

I was admitted. To my astonishment Dottie then fell into my arms and began howling hopelessly. Her long, silvered hair was hanging about her shoulders and she was anything but elegant in a candlewick housecoat. This was a Dottie never before glimpsed; an unimaginable Dottie, bereft of her all-in-one girdle and her warpaint. The hitherto unassailable self-confidence had sunk into the hitherto well-confined flab.

'Oh, Dottie darling,' I said in horror, 'whatever has gone wrong?'

Gently I led her into the sitting room to the sofa, where I let her sob on until she could speak.

'It's Arnie. He's gone. My bed is empty.'

My mind began revolving around the ramifications of that statement: oh dear, Smallwood House could indeed be no longer for sale. 'Do you want to tell me what's happened?' I asked tentatively.

Dottie hesitated, wondering I suppose if I were the right recipient for such confidences and if in fact she should couch these disclosures in the modern vernacular; but if she couldn't tell *me*, who else was there?

'Well, I expect you can guess what's been happening as you seem to be so friendly with all those awful people in Chapel Street. But I've been made to look foolish, made to look cheap. I find that Arnie has been knocking off that frightening young woman with the huge tits. Doing it on a regular basis while I've been supplying the chocolate cake. That creature is running a one-woman brothel, apparently. I think someone should alert the authorities.'

I was momentarily stumped for pleasantries.

'Anyway, I sent Arnie packing, my dear. There was a disgusting scene and unforgivable things were said about my sexual abilities, and a large cheque was demanded to obviate any sordid repercussions in the tabloid press. Extortion, I know, but I decided blackmail was the better part of discretion in such a case.'

A pay-off. I had to hand it to Arnie. He had style. And a good head for business. But I was concerned about the situation with Juliet, the situation with George and Ivy and Smallwood House.

'So, what about your plans to move?' I asked.

'I am not selling,' said Dottie flatly. 'Arnie and I were going to set up home together in a serviced flat in a mansion block off Knightsbridge. We had made such plans. We intended to travel extensively. A small cabin cruiser had been discussed. Arnie wanted it called the *Dorothy Belle*. He said I hadn't lived until I'd done it to the sound of lapping water.'

117

That's a point, I thought. I wonder if Jason knew of any handy lapping waters?

'So you are taking Smallwood House off the market?'

'Yes, dear, that is what I've been saying. You don't seem to be taking much in this morning. Too infatuated with Mr Montgomery's dimensions, I suppose. Normally I would have revelled in a full description of the whys and wherefores, but not today, dear. I am in mourning.'

'You won't be mourning for long, Dottie' I assured her. 'You are a very sexy lady, you know. This is a blip, that's all. Anyway, I don't think Arnie was good enough for someone of your temperament and capacity. There's plenty more men around. How about the president of the local art society? He seemed promising material for a fling.'

'The one with the beard and the irregular contacts in Borneo? All talk, my dear. I fear I am letting you down,' Dottie continued without much remorse, 'and I'm sorry about George and Ivy, of course. A nice little couple in their way.'

'They are devastated,' I said.

'Does losing a sale like this mean a personal loss of money for you, Holly?'

Her sudden question suggested that I, too, might be in for a large cheque to avoid sordid repercussions, but then Dottie said: 'So how about if I let you sell my land instead? The money from such a sale would amply replace what I've thrown away on Arnold Pearson.'

'Oh, Dottie.' I bent and kissed her damp cheek. 'It would help to sustain Mr Montgomery's interest in me at a critical point in our relationship.'

'Then you must have the land, my dear. You've obviously got to keep your end up.'

I drove out to the Suckling Pig in the company car by way of the garage and bought Mother's weekly numbers. While at the counter I purchased a garish card. It depicted two weird animals about to go into a clinch and its message was suggestively double-edged. I added a few more explicit words of my own, knowing this would appeal to Jason's knickers humour. The girl at the counter asked after 'my dear mum' as usual.

118

'You off to see more houses, then?' she continued. 'You are lucky. I get bored sitting here all the week. Still, I don't suppose you get much time for a private life, do you?'

'I'm not grumbling,' I answered with truth. 'I manage to fit in a few extra activities.'

'That's the way,' she called after me. 'There you go.'

I got to the Suckling Pig as early as I could. I was intrigued to know just how broad-minded the landlord was and how far he went to accommodate clients with urgent requirements. Mine were becoming more urgent with every turn of the wheels. The Range Rover was already in the car park when I arrived.

I stepped daintily across to the saloon bar and found Jason, a pint of beer in one hand, hobnobbing with the landlord, Roger. I went up to Jason boldly, and kissed him, lingering deliberately to satisfy myself that his hunger for me was by no means diminished from the night before.

'Thank you for your letter,' I said. 'I've written you a short note in reply.' I produced the weirdo card and gave it to him.

Jason chuckled as he read it. He put his arm through mine and walked me towards a door marked PRIVATE. Here comes the broad-minded bit, I thought in delight, as we ascended a staircase, its treads covered in threadbare brown carpet.

'I love the card, Holly,' said Jason. 'I'll always keep it. I'll sleep with it under my pillow, and,' he continued as he steered me into a small dormer-windowed bedroom, 'you really are the most adorable tart.'

Never bashful and never subtle I whisked out of my blouse and skirt. Within seconds we were on the bed, Jason's spectacles were off and so were his clothes.

'This is a most accommodating pub,' I murmured.

'Didn't you know they did bed and breakfast?'

'The bed's terrific,' I replied, 'So who cares about the breakfast?'

'Roger will be along with some sandwiches soon,' Jason said. 'I've got to keep my strength up.'

'Room service as well?'

'I try to cover all eventualities.'

'You're covering mine very professionally, Mr Montgomery.'

I was vaguely conscious of someone coming into the room, while Jason, unabashed at our occupation, called out, 'Dump the tray over there, Roger, and open the bottle, will you?'

'Is this your idea of informal entertaining?' I asked.

'Shut up and concentrate, Mrs Smith,' Jason answered. So I did.

Later, when Jason padded across the sloping, creaking floorboards to collect the tray, I lay back against the greasy velvet headboard and sighed. 'I do love you, Jason,' I said foolishly.

'I'm fairly partial to you too, Mrs Smith, Have a sandwich.'

'I'd rather have you.'

'Good God, woman, give me a break.' But he leaned forward and kissed me again, his mouth full of smoked salmon. 'Statistically speaking, I don't think I can keep this up.'

I thought then what fun he was, unlike Grover, who nagged, unlike George, who flagged.

'Do you want the good news or the bad news, Jason?' I asked, sipping my wine.

'No bad news this afternoon, sweetheart. This is essentially a good-news day for us.'

'Dottie says we can sell her land.'

'What? You're joking.'

'No, I'm serious. I saw her this morning and she's promised to give it to Montgomery's.' I failed to add that Dottie's promise to sell Smallwood House had not been fulfilled and that being a woman of whim as well as of steel, we could not rely on her word being her bond.

'If this is true, Mrs Smith, then you've worked a bloody miracle.'

'Thank me nicely, then, Mr Montgomery.'

So he did.

Jason dropped me back home about six o'clock that evening. I sauntered up the pathway, giddily singing to myself, filled to the brim with white wine and satisfaction.

A small, and totally unwelcome, deputation awaited me in the kitchen. George, with another bunch of gushing red roses at the ready, and Seth, who was wearing an executive sneer almost worthy of Glossop's.

'Any news on the house, Holly?' George asked anxiously. 'Did you manage to persuade Dottie to go ahead with us?'

'Oh darling,' I replied, wondering whether to ad lib or come clean, 'give me a minute, please. I've had a gruelling day and I'm positively knackered.'

Seth snorted, 'I told you, George, Holly would be useless. Now, if only you had negotiated for Smallwood House through Ash and Spicer, all might not be lost. We can always throw some *professional* weight behind a wavering vendor.'

'But Dottie thinks of Holly as a friend, Seth.'

'That's half the trouble,' said Seth from his negotiating pedestal. 'Holly gets too chummy with the clients. A great mistake. They just twist her round their fingers in the end. She's no idea of what she's doing. I can tell you now, you've lost Smallwood House. But don't worry, Ash and Spicer have a lot of other interesting properties on our books. I suggest you come in and see me tomorrow morning.'

'It's no good, Seth. Ivy has set her heart on Smallwood House. We won't budge her,' said George firmly.

'Come upstairs with me, George,' I said beguilingly. (There was only one way to deal with George at such a juncture.) 'I'm going to have a bath and I need company. You scrub my back and I'll scrub yours. We'll talk it all over in a more relaxed atmosphere. As for you, Seth, you can bugger off. Go and do something against the law with Juliet.'

Obediently George followed me into the bathroom. I stripped and ran the bathwater. Even my winsome nudity failed to bring a response. George just gazed dolefully into the foaming water as I added a spurt of bubble bath.

'Seth's right, isn't he?' he asked.

'Oh, come on, sweetheart,' I cajoled. 'Get your clothes off.' I put my arms around his neck and started kissing him. It hurt me to see his misery.

'I don't know how I'll face Ivy tonight.' he said, automatically undressing.

'Then stay here with me, silly.'

'I don't think I'd better. Ivy's going to need my comfort. And you said you were knackered.'

I was put suddenly on my mettle. Why should Immortal Ivy get all the comfort? I ached to bring a smile back to my dear old George's face. I snaked my legs around him as the water dowsed us in soapy splendour.

'Just forget that old house for a few hours. Dottie may well come round in the end. She's had a bit of a shock, that's all.'

My tactics were succeeding.

'I love you, Mrs Smith,' said George tenderly.

'And I love you, darling,' I said. At that moment I was so happy I loved everybody. I decided I couldn't give George his marching orders now that Jason and I were lovers. After all, George might always come in useful even after I married Jason. For I *would* marry Jason and live happily ever after on the Common Agricultural Policy.

12

I had definitely been put off my breakfast at Tesco's. The usual gang were absent. Only Seth was present, in greasy isolation, heaving sausages, egg and bacon towards his slobbering mouth. He had long since abandoned the healthy diet regime.

'You're rather a picky little eater, aren't you, Seth,' I said with distaste.

He looked at me soulfully above a fork that had just speared a piece of fried bread. 'Glad to have an opportunity of a private chat at last, Holly. You've been so preoccupied with your carnal appetites lately I've hardly had the chance of a talk.'

'I'm sorry. You should have made an appointment,' I snapped, taking a gulp of black coffee to mitigate the effects of Seth's proximity. But Seth in confidential mood was always disturbing. Was the bogey of the flat about to surface again?

'I want you to be the first person to know this,' Seth continued, 'as you are the nearest I shall ever get to a real mother.'

When Seth leaned on our tenuous family connection, I wanted to throw up. But, to be fair to the poor sod, his 'real' mother had gone in search of a brighter future a few months after his birth, leaving him behind in his pram, to the everlasting repugnance of every female who had tripped across his father's horizon thereafter.

'Juliet and I are officially engaged,' Seth announced, to my horror. 'Our love for each other has reached the stage of total commitment. We are ready for Holy Matrimony.'

I felt the cold slap of lost rental income hit me in the face. 'Don't be so bloody mad. You can't possibly marry that raving nymphomaniac.'

Seth put down his knife and fork. 'I can do without your normal abuse, Holly. All I want is for you to give us your blessing and act like a normal stepmother, or even a normal woman. Madge and Steve are over the moon about our engagement and they're your generation.'

'How dare you. I'm not an octogenarian. And although you are too blindly besotted to see it, my reaction could save you from making a ghastly mistake. A worse mistake, this time, than you made the last time when you picked up that other floozie, Sandra. You insisted on marrying *her* too. What on earth gets into you that you must rush these scrubbers up to the altar every time?'

'I have a moral duty to the women I sleep with. But you wouldn't understand about morals, or duty, or any of society's codes of conduct. You can't even look after the cat.'

'What's the cat got to do with it?'

Seth sighed. 'I was afraid you wouldn't comprehend the solemnity of my proposal. You will never be capable of transcending the fleshly union.'

'Well, I don't deny it, I do rather enjoy the old fleshly union now and then. And I gather dear Juliet is not averse to putting herself about a bit. How will you cope with her endearing little trick of tearing the pants of every man she meets?'

'Keep your voice down, Holly,' Seth said in consternation, indicating the small group of riveted breakfasters at nearby tables. 'My wife-to-be may not be entirely virtuous in the orthodox sense, it's true, but her talent and her loins have been fused into focusing her sublime art. Another facet to her existence to which you will be forever unaware.'

I rose to my feet in exasperation. 'I hope you will be extremely unhappy, Seth,' I shouted, 'because you bloody well deserve to be for being such an abysmal idiot.'

'And up yours too, Holly,' Seth said calmly, going in for the kill on another hapless sausage.

There was no doubt about it, summer was over at last. That long-lasting heatwave, the flawlessly blue skies, had ended,

124

abruptly as always, and now there were cool winds rattling the weary leaves. Grim clouds of grey and black cloaked Tinkerstown Church atop the High Street, and when rain wasn't falling, fog was forming. It was all very joyful. However, the change in the weather had presented me with an opportunity to wear my sexy black raincoat and my patent leather stilettos. I looked like the archetypal street-corner tart and Jason took off his spectacles rather a lot and totally failed to keep his hands off me. We made love incessantly. In my bedroom, at the edge of Barty's Field, even in his mother's farmhouse when she went off to London to chair a conference. As Jason penetrated me, I felt I had penetrated to the very heart of the farming community. I was exultant.

That afternoon the Range Rover roared towards the estate of Cavendish Parkes. Old Cav was an acquaintance of the Montgomery family. A well-known, but not much respected, local millionaire whose indecently large funds had been accumulated by means obscure but almost certainly suspect. Jason referred to him jocularly as the Arms Baron. I was intrigued to meet the man, not so much for his money this time, as for his reputation as a womaniser, I was beginning to have expectations beyond my station: Jason's enslavement was giving me overweening confidence in my ability to sexually entice. Although Jason was boringly proprietorial when I was with him, nevertheless the situation held promise.

'Do you think your Mr Parkes will fancy me, darling?' I asked, snuggling against Jason. I was still warmly receptive, having just shared an hour on the dog blanket with my employer.

'No,' Jason said bluntly. 'Old Cav likes 'em young.'

'Thank you very much.' (Seth's earlier jibe concerning my rung on the generation ladder still stung.)

'Cav's not at all like me, sweetheart. I'm hung up on maturity. I'm only taking you with me now because it's business.'

Dottie had come across with her land. She herself had gone on an extended cruise, presumably in search of a replacement soulmate. She had hopes of one of the cabin staff, she told me on a postcard from Tunisia. Jason had brushed aside my builder candidates with contempt. The man to develop this nice little parcel, he assured me, was Cavendish Parkes.

We had the documentation with us, together with Dottie's letter of authority, and we had put a price on the deal that was frankly immoral.

Cavendish Parkes's estate was set in an area of Outstanding Natural Ugliness. As far as the eye could see all was flat, unhedged, unedifying. And, with the great arc of East Anglian sky all broody with the onset of the monsoon season, the landscape offered a scene of unrelieved gloom. Even the rich man's house was a disappointment. I had expected something grand or glitzy. But no, it was in fact a bungalow. But a bungalow of immense size. It had spreadeagled itself about, like a Texan ranch, without appeasement to taste or design. And Cavendish Parkes was as ungainly as his property. A big-boned, loose-limbed fellow with little hair and even less charisma. He eyed me coldly so I decided not to treat him to my sexy pout.

If he were a wow with the little girl brigade, there was no sign of any nymphet cohabiting with him. He led us through a labyrinth of dull rooms floored in parquet with the occasional scuffed rug in evidence, and eventually our dismal wanderings led us to a large office festooned with the equipment of modern communication. A full-sized billiard table was the centrepiece. Its green baize was covered with files and disgorged faxes. Obviously, if you dealt in arms it made for a great deal of paperwork, and my mental picture of glamorous getaways in helicopters from Amazonian jungles vanished.

Cavendish Parkes and Jason were on the best of masculine terms. There was a lot of guffawing and whisky-swigging during the next hour of negotiation. I sat quietly beside the window fondling the ears of the bleary-eyed Irish wolfhound that had been the only male to take notice of my presence.

However, winding up the conversation, Cavendish Parkes turned to me. 'So this is your Holly, then, Jason?'

'Isn't she an adorable tart?' answered Jason.

Cavendish Parkes looked me over with what, I am sure, he supposed to be his connoisseur's eye and said, '*Chacun à son gout*, old boy.'

I did not care for the thrust of that comment, and replied offensively, 'I gather your preference is for little girls, Mr Parkes.'

Jason downed his whisky nervously.

'Not little girls, my dear. *Big* girls.' Cav glanced at us roguishly. 'Shall I show Holly my art collection, Jason?'

'I think we'd better be off, Cav. Holly and I have no liking for art.' Jason was on edge by now.

'Come along, Holly,' Cavendish insisted. 'I'd welcome your reactions.' I was reminded of the bearded president of the art society as old Cav led us down yet another corridor. However, unlike the president, Cav kept his hands to himself. I was definitely not his type.

He took us into yet another rectangular room. Here the walls were thick with line-and-wash drawings, with oils, and with pastels of varying size but singular theme. *Nudes*. Pot-bellied, gigantic-breasted, swollen-buttocked, nauseous nudes. Some cavorted, some reclined, some were entwined in orgiastic revelry. I could imagine this unprepossessing, uncouth man sitting here night after night gloating over his harem and I was horrified.

Jason had obviously never before been invited to view these spoils. His hand shook on his refilled glass of single malt. 'Bloody hell, Cav,' he exclaimed.

Cavendish leered across at me expectantly.

'I am fascinated,' I said. I meant it. The sight of these substantial females had given me an idea. Furthermore, I had at last pleased Cavendish Parkes. He flashed his implants in a grisly smile.

'Your lady friend has unexpected powers of appreciation, Jason.'

'My Holly is an adorable tart,' reiterated Jason heartily, putting a protective arm around me.

'Jason,' I said, 'do these pictures remind you of someone?'

'No,' said Jason obtusely.

'Of course they do,' I said irritably. 'A young lady whose proportions not only rival, but eclipse, those of these female forms.'

'Oh, I know,' said Jason, 'that fat tart who makes the mean fruit cup.'

'Exactly. Her name is Juliet,' I explained for Cavendish's benefit, 'and she is an artist herself.'

Jason peered more closely at one of the oils of two lewdly embracing ladies whose nipples appeared to be the size of dinner plates. 'Bloody hell, Holly, you're right. Do you think she posed for this lot? It's her to the life.'

To our dismay, Cavendish Parkes galloped across the room and kissed first me and then Jason. 'My dear, my dears,' he cried, overcome. 'You aren't teasing poor old Cav, are you?'

We gave him our assurances of Juliet's existence and statistics.

'Come to think of it,' Cav continued, 'I may have heard something about a massive beauty on the old grapevine. Artist, you say?'

'Not only an artist,' I said. 'but, to quote an admirer of hers, she is someone who fuses her talent with her loins, and I know for a fact that she does specialised finger work with oils.'

Cavendish swayed dramatically.

'Steady on, Holly,' Jason warned. 'Cav's got a dicky heart valve.'

'I must meet her, I must,' Cavendish said feverishly. 'This could well be my last chance to possess an odalisque of my own.'

I could see he was seriously excited, and momentarily, I experienced a stab of conscience. 'It's only fair to say,' I went on, 'that Juliet is engaged to a young man who loves her very much.'

Cavendish brushed aside this irrelevance. 'Then I must ensure that she is released from this absurd entanglement no matter what the cost. I can offer such a superlative child every advantage. No young man can match me.'

'I'd wait until you see her, Cav,' Jason said. 'She's a bit of a handful for a chap with a dicky heart.'

'A matter of little consequence,' Cav said airily. 'You see, dear ones, I would be prepared to die for the culmination of a lifetime's ambition like this. When do I get to meet this divine creature?'

'I can get the slag along any time,' I offered generously. 'I'll tell her you are a vegetarian millionaire who wants to evaluate her artwork and she'll be on the hook in a second.'

Once back inside the Range Rover, Jason and I congratulated each other on an afternoon of financial success.

'You are wonderful, Holly,' said Jason, taking off his spectacles.

'I know I am,' I replied, taking off my clothes.

128

It had been tougher than usual to stifle my uneasiness over my actions. I knew I was being unfair to Seth. As for Steve and Madge, what would they think if they knew I was attempting to procure their angel for the delectation of a crumbing old lecher like Cavendish Parkes? It was all a bit sleazy, And would I be struck down for such wickedness? I knew strange things could befall those who subverted the Forces of Destiny.

On the other hand, surely I was doing everyone a favour? Juliet would have a secure future as an early widow. Madge and Steve could bless the bride of a millionaire and Seth would recover. My rental monies would continue and he and I would rub along together in our abrasive tandem, happy as sparking plugs.

Anyway, I had made my play for Juliet's removal and I must run all the way with it. So I stilettoed round that evening to Juliet's stable block. She had a choice, did she not? She could refuse to meet old Cavendish. But I was very sure she wouldn't pass up that kind of invitation.

I approached the stable cautiously. I never knew what moment of artistic frenzy I might be about to interrupt. However, I found the Madonna alone, and fully clothed, slapping some acrylics about and munching a cheese sandwich. She gazed at me blankly before saying huskily, 'Madge is out. Something to do with fund-raising for kittens.'

'It's all right, it's you I've come to see, Juliet.'

'Really?' Juliet was chilly. 'If it's about my engagement to Seth, I don't consider it's any of your business. You are no blood relation, not like his delightful father.'

'If you and Seth intend to get married, it's no big deal for me, although I am surprised you are both so reactionary as to want to tie the knot. Has Seth bought you an engagement ring?'

'Seth and I have no need to exchange silly trinkets. We have given ourselves to each other. A far more meaningful act than the acquisition of a piece of jewellery.'

'I quite agree. How about the wedding then? Church, white dress, choir, all that?'

'Seth insists on a traditional atmosphere. He is smitten with the pageantry of the processional. He wants the ultimate macho

129

glory of leading his prize down the aisle. I can understand that. I am, as even you must acknowledge, quite a prize.'

The woman's touched, I thought. She'll do old Cavendish proud. 'I can't help thinking,' I said confidentially, 'that it's an awful shame for a young girl like you to be tied down so soon.'

'But nothing is going to change for me, Holly. I shall continue my life as I lead it now but from a different base. Also, I shall shed the yoke of Madge and Steve. They are excessively old-fashioned where sexual freedom is concerned. Seth understands that my spirit is not to be shackled and my body remains mine to give as I please.'

'You're a selfish slut, aren't you?' I said sweetly. Then I took a deep breath and plunged: 'Someone I know, someone who is an art collector in a very bold way, someone with loads of money and a reputation for being a rampant roaring old sexpot, wants to meet you. Wants to meet you badly, Juliet darling, engaged or not engaged.'

Juliet ignored me. She splodged two strokes of vivid yellow against a stark, grey background.

'I mean it, Juliet. I'm not joking. This person is beside himself with excitement. You could well be the ideal woman he's spent his life searching for. Anyway, think of the money.'

Juliet changed brushes and spattered brilliant red across the canvas. 'Bugger,' she said angrily. 'Now look what you've done. You are distorting my creation.'

'Perhaps it's a sign,' I cried.

'Don't talk to me like that. You know nothing of creative genius. You are just an envious middle-aged tramp with tits like pimples.'

'I've always admired you, too, Juliet. But don't dismiss this offer. Out there is a millionaire who wants to bang you to death because he likes 'em fat.'

'Has he really got money?'

'Rumour suggests he's big in arms-dealing.'

Juliet stuffed the remains of her cheese sandwich into her large mouth. 'Well,' she said slowly, 'it has always been my philosophy to spread happiness through intimate contact. When do I get to meet the guy?'

'I'll drive you out tomorrow, darling. Anything to foster the erotic arts. Apart from the lust angle, he really does have an amazing porno collection, and everyone of these arty concoctions is a dead ringer for you.'

'My own voluptuous alchemy has yet to be captured on canvas,' Juliet said coyly. 'Seth says it would be beyond human ability to portray it in any illustrative guise.'

'The artist would certainly run out of space pretty soon,' I conceded.

13

It was a now a month since I had delivered a real live odalisque to Cavendish Parkes. And so far retribution had not overtaken me. Juliet's introduction, effected at the old lecher's bungalow, had been an unqualified triumph of flesh over conventional small talk. Cav had fallen on his knees before the stately Madonna. For her part she had lost no time in shedding her flowing covering and, as if I were totally invisible, they were at it before I could make it to the door. I allowed myself one satisfied peek to reaffirm that Juliet had grasped the essentials.

However, if an irrevocable bond had been forged on that occasion there was no subsequent evidence to support it. Seth continued to burble pathetically about wedding plans, although he did admit that Juliet was being evasive about an actual date for the nuptials.

'Understandable,' he kept repeating. 'It's a big step and we both want to be quite sure about it.'

Madge and Steve were already quite sure of it. Madge especially was oozing sentimental clichés on matters bridal whenever we met.

Juliet's parents, who still lived abroad doing their ecological thing in a forest, were unable to attend. Apologies had been received (by fax) and, as no cheque had been received from that source (by any method) my dear little friends were deputising yet again and doing the decent thing for their god-daughter's Big Day. Mrs Angelicus was going to be matron of honour; Sandy was going to be best man. Steve, of course, was going to give

132

Juliet away (no doubt with enormous relief). Seth was handling the invitations and Ash and Spicer were getting them printed (at trade). My ex and classy Philly were being excluded from the guest list. All this preparation caused me considerable chagrin. Evidently old Cav was a man of straw after all. Or had Juliet's generosity proved too damaging to the dicky heart valve? Perhaps this was why retribution had ignored me as an instant candidate for meaty sorrow. However, there was the odd portent or two.

George's attentions, for instance, had waned since my inability to retrieve Smallwood House for him and Immortal Ivy. I had had a postcard from Grover, also; a postcard from Spain, where, he told me, he was enjoying the sunshine, the wine and the mountain scenery. 'We are sitting on the terrace of this charming little villa replete with the good things of life,' he had written. His casual use of the plural bothered me. *We.* Who was the bastard with? A business colleague? A passing tourist? Or some bloody woman who had got her talons into my boy next door. But surely Grover was now a plaything of my past? Oh no, when I saw that spidery handwriting, all the old yearning arose, all the old longing to have him as my husband overlaid my more recent aspirations towards the Common Agricultural Policy.

What with all the wedding furore, I prayed for Dottie's return from the high seas. I wanted a sane and sensible gossip that didn't involve tulle veils, church bells, and heavily iced cakes. Even Alex had gone sloppy on me. The moment the marriage was mooted she had proved herself a tireless authority on etiquette for bridesmaids, the best photographer to seek and car-hire firms specialising in white Rolls Royces.

'Didn't you have a white wedding, Holly?' she had asked. As it happened, I had not. My ex was newly divorced, newly dried out and newly fired from an orchestra. Not surprisingly, I had felt cheated of the pomp and circumstance of such a momentous event in a girl's calendar as the white wedding.

My Big Day had taken place in a register office, not a church, and not in white. My wedding reception had been a thin slice of fruit cake (wrapped in cling film) at a railway station buffet en route to a seaside town where my ex had had a brief engagement at the end of a pier. Even then, stoned again within a week, he had fallen off it and been replaced hastily by a youthful sax-ophonist from a local school who was billed as a child prodigy.

In the middle of all this romantic tomfoolery. I arrived home one evening eager for Seth's presence at the microwave, to be met by him at the gate.

'Cat's been in a car accident,' he announced. 'The widow up the road has taken him to the vet. I don't know the result yet but I've promised to help with the vet's bill.'

Of late the cypress cat had been having thin rations, due to Seth's preoccupation with his bride-to-be.

'Oh the poor little cat,' I cried in anguish. 'Is he badly hurt?'

'Don't know,' said Seth. 'The widow has promised to ring us when she gets back from the surgery.'

We went into the kitchen together. The cat's empty feeding bowl reproached us. 'I loved that little cat,' I said. 'Even though he wasn't mine he made this house seem like a home.'

We agreed to waive dinner. When the telephone rang we both plunged towards it. I grabbed it first.

'You done my numbers?' shouted my mother.

'Get off the line, Mother,' I said unceremoniously. 'Seth and I are waiting for an important telephone call.'

'He never comes to see me,' whined my mother. 'Too busy with women, is he?'

I cut her off in mid-tirade and the next call was from the widow. Would we go round to her house at once? It sounded serious.

'How's the cat?' Seth asked anxiously.

'She didn't say anything about the cat. But if she wants a cheque, Seth, will you write her one, please? I'm overdrawn this month already.'

'How do you get your finances in such a mess, Holly?'

'I screw up everything.'

'Well, you said it.'

The fussy widow two doors up opened the door and com-manded us sharply to 'come in for a minute'.

Fortunately, her attitude was not as ominous as we had feared. The cypress cat was sitting up and taking notice. His injuries were not sufficiently harrowing to have made euthanasia imperative. He had dislocated one hip and had to have cage rest for a month.

134

Indeed, he was already in this weird imprisonment with a litter tray and a bowl of water. He did not look at me. And, as I gazed fondly at him, I knew with a pang, that he would never share my life again.

The fussy widow gave Seth and me a blast of displeasure. 'I don't propose to let my cat out after this,' she said. 'I shall restrict him to my garden by putting up a wire screen. It was foolish of me ever to let him stay with irresponsible people like you. The vet says he was full of fleas too. I dread to think of the condition of your house, Mrs Smith.'

Although I had always disliked the fussy widow, I recognised her attitude was dictated by the distress of the incident rather than an assessment of the circumstances. Nevertheless, Seth and I returned to the mausoleum chastened.

That evening we sat together on the sofa in the sitting room, watching a video. There was no George, no Jason and no Juliet. We had not been so cosily ensconced for many months. Presently Seth observed, 'You've got some settlement in your chimney breast, Holly. Look at that ugly crack.'

'Always ready with the cheery little comment, aren't you,' I replied. I had already noticed the crack and was trying to stifle yet another terror about costly repairs. 'Long dry summers always cause movement,' I said knowledgeably.

At this point in the agents' calendar 'under offers' came floating down like blossom in a breeze. At the back of most of these changes of heart lay a surveyor's report. And after the dry spells of East Anglia, the clay shrank, the cracks appeared and the purchasers took fright.

As the video, which contained a considerable amount of gratuitous copulation, irritated me and underlined Jason's absence. I went to bed – with Gummidge and the gin bottle and a feeling of imminent doom.

The following evening I made a point of calling at the garage and, adopting the stance of a serious punter for once, carefully studied the Lottery form. Hitherto it had been a perfunctory operation but, suddenly, I wanted to atone. I felt responsible for my mother's luck. She had asked me to choose her six numbers in future, after a fierce altercation at the gnome complex.

'How's your dear mum?' asked the girl at the counter.

'She's fine, just fine. But I've got to sort her numbers out for her now. Any suggestions?'

'No, love, none at all. I've never won anything. The odds are too long. It's only a bit of fun, really. Why don't you try birthdays? They seem to do well.'

Birthdays. Whose birthdays? Certainly not Seth's or Mother's, or my ex's. George's, Jason's or Grover's – together with mine? That seemed to turn Mother's bloody numbers into a fun situation at last. I decided to use Grover's birthday. He was two years older and born under Cancer. I liked the idea of a seven in the line-up.

I felt quite smug as I sauntered home. I paused by the fabric shop, sighing over Colefax and Fowler and Osborne and Little. When I married Jason I would bring interior design into his tasteless life. Perhaps it was all down to Dottie's inspiration. I needed an injection of the Smallwood House style. I turned towards her part of Tinkerstown. There was just the chance she was back from her cruise.

As I approached Smallwood House, George came out of the ornate ironwork gate. Seeing me, he blushed and looked sheepish. This, combined with the inherent sexiness he always exuded, made him immediately desirable. I put my arms around him and gave him one of my blatantly provocative kisses.

'Steady on, Holly,' said George.

'I am reminding you of what you've been missing. You haven't been round to see me for ages.'

George apologised. 'I know, I know, I'm sorry.'

'Is Dottie back yet?'

'No. I just called round myself to find out if she's going to sell us her house now she's had time to calm down and reconsider. If she won't, though, my life is ruined. Ivy's a proper old misery these days.'

'Come back with me now, Georgie Porgie,' I whispered, 'and make me cry.'

'Why not?' agreed George. 'Let's not waste any more time.'

And, once we were in George's car, we didn't.

14

Ivy had gone off to her sister's that day, so George felt that he could spend longer than usual comforting me about the cat's accident. Then I had to be comforted about my structural settlement. Then I had to comfort him about the loss of Small-wood House. With such a surfeit of comforting, plus the intake of two bottles of white wine, we both fell asleep about four in the morning and awoke at seven.

'Oh dear,' said George, reproached by my bedside clock, 'Ivy usually rings me at home about now. She'll worry if I don't answer.'

'Tough,' I said, without remorse.

George grinned. 'She'll have to worry, for once. It's been a lovely night, Holly.'

I stretched out my winsome nudity despite the chill in the bedroom air caused by the central heating boiler, not serviced for years, finally failing. For a few weeks now, Seth and I had been relying on an ancient electric fire to keep the frostbite at bay.

George paused in mid-dressing. 'One more time, my love?'

'Yes, please, George. And then a nice big breakfast at Tesco's.'

We arrived at the cafeteria hand in hand; George was growing less circumspect, less concerned about country town gossip. Sandy and Mrs Angelicus were there, a pot of tea between them; Seth and Juliet were sharing a milk shake.

'Fixed a wedding date yet?' George asked them.

Juliet smiled inscrutably. 'Further knots are being placed in our relationship,' she admitted.

Now what sort of nonsense is that? I wondered; why can't the silly cow come out with a definite date – or call the ridiculous affair off? It obviously infuriated Seth too.

'Yes, we have fixed a date,' he bellowed. 'Two months from now. Banns on Sunday. The whole works.'

'Oh Seth,' breathed Juliet huskily. 'Always so upfront.'

'Why a November wedding?' I said. 'Bit bleak isn't it?'

I pondered on what I might wear to look sexy and steal the show. Not easy. The church would be icy and the reception, which it was proposed to hold in the adjacent church hall, would be even less inviting with its sparse complement of calor gas stoves and nothing more warming to drink than herbal tea. On balance, I thought I might skip this bloody wedding altogether. But the other breakfasters were still agog.

'Diaries out, everyone,' cried Sandy. 'Let's all get synchronised. This is going to be an important date. A first for Tesco. Wedding breakfast of the year.'

'Let's drink to this,' said Mrs Angelicus, raising her teacup.

'The happy couple,' cried Sandy.

'The happy couple,' echoed George.

Sod the happy couple, I thought. All my hopes were now blighted. In spite of Cavendish Parkes and his odalisque obsession, my plans to thwart the course of foolishly misguided love had been aborted. The wedding would take place.

As George and I were leaving, Mrs Angelicus took me aside. 'Holly dear, a word in your ear.'

My mood was decidedly unreceptive. 'What now?'

'Your mother seems to be failing. In many small ways I see a lessening of her iron will.'

'That'll be the day,' I said.

'None of us lives for ever, Holly,' said Mrs Angelicus. 'And if anything should happen to your dear mother, you will be broken-hearted, you know. I'm just giving you warning that she may not be around for much longer, so you really ought to come up to the bungalow and see her more often than you do.'

'That's blackmail,' I said resentfully. 'I do her bloody numbers, don't I? I'm even choosing them for her now.'

'Such a small obligation, surely?'

138

As George and I walked across the car park, I said testily, 'That woman is becoming a pain in the bum. I hope Sandy never marries her.'

'Not much chance of that,' said George. 'Sandy doesn't have the appetite that I have.' Impulsively he pulled me against him and kissed me greedily. He really was throwing caution to the winds this morning. The car park could have been teeming with Ivy's chums. I had never known my bit of rough to be so daring.

'This is nice, darling,' I said appreciatively.

'I want you to know, Holly, that I really do love you. Never forget that.' Then he got into his car and drove off. How odd, I thought. Of course he loves me. I had never really doubted that; only Ivy stood in the way of our blissful future together.

'You're looking pleased with yourself,' said Alex. The office was warm and I leaned gratefully against the radiator and accepted the mug of coffee she handed me.

'Everybody loves me,' I said.

'Only yesterday you were afraid no one loved you any more.'

'A slight hiatus in the bedroom department, that's all. I was back on form again last night, I can tell you.'

'Well, don't tell me. I have some news for you instead.'

'Not another sale dropped off?'

'No, this is personal.' Alex looked at me, all dewy and girlish. 'Cant' you guess?'

'You and Mark are going to split up.'

'Oh, Holly.' Alex was exasperated. 'Of course not. We are going to be parents at last. I'm pregnant. Isn't it a miracle?'

This news took some swallowing. I was used to Alex being permanently infertile.

'Well, you might look pleased for me.' She was now in a huff.

'Oh, I am pleased for you,' I answered coldly. 'If it's what you want.'

'You know it's what I want more than anything in the world. We've been trying long enough.'

'I've just got used to your being here, that's all. Looking after everything and all that. Now I suppose you'll leave and I'll have to train someone else. No one will be the same as you, anyway.

139

I can talk to you – or rather I *could* talk to you. From now on I guess it'll be Pampers and play schools all the day.'

'Don't be so mean, Holly. Anyway, what will happen if you do marry Jason? You'll leave me then and play the rich, bored wife, with nothing better to do than count her lovers.'

'I like that scenario,' I said, brightening. 'I might even invite you and your brat for tea occasionally? Or will it be brats? Once you mothers get the bit between your teeth you can't stop filling your wombs.'

'One will do for a start,' said Alex. 'Although there is a history of twins in Mark's family – so I'm hoping.'

'My God. Two for the price of one.'

'I'd be a glutton for that sort of punishment, Holly.'

'Well, yours is the second piece of bad news I've had this morning.'

'What other bad news?'

'Seth and Juliet are tying the knot – they've fixed a date. Banns will be read. Can you believe it?'

'You don't want Seth to get married, do you?'

'Oh, you've noticed? No I do not. I'll miss the sod. And I'll miss his money.'

'Never mind. You can invite him and Juliet to tea as well when you're the chatelaine of the big farmhouse.

'No thank you. They'd spoil the effect of my Colefax and Fowler.'

The telephone rang. To my relief it was Dottie. She was back, she was offering me coffee and she was eager for pornographic disclosures.

'I'm off up the hill to Smallwood House,' I told Alex. 'To see someone who isn't going to get pregnant and ruin my life.'

'I'm sure you're quite capable of ruining your own life, Holly.'

'I shall ignore your spitefulness and put it down to morning sickness. Where's my beloved Jason, by the way?'

'According to his mother he's sleeping off a skinful at the Suckling Pig. You might look in there after you've finished your social rounds and get yourself stuffed again,' said Alex with unwonted vulgarity.

140

After I had recovered from Dottie's effusive greeting, and Buster's aggressive one, I asked her when she had returned.

'Last night, but I went straight round and collected my Buster from the kennels. After that I was whacked and went to bed.'

'I came round here myself last night but found you out. George came round as well. He still wants the house very much.'

'Ah, George,' said Dottie vaguely. 'Well, I've not made up my mind about anything yet. He'll probably get his wish in the end.'

Dottie led me into her kitchen. The dark green Aga warmed my bones. I looked around contentedly. Odd compensations came to pass in life: had George and Ivy bought Smallwood House I could never have luxuriated in its kitchen again. I was not on Ivy's guest list.

'I've brought you back a present,' said Dottie. 'I bought it in a sex shop in Amsterdam. It might come in handy if Jason should flag at any time.'

'*Flag?* My dear Dottie, the man is gloriously inexhaustible.'

To my surprise, Dottie's reaction was neither amusement nor delight. 'I do hope Jason's amorous interest in you is proof against family opposition.'

'What do you mean? Jason adores me.'

'I'm sure he does adore you, my dear. But there's something about these farming families – sort of incestuous inclination.'

'Incest? Steady on, Dottie'

'I mean they are incestuous about keeping farming money in farming families. Still, Jason is strong-willed and he would be an ideal catch, but you'll have to box more cleverly than gratifying your mutual sexual desires. And do watch out for Mrs Montgomery.'

'Do you know her?'

'Met her a few times, yes. Charming, of course, but formidable. She worships Jason, though, so if he sticks up for you, she'll give in eventually. Now, dear, tell me what's happened to that frightful fat person who paints.'

'Oh, Dottie. I've tried my best to stop her marrying my poor old stepson. But a date for the wedding is fixed, despite my having thrown her to old Cavendish Parkes, who seemed such a suitable wolf to gobble her up.'

Dottie yelled in excitement. 'Old Cav – my dear, *what* an inspiration. She's perfect for that old lecher. He's crazy about elephantine teenagers.'

I described the meeting I had engineered at Cavendish's bungalow. 'And that's the unexpurgated version, so I was certain I'd rocked Seth's marital apple-cart. But there it is. Old Cav must have backed off.'

'What a shame. I'd have called theirs a match made in Hades which they both deserve. Perhaps she was too much for old Cav – he's getting on a bit now. A wolf with wobbly teeth, I'm afraid. Anyway, Holly, it was a brilliant try and it might still work. Don't despair. Weddings can be called off.'

After a discussion about Dottie's parcel of land, the completion of which was imminent now that she was back to sign the contract, Dottie said, 'I suppose that's how you came to meet old Cav. Did he show you his abominable art collection?'

'Of course. That's where I got the idea of getting him together with Juliet. It seemed too good a possibility to miss, what with her vital statistics and his addiction to obscene paintings.'

I left Dottie's and, clutching my sex aid, hurried to get the company car and drive out to the Suckling Pig. It was now noon and Jason would be up and about from his hangover. As I drove through the lanes I made a resolve. I would broach the subject of marriage with Jason myself. He was such a slouch at drawing a conclusion. He may not have realised that my aim was respectable – with a farmhouse and designer-fabric curtains to call my own.

By this time I was friendly with the landlord, Roger. After all, he had seen my winsome nudity often enough at my most entangled moments with Jason. But Roger was not only broad-minded and discreet, but at heart uninterested in the sexual athletics of his clients. His love was light railways. His spare cash and his spare time were not given to bedroom capers, but to sleepers, signals and the acquisition of elderly rolling stock. He was the chairman of the local light railway society and his ambition was to open up as much of the defunct branch line as possible. Jason considered it a laudable enterprise (he was keen on playing trains too) and did not begrudge the inordinate payment Roger extracted for the use of his upper room, which swelled the branch line coffers.

I approached Roger, who was behind the bar pulling a pint. 'Jason upstairs?' I enquired.

Roger inclined his head towards the restaurant. In there I found my beloved employer alone at a table, eating steak and kidney pie. I snuggled up to him, while he implanted a gravied kiss on my cheek.

'You adorable tart,' he said. 'I hoped you'd turn up.'

'Statistically speaking, it was a certainty once I knew where to find you.'

'Want something to eat? Packet of crisps?'

'That'll do. Large gin and tonic might increase my sex drive, though.'

Jason produced a twenty-pound note. 'Buy a bottle if necessary, sweetheart. I intend to have some fun in Barty's Field this afternoon. I am somewhat deflated by the turn of events and I need you to put back my customary cool.'

Jason deflated? It seemed unlikely. In any event, Jason's generosity was unexpected so I took advantage of it and, armed with gallons of tonic, a large bottle of London Dry and the sex aid, we set off for Barty's Field in randy anticipation.

Once parked, I lost no time in wiggling out of my clothes and divesting Jason of his, amid much giggling. We were soon interlocked and drunkenly ecstatic.

'I love you, Holly,' said Jason. 'Sex aid or no sex aid, you are terrific.'

This is the moment, I thought. Always get a man to propose when his trousers are down. 'If you love me so much, darling,' I murmured, 'when will you marry me?'

'Bloody hell, Holly, I can't marry everyone.'

I was putting my all into my sexual fervour, as never before. 'I don't want you to marry everyone, darling, just me.'

'Shut up and concentrate, you adorable tart.'

This was not music to my ears, but the moment held its own magical urgency and my plea for wedding bells had to be briefly adjourned. In a calmer moment, while Jason refilled the thermos with gin and tonic, I returned to the theme, placing my legs appealingly around his torso and fluffing out my thick blonded hair. I took one more deep slug from the thermos and plunged into my important, if unrehearsed, speech. A speech to secure a fabulous future of romping and riches.

'Listen to me, Jason. I am quite serious about marrying you. I love you.'

'I love you too. Let's have that bloody thermos. I'm parched.'

'Jason, you clod. I am proposing to you. I want to marry you.'

'I must be a bit squiffy, sweetheart. You want me to marry *you?*'

'Yes I do. I do. I promise I'll make you a good wife. I'll even bake things and supervise harvest suppers and provide luncheon for the guns when you have your pheasant shoots. I know all about country obligations, honestly.'

Jason put his spectacles back on. Then he hiccoughed. 'I feel rather ill,' he said. 'I don't think this is happening to me. Things were bad enough before you started. Marry me? Don't be so stupid, Holly. You can't marry me.'

'Why not? You love older women, you said so. We could always adopt a baby if that's bugging you.'

Jason shook me roughly. 'Stop it, Holly. Stop it, you silly cow. You are only joking, aren't you?'

'Joking? Why should I be joking? Sod you, Jason, I mean it.'

'Come on, sweetheart,' he said, pulling back my hair and kissing me fiercely. 'Just shut up and make love to me.'

With sudden anger, I hit him with the thermos.

'Bloody hell, Holly, what's got into you? You were well away just now, What's the matter?'

'It's your mother, isn't it? She hates me. I knew it. She doesn't think I'm good enough for you. The bitch, the rotten bitch.'

'Don't be rude about my mother,' said Jason, white-faced. 'She doesn't hate you. She doesn't even think about you. Why should she? All right, then. I was going to tell you in any case before someone else did. I am getting married, Holly. And quite soon.'

I was briefly bereft of response. And Jason, realising at last that I was more than slightly perturbed by his announcement, went

144

on haltingly. 'She's someone I've known all my life. She's got two farms and four thousand acres. It's not exactly a love match, but she's not a bad sort. We'll muck along together all right. Anyway, Holly darling, it need not make any difference to us, you know.'

'Oh Jason, don't marry her. Just *don't*. You don't have to just to please your mother. Stand up for yourself for once. Forget about farms and acreage. You've got enough money and land as it is.'

'You can't understand, Holly. Apart from other considerations, I've got to marry her. I've made the bloody woman pregnant.'

'How?' I said stupidly, my mind stumbling.

'The usual way – how do you think? You know me, sweetheart, I tend to put it about a bit and she's always been keen.'

This is a nightmare, I thought. He's too drunk to know what he's saying. It could not be true, could it? I looked at him, my passport to another life, cushioned, sexually fulfilled, socially acceptable, secure to my dotage – and I hated him for snatching it away from me. And for what? Four thousand acres of *mud*. I took aim and struck Jason's face. His spectacles shot off and his nose began to bleed. Alarmingly, he also started to cry.

'Don't blub at me, you bastard,' I said viciously, 'Just get me home.'

'I'm sorry, Holly, I'm sorry. I didn't think you'd care so much. It was only meant to be a bit of fun for both of us. No one ever said anything about marriage. And you are almost old enough to be my mother, don't forget.'

15

Along with the humiliation and the despair, came the severe chest cold. I was confined to bed for a week, slightly delerious, with a temperature, having Gummidge for company and Seth doing his best. Madge came round to hold my hand and feed me milk puddings. Even Dottie turned up one morning, concerned for my welfare. She presented me with a bottle of vitamin pills. These, she insisted, were a cure-all for colds and sexual withdrawal symptoms alike.

'I'm never having sex again.' I spoke with resolve. 'I'm going to lead a chaste and virginal life and wear a vest and long johns when I'm cold instead of freezing to death in bikini briefs to facilitate quick action.'

Dottie squeezed my hot hand. 'That's my girl. Hit back. The men will still be wild for you even in thermal underwear.'

'Spare me from wild men like that sod Jason, or from calculating men like Grover, or old men like my –' I stopped short. How friendly was Dottie with Immortal Ivy? I knew George and his wife were regularly visiting Dottie these days because she told me they called often for a chat and a game of Scrabble, all three being aficionados, apparently. Perhaps I ought to take up Scrabble now? A winter of discontented evenings lay ahead for me. With Seth married I would live alone again. With Jason married I would have no more gratification on the dog blanket. I might see more of George if I could offer him the occasional bout of Scrabble as a corollary to my winsome nudity. But just the thought of these middle-aged pursuits made me tearful.

'Oh, Dottie,' I sobbed, antagonising my already congested nasal passages, 'why is life so unfair? Will I ever have a house that isn't falling to pieces and a love life that isn't in tatters? What's going to become of me?'

'Now, now, Holly. Self-pity at your age is ridiculous. There are plenty more fish in the sea for both of us. Life continues, my dear, life continues.'

Life may continue, I thought bitterly, but not with a dark green Aga.

And, indeed, life did continue. Jason got married, without splendour; a rather hole-on-the-corner affair, people said. Montgomery's continued, with me in charge, still underpaid and underacknowledged. Alex thickened and sang a lot over her word processor.

At least life was peaceful without Jason's interference in office matters. His honeymoon became protracted. The wife had given birth prematurely while on the cruise liner, thus preventing Grandma Montgomery from being in on the arrival.

It was different for Alex, of course. Her perception of such an event was coloured by her new role as expectant mother. Details of the Montgomery offspring were seized with delight. I had to put up with bulletins about the nasty little alien relayed via Grandma Montgomery. What was even more sickening, Jason's mother had taken to 'popping in' to see how 'my son's girls' were doing; these visits were the occasion of small offerings, like booties and bibs, for Alex's ultimate bundle of joy.

'You are just accepting surrogate bribes from the enemy, do you know that?' I said furiously.

'Don't be small-minded, Mrs Smith. Look – isn't this cute?' Alex jerked something pink and peculiar under my nose.

'What is it?'

'It's a rattle, of course.'

'Looks more like a sex aid. And that's what Jason will be needing before long when the novelty of his four thousand acres has worn off.'

'He'll be a changed man when he comes back, you see. Fatherhood will pull him round from his boyish pranks in Barty's Field. He's a devoted papa, by all accounts.'

'Rubbish. He'd rather have a Jack Russell pup.'

'Seriously, Holly,' said Alex, assuming her matronly expression, 'I hope you will behave yourself in future where Jason is concerned. No more Suckling Pig assignations.'

'What do you take me for? I hate the bastard. He'll never get into my knickers again. Not now, anyway. They are thermal and decidedly passion-quenching.'

In the meantime, as irrevocable as snow on high ground, Seth and Juliet's essay into matrimony approached with all its horrid implications. Seth was the good-natured butt of endless jokes at Ash and Spicer's about paternity suits once Juliet was legally his (her reputation had got around); Steve grew even more jittery, fearing some calamitous disclosure arising from her oil and loin techniques; and Madgey became more protectively maternal.

Clothing for the great day was under constant discussion at breakfast. Would Sandy and Steve go to the sartorial extreme of grey toppers, or opt for bohemian garb with a floral waistcoat, or worse, something in the pop star line of glitter and outrage? But Steve could not see himself in sequins and Sandy, although tempted to the bizarre, decided it might prove adverse publicity for a writer formally involved with Royalty. Seth finally put his foot on further excess because of Ash and Spicer disapproval. Juliet, however, was reportedly displeased. She had greatly favoured the *Oklahoma* look.

So formality won, and Madge, Mrs Angelicus, Dottie and Immortal Ivy were all relieved and hard at it in the large departmental stores of Norwich choosing designer outfits – with complementary accessories. In the end even I succumbed to some stunning new clothes. But I was going in black. A blonde is outstanding in black. I had a fake astrakhan beret and thigh-high patent leather boots. I had a military greatcoat with brass buttons and, my one concession to frivolity, an organza blouse through which my tantalising titties could be observed should the church hall temperature permit such exposure.

Then, again, a long wrangle about organists had taken place. This turned out to be one of Mrs Angelicus' specialised areas. 'Juliet must have the *Wedding March*. The organist at St Jude's is quite up to it.'

'Juliet wants to break with such stuffy tradition,' said Seth stoutly. 'She's having country and western.'

'Oh no she's not. The vicar will never give his support to such a sacrilegious sound.' Mrs Angelicus bristled with vigorous condemnation.

'Well, that's where you are wrong,' Seth replied. 'The vicar is anxious to appear modern. It was he who suggested a little folk group. The organist costs a packet anyway, and the folk group come cheap.'

Such economies were now creeping in; Madge and Steve were finding the cost of mounting a white wedding astronomical.

Mrs Angelicus drooped. 'No choir, no organ, no triumphal processing down the aisle to the great chords of Mendelssohn.'

'I know,' agreed Seth soulfully. 'It won't sound the same on the guitars.'

Over an Indian takeaway in the kitchen, as the wedding week came around, I tackled Seth more earnestly than I had done before, knowing time was eluding me.

'Are you sure you want to go ahead with all this, Seth?'

'Don't start. And don't tell me how much you'll miss me. You didn't want me here in the first place, don't forget.'

Seth was in the process of obtaining a mortgage on a typical first-time buyer's gem set on a large estate in a village that was rapidly overtaking the nondescript fields that bordered Tinkerstown to the west. The idea of Juliet settling down to the humdrum of life in such an environment was ludicrous and I had said so on several occasions. But poor Seth, who may have recognised that I was accurate in this respect, still clung to his dream that it was just what Juliet needed to give her stability. Soon the oil and loin technique would give way before the happy couple syndrome. He even took heart about this latest country and western phase with its emphasis on true love and sticking by her man.

'I've grown to appreciate your very real virtues,' I said, trying to emulate Seth's own brand of tacky philosophy. 'Since you became an Ash and Spicer executive, you've been the perfect companion for me.'

'You're taking the piss again.'

149

'No I'm not. And I can only say it again, Seth, you are never going to be happy with Juliet and she isn't going to stay with you for long. You are just being naive.'

'You're the last person to talk about being naive. Look who thought Jason Montgomery would marry her.'

'That's a really beastly crack – stop being unkind.'

'Why should everyone have to be kind except you? I love Juliet. I'd do anything for her. If she still wants to sleep around, then I'll let her. I'll let her have anything or do anything as long as she's my wife. And if it doesn't last,' Seth continued desperately, 'at least I'll have had a wonderful relationship to remember – a relationship that was sanctified by marriage. It may mean nothing to you, but it means something very precious to me.'

'All right,' I said, reeling from so baffling a declaration, 'I won't say another word. I promise.'

And I did not. The week wore on grimly. November was at its dullest with perpetual fog and chill. Seth was in parsimonious mood, saving for the big day and the mortgage and the down payment on a three-piece suite, so the servicing of my oil boiler was not put in hand. I stayed late at Montgomery's to keep warm, and visited Dottie's Aga when I could. I even went over to the gnome complex more often, not to appease Mrs Angelicus nor yet to give joy to Mother, who was as querulous as ever, but because, as the elderly were kept, like rare hothouse plants of enormous value, in consistent temperatures, the bungalow was always at furnace heat.

Jason was still absent although his world tour was coming to a close. He was due home, with wife and baby, the day before Seth's wedding. I dreaded Jason's return to the office, which would bring us face-to-face once more. I knew also that I still ached for the man. It was going to be very embarrassing. Above all, it was crucial that I kept my job. My salary was vital, more so now that commissions were thinning; the onset of winter and the awful threat of Christmas always had a damaging effect on house sales.

Due to the emotional cross-currents, nerves were rubbed raw. The normally placid Seth became agitated: he dropped cups, he spilled wine, he pranged his car. Madge broke down in tears rather too often, while Steve, glassy-eyed, smoked packet after packet of cigarettes with a shaking hand. Sandy, of course, remained detached, but I was peeved at the excitement the event had engendered in Dottie and Immortal Ivy. Those two ladies were forming an unlikely duo. They had gone shopping for their outfits together; they had gone back to the store to change their original selections; they wore each other's shoes, they swapped jewellery. I wasn't jealous, but I was uneasy. With Dottie's ingrained snobbery, Ivy was an odd choice of bosom companion.

The author of all this hysterical behaviour was, of course, Juliet, and she, of every one concerned in the forthcoming fiasco, acted as if nothing of significance were taking place. Regardless of the furore, she went on calmly painting in her studio loft and, on the one occasion I had chosen to call on her, the groaning and gasping emanating from the cubicle gave me cause for reflection. Could it be Cavendish Parkes being thus entertained, or some anonymous punter lured by her dinner plate nipples?

I had intended to berate Juliet. I hated to see the cavalier way in which she had delegated the organisation of her impending bridal bash to poor Madge. Had left that dear woman – overwhelmed by the cost, by the worry, by the work – to cope alone, without so much as an acknowledgement of the effort so selflessly made on her behalf.

I had also hoped for an opportunity of seeing Cavendish Parkes again. Hoped to glean some insight into how matters now stood (or lay) between him and Juliet. But it was not to be. With Jason away, old Cav had dealt entirely with the solicitor over the purchase of the land, and this transaction had now completed. Having acquired Dottie's parcel, it was not his intention to develop it immediately; he proposed to await a surge in house prices. Cavendish Parkes was a greedy man and his greed had been nourished by his success. Anything that took his fancy – land, possessions, property – he amassed; like his gallery of grotesque females, it was all part of his miser's hoard. Still, my share of the commission on Dottie's land was tasty and might have assisted my monthly cash flow, had it not all been pledged on my black widow wedding apparel; the patent leather boots alone had knocked me back into the red.

151

At last the wedding day dawned. A Saturday morning of leaden clouds and thin drizzle. The sort of weather that induced suicidal tendencies in the sensitive. Seth, who had endured the customary stag evening put on by the Ash and Spicer executives, was pale. He had thrown up copiously in the early hours and could not face so much as a water biscuit at the breakfast table. A card of congratulations had arrived from my ex and classy Philly, which further threw him.

'I should have asked Dad,' he said. 'I should have overlooked Dad's behaviour last time and blamed the champagne.' He turned to me, looking vulnerable and frightened. 'I hope I can cope, Holly. I want to make Juliet a worthy husband. I want to be firm without becoming dictatorial. Know what I mean?'

'Too late,' I cried gaily. 'Too late, my boy. Banns have been read. You're on the treadmill again. Remember what fun you had the first time around with the appalling Sandra. So brace up.'

Seth put his head in his hands. 'What can I take for a hangover?'

'More of the same,' I replied, getting down the gin bottle.

'I wish I was dead,' said Seth.

I had ruthlessly purloined the company car, which stood waiting round the corner in the cul-de-sac. I was driving Sandy and Seth to the church. Only two white Rolls Royces had been hired, one for our majestic bride to spread out in her pearl-encrusted tent, skinny Steve slewed to the side; one for Madge and Mrs Angelicus.

At Juliet's request, there were no bridesmaids, pages or other decorated followers of the veil, but a bevy of giggling Ash and Spicer females were attending in garlanded style. Seth's car had been pranged too badly for use as the honeymoon vehicle, so an Ash and Spicer mate had undertaken to drive the happy couple to the InterCity connection en route for the secret honeymoon destination.

The actual service was timed for eleven o'clock at St Jude's. Seth, Sandy and I arrived well beforehand. The musty old church had been bedecked with golden chrysanthemums by Mrs Angelicus and cohorts from the floral group. The folksy trio were assembling beside the lectern and arguing about amplification. They, at least, were wearing cowboy hats.

I left Seth, still looking dangerously nauseated, in the front pew, and selected myself a seat at the rear. The church was filling up. Obviously Seth had been broadcasting the event throughout the Ash and Spicer associated offices. The Tesco contingent, as such, were outnumbered. But I did glimpse George and Ivy, with Dottie, seated nearer the action.

Sadness enveloped me. All my own silly daydreams of weddings and green Agas mocked me. I would have made a pretty bride, too. With Jason gone, would I ever shimmer down an aisle – would Grover ever come back to claim me?

Eleven o'clock came. But not Juliet. Steve was a stickler for timekeeping, for traditions and for ceremonial observance. So I was puzzled. Presently Sandy swept up to me, frowning and on edge with the dawning possibility of disaster.

'What's the hitch? Seth's in a terrible state.'

'How should I know? He should have more faith in his bride.'

Sandy went out into the porch, where the photographer was blowing on his hands, having been waiting patiently at the church entrance to get a picture of the bride's arrival. The Ash and Spicer chaps, acting as ushers, were now posted to the pavement outside, anxiously scanning the thickening Saturday morning traffic.

My dark mood lifted. Yippee – the odious bitch wasn't coming! The unthinkable was actually going to happen. I turned to my heavily fragranced neighbour in the pew and cried: 'I believe in God after all.'

She put a steadying gloved hand on to my greatcoat sleeve. 'Don't panic, my dear. Brides often get these last-minute nerves. I should know. My three daughters were all late for their weddings. It's quite a ritual.'

The congregation was twittering with ill-suppressed speculation. Jilted lovers were always good for excitement. I saw George had left his seat and gone to comfort Seth. The vicar looked bewildered and more than a little sour. The folk group, though, had seized the moment. In proper country and western spirit they had embarked on a doleful ditty of a trucker's doomed love.

At that critical second, Jason appeared in the doorway. A Jason I hardly recognised. He was gloriously changed: tanned to the

153

perfection of a world cruise legacy, and his hair, tumbled and tawny, now reached to his shoulders; gone were his spectacles but not his elegance. He wore a matchless dark overcoat, he carried a sombre umbrella. I stood up, mesmerised. He saw me. The glamour unleashed by that romantic moment was dramatic, spellbinding.

He took hold of my hand and said: 'It's bad news for poor old Seth, I'm afraid. Juliet's eloped with Cavendish Parkes. Bit of a bugger, really.'

16

It had been decided not to deny the faithful their reception. Nor was it thought quite moral, in a world of famine and war zones, to waste the abundance of sandwiches, quiches, trifles and cheesecakes that had been spread out on trestles in the church hall. The herbal teas, I later learned, were considered inappropriate to a wedding party that was now in mourning, so some Ash and Spicer stalwarts had hurried to the nearest off-licence to remedy this aspect. Even the vicar and Mrs Angelicus were in favour of strong stimulants after the debacle at the altar.

But all this came to me second-hand. Jason had led me quietly from the scene to his Range Rover and driven me back to my house. I sat beside him in silence. What was I to say? The normal inanities seemed superfluous.

All Jason said, as he parked in the cul-de-sac, was: 'Statistically speaking, it must be very unusual for a bride to pull out like that.'

'Statistically speaking,' I replied tersely. 'there are not many Juliets in this world.'

We walked sedately up to my front door. In our impressive black garments we must have looked like a double act of undertaker's mutes.

'What now, Jason?' I said, sensing we were poised on the brink of his adultery. He hesitated, so impulsively I kissed him and pulled him into the hall.

'Oh Holly,' he said, 'I still love you so much.'

'I still hate you,' I said, kissing him frantically, as he peeled off my greatcoat. 'But when I saw you in the church just now, looking so handsome, what was a poor simple country girl like me to do but insist you came back to bed with me.'

We made a dash for the stairs and galloped across the landing.

'God, it's cold in here, Holly,' said Jason, shivering in his underpants.

'Come on, sweetheart, be a man, and it's warm enough under the duvet. What's happened to your spectacles, by the way? Or do you prefer to look at your wife through a myopic fog?'

'Watch it – my wife's the one who banished the spectacles. Got me into contact lenses. Damned expensive chap in Hong Kong fitted me up with the things. Mummy's very pleased, though.'

'Sod your mother and sod your wife. Forget all about them. I am the one who matters most to you. Go on, admit it.'

'I admit it, you adorable tart,' agreed Jason readily, jumping into bed and giving me every indication of having meant what he said.

Our reunion was dynamite. I do not think either of us had recognised how erotically important we were to each other. My illuminated bedside clock showed me that afternoon had passed rapturously into evening. From the landing area I heard sounds of Seth's (paralytic) return. Someone was with him, some Ash and Spicer crony, no doubt, so his condition would be monitored. I felt a spasm of guilt. Poor old Seth. But if Jason's loving return were my come-uppance for having introduced Juliet to Cavendish Parkes, I considered the devil's rewards much superior to heavenly intervention.

Jason was now asleep. His tousled, tawny locks made him look cherubic. I felt satiated and triumphant. This was the way to sock it to his wife. I hoped she was distraught at his absence. Mummy might have even sent for the police. Reporters could be on the job already. *Missing husband discovered in arms of his mistress. Scandal rocks farming community.* I giggled, and Jason awoke.

'Bloody hell, Holly. Did I drop off? How disgraceful. I must be running out of stamina. It's that sodding baby. Keeps me awake all night long.'

'Oh dear,' I said gleefully. 'I had heard that you are a besotted father.'

'Nonsense. I could wring the little brute's neck most of the time. All he does is bawl his head off.'

'Perhaps there's something wrong with him?'

'Colic,' said Jason. 'His guts are always full of wind. Poor little bugger doesn't follow me at all.'

'Really, Jason, what other idiot but you would engineer a premature birth on his honeymoon?'

'Why do I love you so much when you're so disrespectful? Remember, I still pay you your salary, so be nice to me.'

'I am being nice to you.'

'Well, be nicer still and I'll get your central heating restored.'

I slopped down to the kitchen the next morning, wearing nothing but Jason's overcoat. He followed me, wearing nothing. We found Sandy, still in his hired best-man clobber, measuring coffee into the cafetière. Sandy glanced at us incuriously. 'Seth's had a rough night,' he said. 'I couldn't very well leave him on his own.'

'Thanks, Sandy, that was kind. I thought he was with one of his Ash and Spicer pals.'

'Let's get some coffee down,' said Jason, gathering three mugs from the dresser. 'This place is like a morgue.'

'I see you're wearing the Emperor's new clothes,' observed Sandy.

'Not much point in getting dressed when I'm with Holly,' retorted Jason. And I thought that comment was one of the most flattering things anyone had ever said of me.

Then the telephone rang. It was my mother, in full spate, and with noises off.

'You didn't tell me you were getting married again.'

'I'm not getting married again.'

'I know you're not. Your gentleman friend jilted you at the altar, didn't he? That just serves you right.'

'No. It was Seth who was jilted.'

'You were marrying Seth?'

'No. Seth was marrying Juliet.'

'Why wasn't I asked, then? You know I love weddings. You selfish girl. I'd have enjoyed seeing someone jilted.'

157

At this point there were sounds of intensive disruption and Mrs Angelicus came on to the line, flurried. 'Oh Holly, I think you'd better get round here, your dear mother's growing restless. And have you any idea where Sandy is? He's not answering the phone at home and I'm dreadfully worried about him.'

'Oh, Sandy's all right. He's here with me.'

'With *you*?'

'Yes, he spent the night here.'

'With *you*?' Mrs Angelicus was outraged. 'How *could* he?' The line went dead.

'Your friend Mrs Angelicus thinks you've just spent the night with me, Sandy.'

'God forbid,' said Sandy. And that I thought was the least flattering comment anyone had ever made about my charms. 'I'd better get round to her and explain. This is not the sort of rumour I intend to foster.'

After Sandy had fled, I did my best to get Jason back to bed with me. But he dressed and became businesslike and responsible. 'I'd better look in on Seth and see if there's anything I can do.'

'Bugger Seth. He brought it all on himself, chasing that abominable female.'

'Have you no conscience, Mrs Smith? No compunction for the suffering of your stepson? After all, it was you who introduced the luscious Juliet to old Cav. If anyone is the cause of Seth's despair, it's you.'

'Don't be so daft,' I said sharply. 'Where's *your* conscience and compunction? There's your poor plain wife sobbing over her missing husband while baby bawls and your mummy is prostrated with worry.'

'No need to bother about them,' said Jason airily. 'They've all gone over to stay with my in-laws. I told my wife I needed a break from fatherhood. It was all getting too much.'

I felt cutting disappointment. So wife, son and mother had not been deserted for my winsome nudity. Jason had merely used me, once more. I had fallen straight into the pig slurry, as usual.

'You are a cold, calculating bastard,' I said reaching for my long johns.

'That's not what you said last night, sweetheart.'

Jason said down beside me and kissed me with intent to disturb. I did not resist. I could not resist. 'Oh, Jason, Jason, where do we go from here? I still love you very much.'

'More than your kitchen fitter? More than the mysteriously absent Grover?'

'Much, much more.'

Jason began to undress. 'I guess it's best not to look in on Seth. He'll be asleep.' Jason pulled the duvet up around us. 'But we've got to do something about your central heating, old girl. I don't want to catch cold every time I come round.'

'Will you be calling often then, Mr Montgomery?'

'Providing you receive me in the manner to which I've become accustomed, Mrs Smith.'

In the end hunger overtook us. Jason said we would go to the Suckling Pig, where they did a creditable Sunday roast. But first came Seth. Jason got him up, helped him dress and finally deposited him in the kitchen. And there he sat, like one embalmed, grey-faced and with the dark-circled eyes of the recently seriously traumatised.

'Do you know where Juliet is now? he asked Jason.

'France,' answered Jason crisply. 'Cav's got a *manoir* out there. They've closed up his place over here for an indefinite period. Look at it this way, Seth. Juliet has done very well for herself. It'll help her art no end mixing with that cosmopolitan set. And lots of painters have actually been French themselves, I believe.'

'I don't blame Juliet at all,' said Seth unsteadily. 'I understand. To be true to her art she has had to be ruthless. I shall always admire her for that.' He stopped, and gulped, 'But I will miss her so much,' He began to cry, the heartfelt tears of a child robbed of its soft toy. Jason and I were at a loss.

'Oh, you're such a wimp, Seth,' I said in disgust. But Jason patted Seth's heaving shoulders and suggested kindly, 'Come and have some lunch with me and Holly. Take you out of yourself.'

I was not pleased. There would be no chance of Roger's upper room if dismal Seth joined us. Fortunately, he declined.

'I think,' said Jason, when we were both in the car, 'that we should call and see your mother now. Poor old tart's a bit confused about things, isn't she?'

159

'I don't want to see my mother,' I said angrily. "I want my lunch. I'm starving. I haven't eaten a decent meal since yesterday.'

'Lunch can wait,' Jason said sternly. 'A mother is more important.'

'You may think so. You haven't had to put up with the garbage my mother has dished out all these years.'

'I like old women. Why do you think I'm so kind to you, sweetheart?'

When we arrived at the gnome complex, we found Sandy had already carried off Mrs Angelicus. We were therefore greeted by my mother from her wheelchair.

'Here comes the jilted bride,' she crowed jubilantly.

Jason bent over and kissed the powder-caked cheek.

'You're the insurance salesman, aren't you? Were you at the wedding too?'

'Yes,' answered Jason. 'Bit of a flop, though. Bride eloped with someone else.'

Mother banged her little feet furiously on the wheelchair step. The fluffy pink pompoms on her slippers danced about alarmingly. 'Don't invent things, young man. I know what happened. *She* got left at the altar. Quite right too. Who'd want to marry her. Would *you* marry her?'

The unexpected directness of the question hit us both. A guilty flush swept up to Jason's sun-kissed hair. And it brought home to me, with sudden cruelty, the fact that Jason was now married to someone else. My fool's paradise, shored up by our recent lovemaking, shattered.

I took stock of my wizened old relative. Yes, Mrs Angelicus could be right. She was failing. Slowly rotting: skeletal, rambling, useless, but still profoundly evil. 'It's no use talking to that devious old crone, Jason. She'll believe what she wants to believe. She always has.'

'You done my numbers yet?'

A wave of weariness at the inevitable repetition of my situation shook me. How many more years of demand and drudgery, of enslavement to the lunatic demands of great age would I have to endure?

160

'Oh yes, I've done your bloody numbers,' I shouted. 'And don't worry, I'll go on doing your numbers for you until the day your own number is up, Mother dear.'

17

Christmas was in the air. Little flurries of festivity shivered up and down the High Street. The gift shops were busy loading up with candles, cards and decorations of outlandish design. The tinkers were present in force, fluting merrily, fluting seasonally with their *Silent Night, Holy Night*, fluting for their Christmas cheer. Their dogs wore improvised coats these days, winter warmers to appease a public vigilant for signs of neglect that could be reported to the appropriate charity.

Montgomery's windows were jolly with paper Santas, embossed reindeer and spray-on-snow, as were Ash and Spicer's windows – only *their* Santas were more portly, their cheeks more ruddy. Arrangements were already in place for the traditional staff luncheon, the anticipated treat for offices everywhere, thus the Suckling Pig was booked to capacity for the weeks ahead. Jason and I had to put up with standing room only at the bar – not that we objected to being pressed together so closely. In fact, since his return from honeymoon, I hardly remembered that Jason was now a married man. For, as sales had slowed down from crawl to stop, we were able to indulge ourselves during the afternoons back at the mausoleum, where, the central heating blasting away again (Jason had kept his word), lovemaking could be done freely in other parts of the house rather than confined to the wraps provided by the duvet.

We had become experimental; we did it to music and we did it in various bizarre positions with the aid of a (remaindered) sex manual I had purchased for Jason's birthday. Married to such a dreary wife, had been my jibe, he would surely need its assistance as the years rolled on.

His dreary wife called often at the office, ostensibly to bring in baby for Alex to fondle. Alex herself was showing her condition quite unmistakably. Twins had been confirmed. Jason's wife was called Jane. This suited her plain ferret-like face, thin and poorly formed, framed by lank, dark hair cut short and fringed. She was skinny and flat-chested. I despised her. She, in turn, although polite, viewed me with agonised suspicion – always checking on whether Jason was out with me and, as we were normally absent, and absent for personal reasons, her suspicions had merit.

Alex, of course, disapproved hotly of my continuing affair. I had to concede it was awkward for her to keep covering up for us, pretending we were run off our feet with instructions when it was clear to an imbecile that we were doing no business at all. And Jane was no fool.

The baby was, frankly, a bit of a runt, an unprepossessing creature. It still howled a lot and had a problem with diarrhoea easily as insistent as Immortal Ivy's, although the latter lady's symptoms were less discussed than formerly.

To be sure, I saw little of George nowadays, apart from one occasion when he had used his key and made free with my person in the most engaging way. But there was a sea change in our relationship for which I could not entirely account. But I had my hands delightfully full with Jason, so I didn't dwell on the possible cause of George's moodiness. In any case, it was Seth who really worried me.

My stepson had never recovered from Juliet's flight to France. He was reverting to an earlier Seth. The executive about Tinkerstown was giving way, in true Jekyll-and-Hyde style, to the grubby layabout I had always known. His purchase of chic microwave meals had ceased. We were back to fish and chips and pot noodles.

'I think it's time you pulled yourself together,' I advised him one evening when presented with something tepid and unrecognisable in a plastic cup. 'Or Ash and Spicer will be dispensing with your services.'

'Then they know what they can do,' Seth replied.

'Oh, come on, Seth. Stop this senseless pining for Juliet. There will be other girls for you. One or two of those Ash and Spicer creatures at the wedding looked quite promising to me. Couldn't you start consummating with them?'

'How can you suggest having it away with someone else?' said Seth gloomily. 'There was only one woman for me. It wasn't just sex with Juliet, it was something sublime. I can never marry now.'

'You do talk a lot of rubbish.'

'Anyway,' Seth continued, 'when you talk about dispensing with services, Holly, you want to look out for yourself. Everyone knows about your liaison with Jason Montgomery. His wife's got clout, mind. Her father is a senior partner at Glossop's.'

Now that surprised me. Jason had not referred to this fascinating fact during our moments of togetherness on the dog blanket. I had imagined Plain Jane's father to be a plain-faced farmer immersed in his arable subsidies. But I could afford to be blasé.

'So what?' I retorted. 'Jason merely did the honourable – if out-of-date-thing and married the silly bitch because of the baby. But he really loves me and one of these days he'll leave her for me. It's obvious she means nothing more to him than a bunch of old muddy fields.'

'I don't think he will give her up,' Seth answered calmly. 'You'll have no better luck than I have. You lost Jason to the lure of wealth and status. I lost Juliet the same way. We are also-rans from the proletariat, Holly.'

'Oh just bugger off,' I snapped, for want of a better expletive and to put an end to Seth's unwelcome sentiments.

It was the week before Christmas and Jason was at last snatched from my encircling arms by family commitment and farming frolics. The party scene for the sons of the soil and their loved ones had hotted up. I hated the thought of Christmas. Enforced jollity and indigestion. It made me despondent, reflective of what might have been. I began to yearn for Grover, my boy next door, the love of my life. Where was he now? The bastard would send me the obligatory Christmas card, he always had done, but one spiky signature hardly warmed my empty bed. George half promised to slip away after the Christmas pud, and this would enliven an otherwise flat hour or so, but the situation was far from ecstatic.

164

That morning I inched daintily down the High Street in my stilettos, ignoring Tesco. I was too late to dally over black coffee and idle chatter and made straight for Montgomery's.

Alex, wide-eyed and white-faced with import, greeted me with the solemnity that befitted her announcement: 'Oh Holly – have you heard the news? George's wife is dead.'

'Don't be ridiculous. She can't be. It isn't true.'

'Oh but it is true. Steve's just rung up to tell us. He got it from someone at Tesco who'd seen it happen.'

I ignored this comment, which had no impact. My mind harped on Ivy's diarrhoea. I found it impossible to accept that it had produced so drastic a result. 'I'd no idea her illness was so serious,' I said weakly. 'Oh God, Alex, and I've always treated it as imagination.'

'It was nothing to do with her health. She was run over, right outside Smallwood House. Killed instantly by a delivery van. She must have been going to see Dottie. But I don't think she could have suffered, Holly. We must think of it like that.'

Far from being shocked at the gravity of the event, my mind raced ahead to an unexpected future. Ivy's immortality had been a myth. Poor George was suddenly a free man, unshackled by a delivery van. Within a few months he could be mine!

The office door opened and Sandy walked in. He was more dishevelled and bohemian than ever, his grey curls wild from the wet wind, his neck swaddled by some grotesque muffler that went on dangling to his waist (no doubt the handiwork of the ever-loving Mrs Angelicus). Sandy paused before making his sepulchral speech.

'Have you girls heard? Ivy has unveiled the last great mystery of life.'

'Yes, we know,' I answered, 'but does George?' It occurred to me that my dear old boy might yet be unaware of his freedom and was still tapping away blithely at some kitchen unit in a far-off village.

'He knows, all right. Dottie told him. She seemed the right person to break the news, having had the ringside seat, as it were, being in at the kill like that. Dottie's pretty unnerved herself. Nasty business to have a friend squashed outside one's own front door. Her little dog went frantic, by all accounts.'

165

Alex gulped. 'Oh Sandy, I feel quite sick.'

'George worshipped Ivy, you know,' Sandy continued. 'He will never get over this catastrophe. Terrible shock. Terrible shock.'

I thought of the last time George had been with me, and found Sandy's obviously sincere statement puzzling. George hadn't evinced any sign of worship where Ivy was concerned that night. I had been busy teaching him one or two of the provocative positions from Jason's sex manual. It had been good fun. George was nimble and innovative for his age.

'He'll get over it, I'm sure,' I said. 'After all, Ivy must have been a bit of a drag sometimes. All that diarrhoea and stuff.'

Kindly, simple Alex was near to tears. 'Oh, Holly, you musn't say such heartless things, not now, with the poor soul robbed of her life like that. Even with diarrhoea, life is still sweet, you know.'

And then I thought of Jason. I must ring him up and tell him. 'The office ought to send a wreath,' I said.

'Flowers – of course,' said Sandy, girding up for action at the florists. 'I must organise a suitable floral tribute from the breakfast group.'

After he had loped away, I telephoned Jason. It was good to have an excuse for contact, even if my message was, of necessity ghoulish. But he was formal, he was curt. Sod it, I thought; his attitude means plain Jane is at his elbow. The happy couple still lived with Mother Montgomery at the farmhouse but they were due to move out early in the new year. One of the family-owned farmhouses had been allocated to them when its current tenancy expired. There had already been much discussion about its refurbishment, discussion that had made my heart heavy. Plain Jane also favoured Colefax and Fowler.

'I have news for you, my lover,' I crooned.

'Come to the point, Mrs Smith.'

So I did. 'George's wife Ivy has been killed by a van in front of Dottie Williamson's house. How's that for drama?'

There was a silence and then: 'You're making this up, aren't you?' Jason said angrily. 'Really, Holly, you are the limit.'

'I'm not making this up. Cross my heart.'

'Bloody hell, that's awful.' Jason must have turned at this juncture to explain to his wife the detail of my tidings, for there were predictable exclamations of horror in the background. 'Better send flowers or whatever. Take what you need from the petty cash. Good publicity for Montgomery's. Shows that we are a caring outfit. Statistically speaking, that sort of gesture does nobody any harm.'

'I love you, darling.'

'Come to think of it, Holly, your kitchen fitter's technically a free man now. So you can marry him, can't you?'

Try as I might to hold on to my desire to wreck Jason's marriage, the realisation of George's amazing overnight eligibility teased me. I did not attend Ivy's funeral. But her widower had not yet come to see me, either at the mausoleum or the office – which was not at all as I had anticipated.

On Christmas Eve we closed for the forthcoming high jinks and Seth and I prepared to spend the boredom of the holiday period in each other's company. A large stock of lager, gin and smutty videos had been garnered to lighten the imprisonment.

Earlier, I had rung Dottie. She was surprisingly cool to me, explaining that she and Buster would be spending the Yuletide at a small hotel in the Cotswolds which catered for dogs. 'I am taking a friend with me,' she added, 'who needs cheering up.' Well, I thought savagely, she might have taken me; if anyone needed cheering up it was the poor bloody woman at Montgomery's who had done so much to secure a fortune for her parcel of development land. All these rich and spoiled people were the same. Having fulfilled your function, you were dispensable. I would vote Socialist in future.

I decided I had better write to George. Evidently he was observing a proper period of mourning before rushing back to my bed. I understood. But I ought to let him know that I would receive his proposal with dignity when he chose to make it, and accept with gusto. Why not? Playing hard to get was a mug's game. We rubbed along together pretty well and he would now be inheriting Ivy's nest egg so the more I contemplated marriage with my dear old boy the more excited at the prospect of wearing Ivy's shoes I became. For what was the point of waiting for Jason, or Grover? Take what Fate had so sweetly offered me and make the best of it.

167

Maybe I was too inebriated to concentrate, maybe I couldn't find words that were apposite, but whenever I went into the kitchen with a gin and tonic and a turkey sandwich to sit down at the table and compose this important missive, I failed to achieve it.

Then I remembered George had said he might pop in over the holiday for a little festive slap and tickle, so I half expected his key in the front door. But, like the letter I never wrote, George and his key never materialised. In the end, I thought a telephone call of condolence, heavily laced with sexual invitation, would suffice. I rang George's number, but there was no reply.

Well, that was not unexpected, either. Of course he would be with supportive friends at such a time, friends like Sandy or Madge and Steve. I felt guilty about Madge and Steve. Ever since the denouement at the wedding, my friendship with that dear couple, once so meaningful, had waned and frosted over. They blamed me for Juliet's elopement. To elope at all, with other than Seth, was bad enough, but to elope with a roué old enough to be her grandfather was, to them, a tragedy of unbearable proportion. The fact that old Cavendish was like a caliph who could grant Juliet's every extravagant *Arabian Nights* wish, had meant nothing. Madge and Steve were unworldly. They had spent lavishly on trappings they understood, trappings they revered, and they were now deprived of the natural result: a happy bride ensconced in a bijou, bright house awaiting the birth of a bouncing baby. But Juliet was lost to them, far away in a foreign land; furthermore a land forever associated with the carnage of war-torn trenches and nasty eating habits. Juliet would never return to her stable studio. Their sacrifice to her artistic talent had been wasted. And somehow they suspected that I was at the back of this sorrow, had deliberately orchestrated their disappointment for some corrupt motive of my own. They had trusted me, maybe even loved me, once.

Christmas was always a time of misery, a time of isolation and regret for those without a family circle. And the new year, with its corollary of better things ahead, was equally a farce. I was longing to get the whole silly season over with, then I could make for the nearest altar with George.

I returned joyfully to the office ready to expunge the sprayed-on-snow and confiscate the hearty red-nosed Santa. Alex was having an additional holiday, so thankfully I would not be regaled with disgusting details about sudden foetus movement. It was also time I heard Jason's voice again, so I got through to the Montgomery farmhouse. Alas, it was Mother Montgomery who answered.

'Oh, Mrs Smith, I'm so sorry but my son's not here. He and Jane have slipped away for a few weeks in Spain while I look after the little one. They deserve a second honeymoon, poor dears – their first one wasn't quite what they were expecting, little one arriving prematurely the way he did, bless him.'

I was livid. 'Jason didn't tell me he was planning to be away again so soon.' (Second honeymoon indeed. What was the bastard playing at?)

'Oh, he didn't know,' Mrs Montgomery continued. 'It was all arranged by his father-in-law. Such a lovely thought.'

'Well, Jason might have warned me. After all, we've got a business to run here.'

'Oh, but he knows what a tower of strength you are, Mrs Smith. Someone of your age is so experienced. I am sure you'll handle any crisis. And business is rather slack at this time of year, isn't it?'

I rang off, almost sobbing in frustration. I could see which way things were moving. That family were weaving a web around my bronzed lover, a web to finally exclude me. With bland, cold-blooded determination, they would stamp on our affair: ferret face had probably been under orders to contrive another pregnancy. I had no illusions as to how Jason preferred to pass his leisure time.

Oh well, at least I had George. When I could trace him. I rang his number once more, but there was no answer. I tried his mobile phone, which was dead. I was perplexed. It was not in character for him to ignore me for so long. With Immortal Ivy cremated and scattered, I expected him to seek my solace at high speed. The delay posed sinister possibilities: had the shock of Ivy's removal rendered him impotent? Had he turned to God and become prudish? Was his conscience preventing our reunion?

To add to my feeling of impending doom, a light sleet was falling on the pavement outside. Hardly anyone was in town. Certainly no purchaser was likely to burst into the office brandishing gold bars. I must be sensible and not give in to this flush of panic, but behave in a rational manner – lock up and go home early. Passing the bakery at the top of the hill, on an impulse I bought a bag of fruit buns. I would light a fire in the sitting room and toast them in front of it. If George called (and why should he not?) this set piece would present an idyllic scene of homely comfort.

And, when I saw that the lights were already on in my house, my heart gave a grateful leap. George! The old bugger was already there. I ran up the path and dashed along the hallway into the kitchen. But it was Seth at the table, not George. No gushing red roses flown across the Channel at the behest of George's credit card. Just bloody Seth looking glum and greasy.

'What are you doing home so early?' I asked irritably.

'Same as you. Skiving off.'

'I've been left in charge of the office, my boy. I can do what I like. But I'm surprised at Ash and Spicer being so thoughtful in your case.'

'Ash and Spicer have given me the push and have rather thoughtfully decided I need not work out my month's notice. I am considered superfluous to their requirements and in their opinion I have developed certain personality flaws, all of which leaves me a free man as of tonight.'

'Oh Seth, I'm sorry,' I said lamely. 'But don't worry. Give yourself a good wash-down and you'll get another job.'

'I shan't bother for a bit. I'll get benefit for a few months anyway. But actually, Holly, I've had this town. I want a change. I'm going back to Dad for a spell. Philly's moved out. Dad's Christmas binge was the last straw, apparently.'

I felt momentarily bereft. I realised I would miss, really miss, the presence of the loathsome lad. No one left for me to bait, no one to lean on, no one to shore up my ever-diminishing finances. Still, come to think of it, things were working out quite neatly – once George and I got together, Seth would be supernumerary.

But we spent a last companionable evening together. We toasted the fruit buns in front of the fire which threatened the safety of the chimney; we ate pork chops, grilled, and defrosted a cheesecake. We also consumed three bottles of wine, which put us on the best of maudlin terms.

'It's been great having you here, Seth,' I said. 'Really great. Life won't be the same without you.'

'It's been a lively old time, hasn't it,' Seth agreed. 'I miss the cat, though.'

'Let's drink to the cat.'

'Bloody nice cat.'

Then I ventured, with drunken insensitivity, 'I blame your vile Juliet for everything. She's at the bottom of it all.'

'She did have a stupendous bum,' said Seth in wishful remembrance.

'Nothing's gone right since she came into our lives,' I went on. 'Even Grover predicted she was bad news. She cast a spell on Tinkerstown and none of us will ever recover.'

Seth poked the fire, gazing soulfully at the reawakened flames. 'Juliet was an angel,' he said. 'But as you're such a devious cow, Holly, you couldn't possibly understand purity such as she possessed. But you're right in one way. None of us will ever recover. She was our catalyst.'

'I may be a cow on occasions, but I am *not* devious,' I said belligerently. 'I am simplicity itself. I don't want fame, I don't want fortune. I just want fun. What could be more straightforward than that?'

All I really wanted at that moment was George to give me a regular orgasm and cope with the tyranny of the household bills: for that much I would forego the dark green Aga, the designer soft furnishings and settle for do-it-yourself and Artex ceilings.

The next morning, early, Seth was in the kitchen, holdall packed. He was wearing the T-shirt in which he had arrived and which had never been subsequently washed. Over this he wore an anorak he had kept screwed up at the back of a wardrobe. It was now rumpled and stained and barely stretched across his bulging abdomen.

'You look like the King of Cardboard City,' I said brutally. But I was unaccountably sad at his departure. I surprised myself by putting my arms around him and kissing him on his unshaven cheek with the fervour of genuine emotion. 'Look after yourself, my love,' I said.

'You too,' said Seth, adding with a faint-hearted attempt at mimicry. 'You adorable tart.'

I went with him to the front door to see him off. From the path he said absentmindedly, 'Oh, by the way, George has given his house to Ash and Spicer to sell.'

'George has *what*?'

'Asked them to sell his house. Too embarrassed, I suppose, to offer it to Montgomery's, seeing how things are. Anyway,' Seth said with one last flourish of executive loyalty, 'Ash and Spicer are a much better agent than Montgomery's.'

A horrid fear caught my throat. A fear that had been fermenting ever since Christmas, bubbling away uncomfortably at the back of my reluctant mind. 'But where *is* George?'

'Oh, he's still away, of course. Sandy had the key to his house.'

'Away?' I repeated like a zombie.

'In the Cotswolds with Dottie. They got married yesterday – special licence, presumably. They didn't want everyone knowing. Funny old world, isn't it? Now maybe you'll understand how I felt when I lost Juliet due to your bloody scheming with that old sod Parkes.'

Seth suddenly gave his all to a spasm of laughter, laughter rare to one of his girth and impassive nature. And I could still see his shoulders shuddering with this unaccustomed mirth as he passed out of my sight down the hill.

18

I was not alone in being stunned by George's unbridled celerity. For quite differing reasons, each of the breakfast group thought his remarriage showed an unparalleled lack of restraint.

I had cause to take it personally. George had been my undercover lover for two years. He had avowed his passion for my bodily charms repeatedly. I had had every reason to take for granted that I would become the successor to Ivy's shoes. It hit me hard. All the more so since Jason had discarded me as a candidate for a farmhouse and a dark green Aga.

Mrs Angelicus spoke up predictably. 'Poor Ivy's ashes scarcely cold. It's most unchristian behaviour.'

'Something was already going on between them,' Sandy assured us. 'Dottie always struck me as being, well, eager for the animal outlets, shall we say.'

'I blame the water in East Anglia,' Mrs Angelicus continued darkly. 'Hormones. Hormones from the chicken factories.'

'And we always thought George fancied you, Holly,' Steve said hurtfully, an intentional barb, I was sure. 'It seems we were wrong again.'

Back at the office, Alex, sensible, infuriatingly accurate Alex, put her finger on the wound. 'It was obvious, Holly, when you think about it. Given Dottie's obsession with sex and George's willingness to oblige, it was a foregone conclusion. Add in the ingredients of Smallwood House, Dottie's wealth and their being the right age for each other and the marriage was inevitable. Anyway, Holly, what have you really lost? George was too old for you. You would have tired of him in the end.'

'It would have worked out, I know it would,' I said miserably. 'George was so handy he would have tackled all the repairs my old house needs. And I could have had new kitchen units at trade. It's not fair. How could I compete with Dottie's investment portfolio?'

'You couldn't,' Alex said simply. 'We are both poor, Holly. We'll never have real money. I worry about my babies sometimes. Will we be able to educate them? As it is, the house is too small for twins.'

'You should have thought of that earlier,' I said, not caring if I bruised a nerve. 'Breeding carries responsibilities.'

'You're right. I know you're right.' Alex looked weary. 'We've probably been selfish. But I wanted a baby so much and we were getting older every year, hoping for a break, hoping to be able to move to a larger house with a nice garden. But my poor Mark never gets promotion.'

Jason's return from his second honeymoon had been delayed. Like the baby's arrival on the world cruise, this time it was Jane's bacterial infection from eating contaminated paella. Then Jason had a mild attack of heat stroke. Then they both had to stay on to recover. I longed for Jason to be under the duvet with me once more. I was lonely with Seth gone, George gone, the cypress cat gone. I began to hate my crumbling musty house, my disintegrating lifestyle.

Business was grim. The property market atrophied. I had only two new instructions and they were hardly of the Glossops's calibre (more likely Ash and Spicer rejects), and I had made no sales at all. Without Seth to keep me abreast of the Ash and Spicer sales graph, I could only guess at their current success – or lack of it. Their thrusting young negotiators still strutted about Tinkerstown with smug importance. I did my bit for Montgomery's too, clicking around the High Street in my stilettos, tits pushed forward and clipboard in hand, but in my heart I was hoping to attract the attention of a prospecting male, rather than a hesitant vendor.

I often hobbled my way up to Smallwood House. It looked spruce and inviting but so far I had not had the courage to approach the glossy green front door, although I was curious to know what Dottie's reaction might be. Had George ever divulged our intimacy? He still had my key. I thought it unkind of Dottie to have dropped me. I knew the couple were back from their Cotswold idyll; I had heard Buster's unmistakable barking in the park one evening. Or was Dottie ashamed of having grabbed the piece of rough before Ivy's ghost had been laid to rest?

I suppose I still expected George to come back to my bed one night, gushing red roses at the ready, mouthing devotion and showering me with the flattery of the two-faced as he brushed aside his conduct by explaining it had merely been the means of giving a kitchen fitter's pension a boost. But weeks passed without a sighting, without a word. And that made me vindictive.

The trouble was I knew Dottie was a swinging old doll She was capable of keeping George occupied day and night. But that did not excuse his actions. He was being particularly craven. He no longer came to Tesco either. The breakfast group (what was left of it nowadays) agreed with me: George had let the side down.

One day, then, I promised myself, when I was feeling sufficiently bolshie, I *would* call at Smallwood House and collect my front door key for myself.

Meanwhile, Jason was at last flying home. Mother Montgomery called into the office bearing these tidings, along with Jason's son, swaddled to his bald head in blue woollies. At the sight of this brat, Alex let out the strange squealing she reserved for pre-play school tots and begged to cradle the creature that was now puckering up for a good bawl. I escaped briefly to the kitchen to make coffee.

Mother Montgomery was up to something. As I emerged with the tray of steaming mugs, she bestowed upon me the sweetest of Giaconda smiles.

'I expect you've missed my son,' she said to me pointedly as I dumped a mug in front of her.

'Well, it always helps to have a man around,' I replied.

'I am sure you feel more secure with my son here, of course,' she continued, 'although this office is so cramped he must frequently be on top of you.'

175

The cow, I thought, she knows everything. 'Oh, we manage very nicely,' I answered innocently. 'This office may be small but it's ever so cosy. The three of us muddle along happily, don't we, Alex?'

'But Alex will be leaving soon to have her little babies. When's the date. Alex?'

Alex was alarmed. 'Not for a bit yet. And I'm staying here until the very end. I need the money. I may even give birth here in the office.'

Mother Montgomery laughed. 'Such loyalty, Alex, although I don't think Jason would mind one scrap – he so adores babies.' She glanced across at me, her manner coy, but her import vicious. 'As a matter of fact, there's going to be another happy event. Our dear Jane is expecting again. Those silken Spanish nights rather went to their heads, naughty children.'

This news struck me straight to my heart, drawing blood. 'I understood the Spanish nights had gone to their bowels,' I said crisply, 'and that they were both too ill for hanky-panky.'

'Oh, Mrs Smith, you're such a wag. I know Jason has always appreciated your sense of humour. But, then, you of all people should know what a loving nature my son possesses. Despite his professionalism, he's all heart.'

'He's all balls,' I said furiously.

Alex went white and piped, 'I feel sick. Please excuse me.' She hastily passed back Jason's bundle of joy to me, and blundered towards the lavatory.

The baby, who had calmed to a grizzle while with Alex, now set up a wailing to unnerve the dead as it met my gaze.

'Please give that child to me,' said Mother Montgomery, all trace of former pleasantry erased. 'And don't think I am ignorant of your unfortunate influence over my son. You have the morals of the gutter, Mrs Smith. And if you imagine you are going to get away with Jason's paying any more of your household bills, you are much mistaken. We don't run our farming account to pay a prostitute's demands.' And with that uncalled for libel she decamped.

Good God, I thought, the woman is more enraged at my inroads into their farming subsidy than she is about my affair;

176

she doesn't fundamentally care whether her son bangs me or not, it's when he parts with money that she responds. She understands sex after years of keeping livestock, but one small handout from my lover and she's on the warpath.

Alex's tear-stained face appeared around the lavatory door. 'Has she gone? Oh Holly, what's happening? I feel frightened.'

I put my arms around her as much for my own comfort as hers and we clung together, knowing our world was crashing around us.

'I think we are going to lose our jobs,' Alex said. 'What shall I do?'

I felt dreadful. Had I jeopardised Alex's future along with mine? 'There's such a thing as wrongful dismissal and tribunals and all sorts. Don't jump the gun, Alex. Anyway, it's me Mother Montgomery is aiming for. She dotes on the fertile so believe me, you are safe.'

'Are you surprised at her attitude, Holly? You really are a babe in arms sometimes. You never see it coming.'

'But Jason loves me,' I said stubbornly. 'And she knows it too.'

'All she knows is that he's stuffing you for dear life and she's got to put a stop to it. You are not just a threat to the marriage, but a threat to her respectable farming empire.'

'Am I?' I smirked with a rush of self-confidence. 'You could be right. And I do intend to get Jason by any means, however foul. And that old cow knows it.'

'You won't get Jason, Holly. Do stop playing silly games. She knows he won't leave Jane now that two babies are involved. But she is afraid he might have to settle some money on you one day.'

'Is there such a thing as a common-law mistress?' I asked. 'Perhaps I could sell my story to the *Farmer's Weekly:* STRIPPER WRONGED BY LANDOWNER.'

'Stop it, Holly. This is serious. If we were selling masses of houses, you could hide behind the sales figures. As it is, you are on your own. You need to be sacked now like you need a dose of clap. And knowing the way you go on, they are both strong contenders.'

'Do you mind? Is everybody insulting me this morning? Mother Montgomery has just suggested I'm on the game.'

'Well, from her standpoint your morals are slightly flexible. I wish you could meet a decent man for once. I wish your Grover would come back again. I liked him and I felt he loved you in his funny way.'

'His funny way was just like all the others,' I said bitterly. 'Legs apart and raring to go.'

It was like waiting in the tumbril, next in line for the guillotine. I knew I was condemned. I didn't want to lose my precious job. Or lose my precious Jason. In the deadly wee small hours before dawn I hugged Gummidge and trembled under my unwashed duvet. What was I to do? Where was I heading? Middle-aged, childless, in debt and a without a husband in my sights and soon to be on benefit. I cried myself to sleep more than once.

And then the blade dropped.

'Are you there?' Jason had hurled through the office that morning, casting no amorous glances my way. It was going to be a fraught interview. 'Sit down, please,' Mrs Smith.'

I decided against humility in the face of management hostility. I would be brazen – as brazen as my black lace briefs that I had taken to wearing again. I crossed my splendid legs and gave Jason the old flashing technique. The gesture had never failed me. I saw Jason wince.

'I may as well come straight to the point, Mrs Smith. I've decided to close the agency. I'm selling out to Ash and Spicer. Business isn't that appealing, these days, and frankly I've had a better offer, which is going to stretch my skills and broaden my experience.'

'What does that mean, exactly?' I asked, frozen with shock.

'I've been offered a partnership at Glossop's.'

'Oh, I get it,' I seethed, the icy shock giving way to red-hot temper. 'String-pulling father-in-laws. No wonder you've impregnated ferret face again. Every time that skinny bitch gets in the family way you take first prize. Not only four thousand acres, but now Glossop's as well. Will you stop at nothing you bastard? What about me?'

'Don't be angry, Holly,' Jason pleaded suddenly. 'You'll be all right. I'll give you a good reference.'

'A good reference for what? A quick legover?'

'There's your redundancy, and I'll see to it that it's topped up a bit from my own allowance. And I'm also giving you the company car. It's a generous package, darling. We were bound to break up one day, you know. It was too good to last. I'll never forget you, you adorable tart.'

I stood up. I was feeling sick, acutely sick. As I got to the door Jason bounded in front of me and barred my departure.

'Don't go like this, sweetheart. You know what we do to each other. You're like a drug to me. I don't know how I'm going to manage without you.' Deftly he unzipped my skirt. 'Once more darling for old time's sake.'

His trousers had reached the floor when I caught him in his tender, over-active, prizewinning parts, at the same time as I struck him in the face. A good crack, with all my despair and disgust behind it.

Jason gave a howl. I carefully pulled up my skirt and left the room.

Alex looked across to me as I struggled not to cry and swallowed hard to still the nausea. 'It seems I have lost my job,' I said, my voice unsteady. I grabbed my coat, my handbag, and made for the outer door. 'Be seeing you, kid,' I called, and stamped away in the direction of the park.

I walked about aimlessly until dusk. It was a nightmare turned fact. I now knew for certain that I had joined the swollen ranks of the unemployed. Possibly, the unemployable. Ash and Spicer would not take me under their aegis once they held the reigns; middle-aged females were anathema to them. I was going to end up selling, not houses, but cream cakes at the bakery up the hill. Or packing chicken legs in the factory down the road.

I looked into the rippling waters of the lake muddied from too many mallard. My future looked just as murky. I contemplated a quick dive, face first; after all, who was there to mourn me? But it seemed a senseless waste of such good legs and expensive tombstone teeth. Grover might yet come back. He was my last hope. Retribution had arrived, as I had superstitiously feared it might, for my sin concerning Seth.

As I dragged myself listlessly up the hill, a lone tinker, under the street lamp beside the church, was at his solitary fluting. He was the one I passed regularly; he was always faltering through a melancholy repertoire, and his rendering of *Are you Going to Strawberry Fair?* now assailed my ears. It was too painful. Tears drenched my cheeks. Desperately I turned at the appropriate corner and went on up to Smallwood House. Mellow light beamed out from the sitting room window (Dottie had always considered net curtains suburban) and the interior looked plushy. I felt like some Victorian beggar on my way to the workhouse. What injustice! I belonged in a Colefax and Fowler drawing room. Without prevarication, I marched up to the green front door and knocked impetuously.

It was George who appeared. My sexy old lover had been refurbished. He was dressed opulently in a velvet smoking jacket with velvet carpet slippers to match. Ash dripped nonchalently from a cigar in his left hand, a hand which disclosed a bulbous wedding ring that now adorned his finger. I had always found George's hand attractive and I remembered vividly in that moment how expertly he always used them.

At the sight of me, George looked stricken. 'Bugger it, Holly,' he said. 'What are you doing here?'

'You bastard,' I cried, hitting him with my handbag and sending the cigar flying. 'You absolute sod.'

'Careful, Holly,' he warned. 'I don't want Dottie upset.'

'And sod Dottie, too,' I screamed. I pushed into the hall, which, even in my agitation, I noticed had not been attacked by George's everlasting magnolia emulsion, but had been redecorated in a striking designer wallpaper.

'You haven't been drinking, have you?' George asked, putting a timorous hand on to my arm.

'Never been more sober,' I hissed, kicking his ankle.

'Steady on, for God's sake,' cried George, now truly discomposed. 'This isn't the time or the place, Holly. I did intend to come round one of these days and have a chat —'

'Don't bloody bother.'

At that moment, Dottie, naked under a diaphanous housecoat through which her ample boobs and other (albeit mature) enticements were adequately disclosed, came gliding down the stairs.

'George darling, what *is* going on?'

'Holly's just popped round for a few minutes,' said George in a fragile attempt to maintain the social mores.

'Oh. How very odd, Mrs Smith. I don't recall inviting you.'

'On this occasion, Mrs Williamson, I've decided to dispense with the formalities,' I said venomously. 'But as you have referred to the odd habits of the underclasses, perhaps you like to cop this one. I've actually come round for my key. The key to my house, Dottie, that George has been using for the last two years. Despite his devotion to his ailing wife, he's managed to have it off with me in my house, in my office and in the local car park. So come on, Georgie Porgie, hand it back. I realise you've been keeping it for a rainy day when Dottie's overripe charms begin to pall, but my shutters have come down for good, chum.'

I had to give full marks to Dottie. Without flinching, she said quietly, 'Give the lady back her key, George. You certainly won't be needing it again.'

George fumbled in his trouser pocket and brought out a keyring from which he extracted a Chubb. Then he and I exchanged one look before I left, and in his face I saw regret and foreboding in equal proportion. A sight which gladdened my aching heart somewhat as I walked away.

19

I had never been noble of spirit. No turning of cheeks, no stiff-ening of upper lips. I sulked, I languished. I did not return to the office to work out my notice. I never wished to meet Jason again. I hung about at Tesco drinking coffee; or I moped at home, drinking gin. Alex kept me informed. She called, with her Mark, most evenings, to make sure, I suppose, I had not taken an overdose, for I had been threatening the tablet formula for a histrionic exit more than once.

In any event, everything happened very quickly. Within a few weeks Montgomery's bore a newly emblazoned logo in the Ash and Spicer colours and our erstwhile office boasted two Ash and Spicer male executives, brisk of manner and wooden of countenance. Alex now worked in the back office with her word processor, alongside another young woman dexterous in the communication skills.

My redundancy cheque was in my bank. I had signed on at the Job Centre, and the company car, still stationed in the car park, was legally mine with its concomitant expenses and its looming MOT.

Jason had now taken his rent table to Glossop's and was fast acquiring the icy shimmer required of their senior personnel. I was now pensioned off to the back street of his memory.

Smallwood House was on the market again. Rumour had it that George and Dottie had decided to make 'a fresh start' in another part of the country. Dartmoor had been mentioned. I could imagine George tramping Buster through the soulless scrub, bereft of opportunity to practise his sexual prowess on anyone else but the widow Williamson.

With time on my hands, I visited Mother once a week. It was a penance I undertook in hopeful expiation of the calamity that had befallen me.

'You're giving your mother so much joy,' Mrs Angelicus declared. Well, that was true. The old Barbie doll was extracting every ounce of pleasure from my dethronement.

'Got no new men, have you?'

'No. I am on my own.'

'Got too old for those dirty habits now, haven't you?'

'Probably.'

Mother cackled merrily. 'Raddled with drink and disease. I knew you would come to this.'

'My aim was always to please you, Mother dear.'

I also continued my chore with her numbers. I toiled across town to the garage every week to slot in Grover's birthday, my birthday.

'You really should take out five weeks at a time, love,' said the girl behind the till. 'Save your legs.'

'Good idea,' I mumbled.

'I'm sorry you lost your job,' the girl went on, hushed and overcome with feigned sympathy. 'Must be hard at your age finding something else. Such an exciting job you had too. I bet you miss seeing all those lovely houses, don't you?'

I did miss seeing the houses. Once in property, always in property. Evaluating bricks and mortar got into the very bloodstream. There were a lot of early Victorian dwellings in Tinkerstown. Many of these elegant terraces, with their arched doorways and their haughty sash windows, survived with their original façades. But, inevitably, some had been robbed of their symmetry with later 'improvements'. The horrendous intrusion of the builders' merchant had taken its toll on many a front door, while UPVC double glazing of various styling had further raped those houses unprotected by a Grade II listing or an owner sensitive to the period proprieties. The exteriors were all that were left to me to look upon and judge; the interiors were indeed behind closed doors as far as I was concerned. The days of dark

183

green Aga discovery were denied me. And that part of me, forever inquisitive of decoration and possession, went unsatisfied.

As did my sex drive. In fact, life had become a total deprivation. I drifted, purposelessly. My tights were laddered, my nail polish chipped, and my roots were hinting strongly that my once bright yellow hair was not entirely natural.

Alex, on one of her well-meant missions, broke down. 'Oh Holly,' she wept, 'I hate to see you like this.'

'Like what?' I slurred, having had access to the gin bottle for an hour.

'Like some fading old pop star,' said Mark, always ready to uplift the spirit.

'What do you mean, *fading*? I'm only forty-four, not a hundred and four.'

'You're letting yourself go,' Alex said. 'It's not like you. You'll never get another job if you don't take trouble – and you'll never get another man, either.'

'Thank you both for making my future sound so rosy. It's a real treat having you two around. I'm beginning to need counselling after your visits.'

'Holly,' Mark said sternly, no doubt coached by Alex, 'as your friends it is our duty to be truthful. You are on the verge of the Tinkerstown equivalent of Skid Row –'

'Skid Row?' I echoed in disgust. 'How dare you? Bugger off.'

This response nettled Mark. 'You drink too much. Your house is a pigsty. You are not serious about getting another job. Your redundancy money isn't going to last indefinitely. Your gin bill alone must be astronomical –'

I was livid. 'I don't need this verbal abuse,' I said. His crack about money, and the constant draining fear of its evaporation, really went home. I was terrified to inspect my property too closely. The settlement crack was widening, and a quick search through the relevant file had disclosed that I had overlooked the premium due on my structural insurance policy and I was therefore now out of cover.

Mark returned to the attack. 'Alex and I think the best thing you can do is to sell this house and rent a small flat somewhere. You don't really need a place this size. Get wise. Conserve your capital. And start being your age. It's not funny to act like a wayward teenager when you are over the hill.'

'Do you really think you are the right person to lecture me?' I shouted. 'You want to look at your own life a bit more closely. You are living in a two-bedroomed house with a wife who is expecting twins. The road in which you live is a slum with a reputation for druggies. And don't get too smart with your own career prospects, either. I hear they are always laying people off at the factory you work for.'

'Stop it, stop it,' begged Alex. 'Don't let's quarrel and say such destructive things to each other. Holly's right, Mark. We aren't clever people. We are all in the same boat, struggling and fearful for our futures.'

'Have another gin,' I suggested.

'I shouldn't really drink at the moment,' said Alex, tempted. 'But oh, all right, then. Pour me a big one.'

Every week at the Job Centre I passed half an hour or so in very pleasant, mixed company. The centre had its regulars. Some were beyond hope, some were lively and optimistic, some had better-than-average qualifications. But I refused to identify with any of them. I was an executive, briefly down on my luck. It was to the interviewer behind the desk that I addressed my better nature. She and I had formed quite a rapport. It was Holly and Avril now. She, like me, yearned for a dark green Aga.

'How about receptionist to an optician?' Avril suggested that morning. 'They really want someone of twenty-five, but they might stretch a point.'

'The idea doesn't elate me,' I replied.

'Manageress of a shoe shop? Very good discounts.'

I shook my head. Shoe sizes would remind me too poignantly of George and his foot fetish.

'Hullo.' Avril peered excitedly at her computer screen. 'This is right up your street. Housekeeper to one single gentleman.'

'Now you're talking, girl. Lead me to him.'

'Oh – wait a minute. He's ninety-five and has special requirements. Some nursing experience needed.'

I groaned. 'Not my week, Avril?'

'Not your week, Holly. Sorry.'

I had not been back at home long when the front door bell rang several times in peremptory peals. Puzzled, I slopped along the hallway, spilling my gin and tonic.

It was Sandy and Mrs Angelicus.

'May we come in, Holly?' Sandy said, pushing past me and making for the kitchen. 'We've been trying to get you on the telephone. You haven't had it cut off, have you?'

'I can't remember paying any bills for ages,' I admitted. Perhaps Mark was right, I was beginning to slide into gin-soaked oblivion. 'But don't get on to me, Sandy. I lack motivation. Nobody loves me any more. And the cat left home as well.'

'Oh God, she's drunk.' Sandy pulled me by the shoulders, not ungently, and sat me on to a kitchen chair. 'Now listen, Holly. I'm afraid it's very sad news.'

Mrs Angelicus, hovering alongside, added, 'There's no easy way to tell you this, dear. Your mother passed away at coffee time. It was very quick. She just dropped her biscuit, that was all.'

First Ivy, now my mother. These swift removals took some grasping. 'Are you sure she's *dead*?' I asked suspiciously.

'Gone to the Higher Glory,' Sandy confirmed.

'She was continent to the end, you know,' said Mrs Angelicus proudly, as if bestowing the only accolade in her remit.

All that I could think of at that stunned moment was that I had just handed over five pounds for Mother's numbers. I wondered if the Lottery people gave refunds.

Death left the living breathless. I ran the gauntlet of the Registrar, the pension and benefit offices, the solicitors, the bank, the funeral directors. The Barbie doll lay in wait in their parlour. There had been a seasonal rush of interments due to the biting winter weather. Snow had hit East Anglia. Crisp and deep and even, it spread its muffling fingers across the region.

On the day of the funeral, the few mourners gathered in the little crematorium: Sandy, Mrs Angelicus, Steve and Madge, and a carer to whom mother had promised her one good gold brooch. Mrs Angelicus shed the obligatory tear. Madge, avoiding my eye, cried in earnest. I wore my black greatcoat and patent leather boots, my undyed hair pushed into a headscarf. In the face of the grief around me, whether assumed for my benefit or felt with any degree of sincerity, I maintained a stony front. I had declined, furthermore, to undertake any form of buffet back at the mausoleum, even though Mrs Angelicus had offered me her savouries to swell the feast. Instead, we all went on to Tesco afterwards, and ordered cream slices and a pot of tea.

I was now truly a pariah. My mother's death had not had the anticipated effect on me. I was not racked with irrational guilt or ravaged by remorse. No childhood idyll was recalled with nostalgic dismay. Instead I was chuffed. Uplifted. Was the unremitting bad luck of my present circumstances about to give way to more joyful prospects? Was Mother's end my beginning?

The snow lingered over Tinkerstown, deadening reality, silencing the days, cutting off the nights. A lot of the time I felt lightheaded. I saw myself sometimes as the heroine of an old classic black and white movie: the rejected mistress, the archytypal Camille, dying daintily of consumption. I had no clear vision of tomorrow any more. Even Grover's return had assumed a ghostly mantle. He had not sent me a Christmas card. He was gone too, just like my other lovers, gone to the arms of women with wealth.

Money taunted me now. I was haunted by poverty. I went to bed early to keep warm, and in the dark to save electricity. Poor Mrs Smith, I kept repeating, poor Mrs Smith, what is to become of her?

One morning I was awakened by something cold splashing my face. I looked up from the pillow to see water dripping from the ceiling. The thaw had set in and, from a loose slate in the mausoleum's roof, unfelted and uninsulated, the snow collected on the joists had melted. That was all I needed. I would have to do something about repairs, even if it meant consuming my entire redundancy monies. Then I would have to sell up and seek some squalid little flat on the wrong side of the tracks. I must go speedily in search of Ned, the jobbing builder. He would do me a quick tart-up for a low price. Maybe, if he still fancied me, he would mend my roof for nothing but an hour's legover. It was worth a try.

My dressing table mirror showed me a woman I didn't wish to acknowledge. I looked rough. Were those *bags* under my eyes? My skin had coarsened, my hair was lank. Surely my tombstone caps hadn't always been that pronounced shade of ochre? I ran across to the cheval. My legs were still all right, the best in town. So it would have to be my obscenely short skirt and dark glasses for my encounter with Ned.

I went down to the car park to retrieve the company car. After a lot of coaxing, it started. The road fund licence had expired (too bad). There was only a spoonful of petrol registering on the dashboard (oh bugger). I juddered round to the garage to fill up. The girl behind the till looked at me and her earlier sympathy intensified.

'I'm ever so sorry to hear about your dear mum,' she said. 'Been just over a month since she died, hasn't it? You must miss her so much, being an only child and all. I know it's hard, but you'll get over it, love. Believe me.'

'Oh, I believe you,' I replied truthfully. 'And I won't be buying any more of your bloody Lottery tickets either.' As I drove away I wondered, vaguely, why Grover's birthday and my birthday had been written in large numerals on a board beside the kiosk selling chocolate bars.

I was probably on a fool's errand. I hoped I might find Ned at work at Rose Cottage out at Garbage Green, although the recent inclement weather could have sent him on a package holiday to warmer climes. But I had to have action before the bulging ceiling despoiled my master bedroom.

The lanes leading to Garbage Green were treacherous with slush and mud and the earlier activities of the sugar beet lorries that seasonally churned and rutted the highways. It was not until I had slithered halfway down the track to the cottage that the significance of the posted numerals hit me.

Wait a minute – did those numbers indicate a connection with the jackpot?

I stalled the engine in my agitation. My hands began to shake on the steering wheel. My heart thumped and I felt an uprush of nausea. I swallowed and gasped. I must find Ned. He would know about things like jackpots: his was a world of boxing rings and race meetings. I stumbled the rest of the way to the cottage on foot, cursing my stilettos, which were far from adequate for this exercise.

There was no sign of Ned apart from a piece of grubby paper stuffed into the letterbox which advised me that he would be back after lunch. Which lunch on which day in which month was not specified. I seized the note and scribbled across it: *Ned. I need you desperately. Holly Smith.* I pushed it back into the letterbox. Ned could misconstrue that message to his heart's content. But it should produce a result.

I failed to back the car in the morass of half-melted snow and muck, so I had to swing it round across the deep front garden. The vehicle was used to being manhandled in irregular rural situations, so it bore up gallantly. I had to get back home and find that lottery ticket.

Since the funeral, I had been so inactive, so preoccupied, that the intervening weeks were hazy. I had no memory at all of that vital piece of paper. My mind was blank. It could be anywhere. I could have dropped it. I could have destroyed it. Someone else might have claimed it by now. I never filled in the name of the purchaser; not Mother's, not my own. Thoughts I never expected to pass through my consciousness did so now. Had I, in my self-absorbed misery, my gin-induced hallucinations, thrown away the chance of riches, riches that were incomprehensible?

I stood in the ruin of the sitting room where I had tipped out drawers, thrown off cushions, scattered the ashes of last month's fire. No burglar could have done a more deliberately chaotic job. Little pieces of paper were so readily lost. They lacked presence, they were *trivial*. I went on searching, searching upstairs, downstairs until I was weak and tearful and the day outside had dimmed to darkness. At this point I felt defeated. And then violent. I shook my fist towards the ceiling and berated the Almighty roundly. 'Don't do this to me as well. Are you never satisfied?'

I ran into the kitchen and reached for the gin bottle on the mantlepiece. It was empty. So I unlatched the cellar door to get out the last green bottle that was hanging on the wall, for my stocks had run disastrously low. The cat bowl, relic of my dear

189

cypress friend, stood on the shelf alongside. And, folded up inside that cat bowl, was the elusive Lottery ticket. Grover's birthday, my birthday.

So my mother, my disliked, my monstrous, mother had been the unwilling vessel that had provided her only daughter with a legacy after all.

Which was not at all what she would have planned.

20

Typically I only made five million. A breathtaking, a heart-warming five million. It was a week when there had been other claimants for the jackpot. But as I achieved a dazzling fiscal goal, I could afford to be magnanimous towards the other winners.

I rode the impact of my windfall blandly, calmly, having had so many shocks and reversals: losing Jason, losing George, losing Seth. Having seen Ivy cremated and my mother cremated. Having said goodbye to my job, to my friendship with Dottie, to the cypress cat, I was cocooned from dramatic incident, however unprecedented.

There was no dancing in the street. I told no one. I made no extravagant gesture. Initially, I sat alone in my house, day after day, making only one small concession to Dame Fortune: I now ran the central heating all the time. I also took to eating dinner, a proper diner's dinner, with meat and two veg, in the neat hotel at the bottom of the hill. Again, alone and demure, I chose a table for one in the most discreet corner of the restaurant, my sexy legs tucked well underneath the tablecloth. For I had already appreciated, overnight, that I was changed. Money, the genie that it was, had changed me irrevocably. I needed time to pause, to let the tension ebb away. A time for decision, unflurried by urgency, for time was no longer my enemy, but a warm and helpful friend. 'Take your time, Mrs Smith,' the bank manager had urged me, 'Don't rush into anything. Don't do anything rash.'

A barrier, as solid as an iron sheath, had fallen between me and the life that had gone before. I was separated for ever from the Holly Smith of yesterday, the adorable tart who tripped so bravely around Tinkerstown, dreaming her tawdry dreams of wedding bells and Aga cookers That Holly Smith had had no other armoury but her legs and her tits and her willingness, and that, as Grover had said, was not enough. The reborn Holly Smith now moved in the world of money. And the world of money, I had found out, ran parallel to the world I had once inhabited, but never touched it. And, in truth, there was no meeting point between parallel lines. I could not return. I would have to start all over again.

Ned arrived one evening, bemused by my message but hopeful of a romp, because he had brought with him a bottle of wine. I ushered him into the hall and took him, without preamble, straight upstairs to my bedroom. His hopes must have soared. I am sure he thought the sagging ceiling was merely an excuse for me to get inside his trousers. I looked at him coolly. He was not unattractive, a decent bit of rough, really. But I had no interest in the man, other than to get him stuck into my remedials; the desire to have him stuck in me was lacking. I could now buy much better men.

I got Ned to give me a quotation to repair the mausoleum from roof ridge to foundation. I already had a plan. When the house was shipshape once more I would seek a solicitor and make it over to Alex and her Mark and their imminent twins. I had no further use for it and they could play happy families under its umbrella for many years. I intended to be far away when they were apprised of this largesse. I didn't want to play Lady Bountiful, but I had always known Alex loved my house, had wished she could have one like it. Well, what was money for but to make dreams come true? And Alex, my good-hearted, simple, surrogate sister, deserved a fairy-tale ending.

I sold off the furniture, as junk, but left the good antique tallboy *in situ* on the landing. Alex and Mark could have that also. But I packed dear old Gummidge, of course. I was not prepared to hurt his feelings by leaving him behind. As I intended to travel, Gummidge would be my mascot. America, the Far East, India, Kenya – the world belonged to me. Ultimately I foresaw buying a home in Europe. I liked the idea of Tuscany and the dreamy

Italian men; attentive, obsequious, olive-skinned men with thick thighs and long probing fingers. I wanted endearments in the night to be uttered in a foreign language. I had no need of George's cockney bedroom obscenities any more. Dottie could have them, along with the Dartmoor gales.

Since my mother's funeral I had seen nothing of, heard nothing from, the Tesco breakfast gang. Had my inability to sob brokenly as my mother's coffin made its last journey disturbed their collective equilibrium? More probably, since I was erased from the High Street scenery, I was being eased from their memories.

But on my last morning in Tinkerstown I was filled with fond nostalgia for them. I made my way towards the familiar cafeteria. The park, as I crossed it, looked lush from recent rains, cleansed from last summer's excesses and sparkling its way towards springtime. The lake glittered under the azure sky. The squabbling mallard were preening and grazing the turf, their bead-brown eyes alert for an early snack. I passed my old office, where, in the front, the young men bustled self-importantly, shuffling papers and making telephone calls.

I had ordered a white Rolls Royce from the hire firm that had been approached on the occasion of the marriage that never was, and this splendid limousine was already parked close to the entrance of the supermarket cafeteria, chauffeur in place. The car would take me to Heathrow when I gave the signal. I would leave Tinkerstown in style.

But first I hoped to see Sandy and, more particularly, Madge and Steve. I wanted to say goodbye to these special friends. I would tell them nothing of my extraordinary financial upturn. I would leave them nothing but conjecture. For they would conjecture. I knew I looked smart. I knew I looked different. I had had one exhilarating splurge in London, when I had visited a designer boutique, had my hair recoloured to a shade less brash and acquired an indecent amount of cosmetics. Gone also were the cheap, cracked stilettos. I was shod by Ferragamo and accessorised by Gucci.

I would have knocked them cold. But at breakfast at Tesco's that morning there was no one I knew. I queued up and bought my cup of black coffee and sat down by myself, deflated and disappointed.

193

My back was towards the entrance, so I did not see him come in. I didn't know he was there until he said, 'So here you are, Holly. I hoped I'd catch you at Tesco as I couldn't find you anywhere else.'

It was Grover, immaculate Grover, the boy next door, the love of my life.

'What happened to my Christmas card, you bastard?' I asked coldly.

'Oh gosh, didn't I send you one? Sorry, my darling, but I must admit I've been somewhat preoccupied these last few months.' He leaned over the table and pecked my cheek.

Self-absorbed as ever, I don't think he noticed the expensive scent, the texture of my peachy skin, the perfection of my hairstyle, the fact that the brooch in my lapel was from Cartier and the diamonds were for real.

'What's been happening, Holly? I began to be seriously worried. Your house is empty and shuttered up, Jason's obviously sold out. You must fill me in, darling. I'm bursting for the information. Shall I get you another cup of coffee?'

'Thanks, that would be nice.' I watched him walk back to the counter. Tall, starving-thin, but still attractive, still set apart from the Georges and the Jasons by some indefinable chemistry. Grover was as elegantly set up as I was; neither of us belonged in a Tinkerstown supermarket. Grover looked as if he, too, had come into money. One of his PEPs must have matured.

'Now then,' he said, returning, 'where's old Seth? What happened with the artistic damsel in the end?'

I told Grover concisely about Cavendish Parkes and the elopement.

Grover whistled. 'Didn't the Prophet Grover tell you it would all end in tears for poor old Seth? I must say I've often thought about that Juliet. What a whopper. Still, the girl had horse sense. She went for the money.'

'She did indeed.'

'Do I take it you are working for someone else now, Holly? I gather the hulk Jason married some farming connection after all. Only to be expected, really. Farmers usually marry farmers. Keeps the money in the land.'

194

'I'm not working at all, actually. I'm considered too old to get another job. No use in concealing my age from you, sweetheart. I'm forty-four and fading fast.'

Grover groaned. 'Oh, Holly, darling. I knew this would happen one day. Didn't I tell you to salt something away while you had the chance? What the hell are you going to do?'

'I don't really know, Grover. You know me, I haven't given the matter much thought. I might travel a bit, or write a steamy novel, or open a sex shop, or just wait around for you to marry me and take me away from it all.'

'Oh grow up, woman. What do you propose to live on? I suppose you'll haunt the benefits office from now on. You've always been a drifter. I've always been afraid you'll wind up on the scrap heap of humanity. I can see you, my pet, in twenty years' time on the street corner, the oldest hooker on the Tinkerstown circuit.'

'You make my future sound so alluring, sweetheart. And I thought it was always your intention to make an honest woman of me, too.'

Grover looked at me sharply. 'Maybe once upon a time, Holly, there might have been a chance for us. God knows, I've kept coming back to you over the years, haven't I? But I've had to wash my hands of you. You are a lost cause. Look at you now, without a job, without an income yet still profligate. What do you do? Go out and buy yourself a new outfit – and one that looks as if it cost a fair amount, to me.'

'Oh darling, you've noticed at last. I try so hard to make myself presentable. They tell me its easier to pick up men on the street corner if you look clean and nicely dressed. The punters pay more that way.'

'Good God, Holly, you aren't already on the game, are you?'

I smiled enigmatically. 'Not quite, no.'

'Look here, if you're really short of funds, I could manage a small cheque.'

'Oh, Grover,' I exclaimed. 'I've never known you in such a generous mood before. My plight must have touched a chord. Or have you come into money?'

Grover seemed momentarily embarrassed. 'That's why I'm here, Holly. I promised I wouldn't disappear from your life without an explanation, not after all these years of quite a, well, strong friendship, shall we say?' He put both his hands over mine. I did not snatch my hands away. I had always loved Grover's lean hands. I gazed at them now, wondering. 'I've made enough money at last, Holly, and I intend to retire. My single-minded policy has paid off, you see. And,' he hesitated, 'and I've met someone recently that I think I can persuade to share my life with me.'

He looked sheepish and a little coy. 'Her name's Annabel. She's about our age and she's very pleasant and —'

'She's got money,' I said. Enlightenment came easily where Grover was concerned.

'Yes,' he said, increasing the pressure on my hands. 'Yes, she's quite well off, really.' There was excitement in his voice now. 'She's recently been divorced and the settlement was very generous. Quarter of a million, actually.'

'I don't call that a lot of money,' I said dismissively. (And I should be the one to know.)

'Don't be so bloody ridiculous. That's always been your problem, you're too casual about money. Do you think even now that it doesn't matter? Now that you're scraping along, scratching about, clutching at God knows what straws? Your attitude has always infuriated me. You never grow up, Holly. You are the perpetual girl next door waiting for Prince Charming. Now Annabel, there's a sensible girl, practical about investment, smart on relationships, takes advice from the right City people. You would never find her going out and spending a fortune on some silly jacket. She keeps her money tied up, makes it work for her.'

I looked hard at Grover then, with sadness yet with the same old longing, the drug of that girlhood crush still potent. But I said, 'Well, bully for Annabel. She sounds the ideal companion for you, Grover. I'm sure you'll both be very happy mulling over the *Financial Times*.'

'Don't mock, Holly, not at this moment. I'm sorry, in many ways, that it never worked out for us, but you are really a mess, darling, and why should I pull you out of your mire? I don't wish

196

to be attached to a loser. In this life one can't afford to be sentimental.'

I smiled. All I had to do was tell him. Tell him about the jackpot. Tell him poor penniless Holly Smith was now rolling in the heady stuff of his aspirations, far richer than Annabel would ever be with her careful City plotting. It wasn't only Annabel who could buy my boy next door. I could buy Grover too. In fact, any woman with the right bank balance could buy the love of my life. I had that choice, but I chose to say nothing. How could I say anything, when he had said so much?

'For all that,' Grover added, 'you're not a bad old tart, Holly.'

'I'm an adorable tart,' I said wryly.

He stood, releasing my hands, releasing me. 'Got to go. Annabel and I are house-hunting at the moment. We're thinking of looking around Dartmoor. Pretty part of the world.'

I was amused. How many more of my ex-lovers were heading that way? 'Before you go, Grover,' I said. 'I would be grateful for that small cheque of yours.' I wondered just how much he thought I had been worth, how much for all those nights of shrieking joy I had given him since we were young.

Grover was displeased. 'Oh yes, all right. I did offer, didn't I?' With reluctance he pulled out his chequebook, his spiky handwriting filling in the appropriate spaces. 'Here you are. It's not exactly that I begrudge this, Holly, it's just that I know you'll do something daft with it. I don't like to think of good money being wasted needlessly.'

'I shan't waste it,' I said earnestly. 'I've learned my lesson at last.'

It was my keepsake. I would frame it, one day, to remind me of much folly. I had loved too unwisely and far too well. (The cheque was for fifty pounds.)

Grover said, 'Don't cry, Holly. After all, we may meet again one day. Who knows?'

'Goodbye, love,' I said. 'See you on the street corner.'

'You're incorrigible,' he answered, smiling but still with faint anger. Then he kissed me lightly, and left. Through the glass windows of the cafeteria, I saw him walk away out of my life, striding past the white Rolls Royce to get to his hatchback, parked nearby.

To my chagrin, I did start to cry. I ran to the lavatories at the far end of the supermarket while shoppers looked at me and paused, puzzled, at the checkouts. I locked myself into a cubicle and, sitting on the lavatory seat, sobbed uncontrollably. Sobbed as I hadn't sobbed when Jason left, when George left, when Seth left, when my mother died.

It was a salutory purge, and when it was over I repaired the damage at the mirrors above a spotless white basin. Then I clamped on my dark glasses and walked out of Tesco. The chauffeur was at his post. He jumped out deferentially, swinging wide the door of the Rolls Royce at my approach. A small group of onlookers gawped. I smiled at them graciously, remote and set apart – and I felt suddenly appreciably *younger*.